THE BRIDGE

JANE HIGGINS

Tundra Books

Cover illustration by Sebastian Ciaffaglione
Map by Bill Wood

Published in Canada by Tundra Books, a division of Random House of Canada Limited, 75 Sherbourne Street, Toronto, Ontario M5A 2P9

Published in the United States by Tundra Books of Northern New York, P.O. Box 1030, Plattsburgh, New York 12901

Library of Congress Control Number: 2012930536

Library and Archives Canada Cataloguing in Publication

Higgins, Jane
    The bridge / Jane Higgins.

Issued also in an electronic format.
ISBN 978-1-77049-437-4

    I. Title.

PZ7.H5349545Br 2012   j823'.92   C2012-900390-5

We acknowledge the financial support of the Government of Canada through the Canada Book Fund and that of the Government of Ontario through the Ontario Media Development Corporation's Ontario Book Initiative. We further acknowledge the support of the Canada Council for the Arts and the Ontario Arts Council for our publishing program.

Printed and bound in the
United States of America

ONTARIO ARTS COUNCIL
CONSEIL DES ARTS DE L'ONTARIO

1 2 3 4 5 6   17 16 15 14 13 12

For Paul

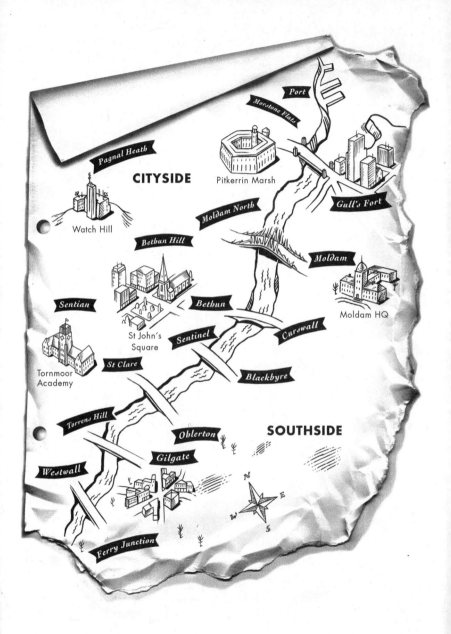

PROLOGUE

We rode to war in a taxi-cab. Dash found it in Fettlers Lane, near the old greengrocer. We'd gone there looking for food. We were fierce hungry and would have taken anything on offer, but the hostiles had got there first. The place was destroyed. The till was thrown through the front window, the shelves were ripped off the walls. Our feet crunched on glass, and everything reeked of smoke from someone lighting a fire in the back room.

They'd stripped it bare before they'd done the damage – not a tin of beans, not a bottle of water, not a crust of bread. We were scrabbling around in the rubble when Dash yelled and we all charged outside.

The cab was one of those big black hulks – beetles, we called them. This one had a smashed back window, a door torn off, blood spattered across the windscreen and a broken fuel cell: dead, by the looks of it. Bad news for us, because without wheels we were stuck in the city, easy prey for the hostiles. So Dash and Jono had this argument about whether the fuel cell was fixable and I said couldn't they just try for half an hour and see? And, surprise, Dash stuck her head under the bonnet and fixed it in twenty minutes flat, while Jono muttered and shrugged and the rest of us watched up and down the lane and chewed our fingernails.

When Dash yelled 'Done!' we all piled in and took to the road. We didn't think we were riding to war, of course. Who in their right mind goes to war with an eight-year-old kid in tow? No. We thought we were getting out.

CHAPTER 01

Two weeks earlier...

ISIS came recruiting on Victory Day. Two agents from the Internal Security and Intelligence Services were standing in the shadows at the back of the chapel when we all trooped in for morning prayer. The sun was barely up and we were fasting, but for once we weren't grumbling. You didn't grumble when ISIS came to call.

We passed these agents, a man and a woman, on the way in. Tall. Fit. Head to toe in black. And sharp, from their razored hair to their battle boots. Alike as peas in a pod, as bullets in a belt.

We were craning our necks to look at them and whispering to each other, and Dr Stapleton had to rap on the lectern (which meant trouble down the line) to launch us into the city anthem: 'God bless these ancient city walls and all who dwell herein...'

God hadn't been doing a great job of it recently, and ISIS had to make up for that. So here they were at school, Tornmoor Academy, recruiting for their labs and their surveillance ops: they wanted smart, so every year they checked out the top senior grades in physics, mathematics, and computing, and in scripture study because they wanted dedicated too. This year we were it, the senior year, ISIS agents-in-waiting.

Dr Stapleton read out the Victory Day message from the General. It was the same message every year: *Never forget, never forgive. The invasion of our city will be repelled. The massacre of our people will be avenged. We will not rest until Southside is reclaimed.* And the punchline: *Remember, always, God Is On Our Side. Victory Is In Sight.*

I don't think anyone actually believed the victory being in sight bit anymore. Not when the latest news upriver was of five brave, stupid church workers who'd ventured over the river into Southside to bring aid or something to the heathens, and who now swung from Westwall Bridge, turning slowly above the water. We'd seen the grainy pictures in the *City News*. We'd listened to broadcasts of attempts to retrieve the bodies and heard the hail of sniper fire that greeted rescuers every time. Meanwhile, downriver, hostiles had hacked into the flood protection system just in time for a storm surge to meet a high autumn tide and drown Morstone Flats. Hundreds killed, they said. Thousands homeless.

So, no. No one believed that victory was at hand.

Stapleton droned to a halt and Dash was called up to read something from Scripture about battles and bloody vengeance. I wondered what the agents saw when they looked at her. An ideal recruit for sure: tall and sporty, she'd take you on at anything and play hard; blue-black eyes with a seriously sharp brain behind them; thick fair hair clipped close; a way of standing with her neck and shoulders held straight and fine; and this way of lifting her chin when she was on shaky or dearly held ground. Which is what she did as she finished the Scripture reading, as if to say, *Go on, disagree – I dare you.* But I couldn't, because I hadn't heard a word of it.

Dash and I had battled each other for top spot in our year all the way up from junior school. She beat me at applied physics and engineering – she could take anything apart and put it back together better than it was before. I beat her at mathematics and programming. Mostly it was a close-run thing either way. Which meant everyone expected us to be together. And we were. Which was also fine.

We prayed some more. We sang. But mostly we thought about being chosen for ISIS, because that was the prize we'd worked for from day one. Those who missed out would be sent for compulsory service in the army, the factories, or the farms – a grim, boring slog, and long. If you didn't have family to find you a different job, or claim they needed you at home, you could be stuck for years.

But the chosen ones were in for the ride of their lives. ISIS was the brains behind the war. Its agents worked in hi-tech, often high-risk, operations in surveillance, cryptography, and forensics dedicated to outwitting and defeating the hostiles. What better way to avenge the people we were now about to honor.

The thirty students chosen this year to commemorate their murdered loved ones were stepping forward under Stapleton's ferrety eye. Everyone was on extreme best behavior now, standing straight and serious and repeating the response after each name: *We will remember them. God bless the city.* In twelve years at Tornmoor I'd never once been up there to speak my parents' names. They'd been killed in a bomb blast when I was a little kid. Not being chosen year after year didn't bother me, and, to be honest, I didn't remember their first names, exactly, which was why, maybe, I'd never been chosen. But *Stais, Mr and Mrs,* that would have been okay.

We filed out of the chapel's dark, ancient spaces into the bright auditorium where Dr Gorton was practically having a seizure trying to get us organized. He scurried up and down the stairs beside our rows, muttering and gibbering, 'Are we ready? Are We Ready?' He stopped beside Lou, who'd unwisely picked an aisle seat. 'Hendry! Is that gum? You are chewing gum. Few are called,

Hendry. Fewer are chosen. You will never be one of them. Get Rid Of It.' Slap, slap, slap on the back of Lou's pricey haircut. Lou ducked, winked at me, and grinned. He had no intention of being chosen for anything other than an easy life in the soft bed of family trust funds and parental doting. But I was a scholarship kid. A few brain cells were all that lay between two futures for me: working with the most brilliant minds around to win the war, and being sent upriver to batter hostiles into submission with a life expectancy I wouldn't like to speculate about. This was my chance. I intended to grab it.

'Senior Year, stand!' said Gorton. 'And forward!' Forty of us marched down to the floor of the auditorium.

Stapleton, who was having a good day, front and center in everything, gave his annual lecture about what a great moment this was. He wittered on for so long that when the ISIS guy finally had his chance at the podium he didn't bother with introductions or niceties, he just cut straight to it.

'Make no mistake about why I am here. We are in a fight for our lives, against an enemy with no soul. Everything your parents and grandparents built in this city, everything they fought for, is at stake. This enemy craves our land, our homes, our livelihoods, our way of life. They crave our annihilation. Those of you chosen today will join the fight: together we will drive them into the desert. It will be challenging, even for the best of you. You will be expected to give everything of yourselves, and more. But have no doubt: we will win this war.'

He flicked on his notebook. The Tornmoor senior year held its collective breath.

'When your name is called, come forward. Form a line in front of the stage.

'Ashleigh Bannister, outstanding in physics and engineering.' Dash beamed at me and strode forward.

'Stephanie Domaine, outstanding in organic chemistry, applied mathematics, and scripture.'

'Christof Freklin, outstanding in genetics and scripture.'

And on he went: Steve, Alistair, Jono (which drew an audible but unrepeatable crack from Lou), Ellis, Gaby (nods of approval all round), Mark, Jenna.

'That's all. God bless the city.'

That's all. My brain jammed on *all*. That couldn't be all. He was supposed to say, *Nikolai Stais, outstanding in…* I didn't care what, as long as he said my name. But instead he was nodding to Gorton and Stapleton. He was clicking off his notebook. He was saying something to his new charges. I couldn't hear what because my heart was pounding in my ears. Then he was walking towards the door and my classmates were marching behind him, already squaring their shoulders and walking taller. Some of them turned around to look at me, but the female agent said something and they turned away and then they were gone. The door slid shut with me standing on the wrong, wrong side of it.

Lou was saying, 'No, hell no! That can't be right.'

Gorton said, 'Hendry, be quiet. Stais, sit down.' Everyone else was heading back to their seats and I was still standing, gawping at the door.

'But what about Nik?' said Lou, loud enough for the entire auditorium to hear.

'You heard me,' said Gorton. 'Be quiet! Stais! Don't make me tell you again.'

And that was that. A key moment, maybe *the* key moment in my life, gone. You can't apply for ISIS. They choose you. Or not. I went back to my seat, heart still pounding. The whole auditorium had got too bright and hot. Lou was muttering furiously beside me but I didn't hear a word.

People steered clear of me for the rest of the day, the way they do when you're deep in it and no one knows what to say. Or maybe they do know what to say but they don't want to say it when you're around to hear.

We all landed back together in the dining hall that night: Lou and Bella, Fyffe and Jono, Dash and me. The lock-down siren had sounded so we were on generator power. The hall was the same vintage as the chapel, and gen-power made the place feel like a drafty old ware-house, all dark corners and dusty stores where the walls were lined with portraits in thick cracked paint, forgotten by their owners. The gargoyles grinned and screamed silently from up in the gloom. Everyone's face was shadowed, everyone's voice muted, as though turning down the lights turned down the volume as well. But at least gen-power made it hard to see what we were eating.

Dash was bright and buzzy, but trying not to show it. Jono just sat, pleased with himself and the world, and didn't say shit. Fyffe pushed her bowl of stew away and tried to change the unspoken subject. 'That's *so* disgusting! Whatever happened to real bread and butter? And roast potatoes, remember roast potatoes?' She looked around at us but she got nothing – just some nodding and mumbling. She crushed her cracker and pushed a finger through the crumbs.

We looked at the watery custard and pseudo-fruit something that was supposed to be dessert and everybody passed, except Jono, who'd eat anything that wasn't actually moving. Another silence arrived, so I said to Dash, 'When do you start, then?'

'Straightaway. Tomorrow.'

'Tomorrow!' Bella peered over her horn-rims. 'That's some hurry they're in.'

Dash nodded. 'Well, it's escalating isn't it. You heard the man. I know we're supposed to think the army's on top of it all, but ISIS knows the real score. They need everyone they can get.'

'Yes they do.' Lou looked around at everyone, but no one looked back. 'So, if they're desperate, why'd they pass on Nik?'

'Doesn't matter,' I said.

'Sure it doesn't.'

'Maybe there'll be a second round,' said Fyffe. 'You know. Later in the year.'

'Oh, yeah,' said Lou. 'Because Nik really needs that chance to improve his grades, doesn't he?'

Jono woke up. 'Don't take it out on Fy. It's not her fault.'

'It's someone's fault,' said Lou.

Fyffe and Lou Hendry – and Sol, their little brother – were as close to family as I had. Their parents had a house out in the country: a huge place, sprawling like you wouldn't believe, with about twenty-six bathrooms and a front lawn the size of a football field and you had to travel for about a day and a half just to get down the driveway. They were the Hendrys of Hendry fuel cell fame – wealth-on-wheels, literally, since their cells powered all our vehicles and more besides. We'd had a normal enough start, Lou and me: rich kid wants assignment done, tries to beat not-rich kid into doing it for him. That didn't work, but bribery did. His hampers from home were mind-boggling, packed with chocolates and biscuits and fudge and apples and plums and you-name-it, turning up fresh and frequent every term. Fyffe arrived in school a year later and was so primly shocked by this arrangement that she shamed Lou into inviting me home. I'd been going home with them for holidays ever since.

I pushed my chair back. 'I got work to do. I'll see you later.' I tried to smile at Dash, and escaped. Crowds parted for me like I was Moses walking the Red Sea. They closed behind me though, whispering, like crowds do. I lay on my bed and went over it again. I'd stayed behind in Gorton's class that afternoon, but he took one look at me and held up a hand. 'Don't ask, Stais. It's not for me to say.'

'But, sir…'

'What did I just say?'

'Did you know?'

'Did I know what?'

'That they wouldn't take me.'

'Of course not.'

But you know, Dr G, you're avoiding my eye. I don't believe you.

CHAPTER 02

When people started drifting into the dorm I left – hurried down the stairs hoping not to be noticed. As I landed in the hallway, an arm shot out from under the stairs and pulled me into the shadows where the cc-eyes couldn't reach.

Dash.

I muttered, 'Hi,' and didn't know where to look.

She put her arms round my neck and rested her forehead on mine, studied me with that blue-black stare. 'What's going on?'

'How do I know?'

'Nik!' She gave me a shake. 'Think! Something's wrong – a mistake in their records, or you've done something…'

'Like what?'

'I don't know. Anything! It could be anything. This

wasn't meant to happen!'

When I didn't answer, she did what she often did when she was nervous: fished out the talisman I wore round my neck, breathed on it, and gave it a polish. It was silver, an elongated S with a long narrow hole at its center. It had belonged to my mother – it was all I had of hers. When I was little I used to think the S stood for Stais. Dash kissed it and put it back inside my shirt. 'We'll fix it,' she said.

I shrugged.

'Don't do that!' she said. 'Don't you give up. I said, we'll fix it.'

'Will you? You and your new buddies?'

She pulled away from me. I felt sick. 'Gotta go,' I said.

Macey was on duty at the main doors. 'Lord, boy, slow down there –' He put out a hand as I went past. 'Hold up. You're not going out. You heard the siren.'

'Yes, I heard it. So?'

'So that means you're stopping here for the night. There's a cell been busted up near Torrens Hill – six men, guns, ammo, explosives, you name it. No one's goin' anywhere tonight, not even you.'

'Gotta get out, Macey.'

'Well, not through these doors, son.' Okay. I headed for the kitchens.

'Nik!'

'Mace?'

'Watch how you go.'

'Yeah, Mace.'

I've known Macey since I was five, but he'd guarded the doors for years before then. He used to walk in the grounds after his shift, smoking cigarillos and I'd follow him because I liked the smell – warm and dark and kind of cozy. After a while he gave up telling me to beat it and let me walk with him, and a while later he gave up the cigarillos, but I still walked with him. He was a Southsider and he talked a lot about his family across the river: two girls, a wife, and his old father. No mother; she died in an upsurge in fighting a few years back. He told me that one day he'd bring them all over. He was saving till he had enough to buy permits for them – that was a lot of money to save. *One of these fine days,* he'd say. *One of these fine days, Nik. You'll see.* He was full of plans, old Mace.

He taught me a few Breken words. That's what Citysiders called Southsiders: the Breken, the speakers of broken language, because of the mutilated Anglo they spoke across all their different groups. Mace had grown up speaking it. Sometimes, when there was no one else around, we'd talk to each other in Breken. But we were careful. It was the language of the hostiles, so you didn't want to be caught speaking it, or even knowing it.

Years ago he'd told me the lock code for one of the

kitchen doors in the dorm wing – *just for when you want to get away, lad, and no one to know.* So before anyone could say, *Where the hell do you think you're going, Stais?* I was out. I wandered down the walkway between the wall and the dorms and came around into the grounds.

Lockdown blacked out the school so I was alone in the dark, which suited me fine. I sat on a bench, thought about ISIS, thought about Dash, walked under the old oaks that lined the walls, listened to the wind rustle their autumn leaves, thought some more about ISIS and wished I hadn't said what I'd said to Dash. Now and then a siren wailed, and sometimes gunfire crackled down near the river. But mostly it was quiet out there, the way cities ought not to be.

Cold too. Autumn had come early. Penance, it felt like – payment for the summer just gone. It had sweltered, pavements baking from early morning till sundown, with no let-up after dark because then the city breathed it all back out in one long, hot, pent-up sigh.

I'd roamed the streets that summer. Everyone else had gone and Lou wasn't allowed to bring anyone home while he made up for his bad grades with a private tutor. I stayed at school. Same old story: you watch parents arrive and gather up their kids, and for all that everyone complains about families, the kids look pretty happy slouching out of school towards summer in the country house and the parents look proud. I tell myself every time not to watch, but it's like picking a scab. You know it'll bleed and take longer to heal, but you can't resist.

Once they'd gone it wasn't so bad. I played football with the little kids in the alleyways around Sentian and Sentinel Park, which made me popular with the kids and their parents. No one ever left their kids to play outside unsupervised – there were too many stories of them being grabbed by hostiles. The kids from rich families might make it back home, because rich kids were ransomed, but others were lost forever, sold Oversea or into the Dry. Little kids were prized by the hostiles because they were 'pure' – uncontaminated by drugs or disease. White kids, especially. The hostiles thought their blood and organs held some kind of life-giving power. A white kid was worth a gruesome fortune over the river. Which meant everyone watched their kids every minute, and felt frantic about letting them out of sight. And everyone was happy to let me organize football in the summer.

At the end of each day I'd go and sit on Pagnal Heath and watch the sun go down over St Clare Bridge, make plans for when I got picked by ISIS, and wonder about the shadow city over the river.

Then summer was gone. The school gates were locked with the early dark and while a few of us were allowed out now and then, we had other things to worry about. Like getting the grades we needed to catch the ISIS eye.

We were told, all this time, that the fighting was going well, but we heard rumors too, of how deep the hostiles were reaching into the city. The worst unrest was upriver. Locking the bridge gates and seeding the river with mines hadn't stopped them crossing over. Kenton Woods and Boxton out on the western perimeter had copped it bad in the last few months: those church workers hanging from Westwall Bridge, a nail bomb ripping into a crowd queuing for bread, and a church graffitied in blood. The powers-that-be said these were flare-ups that happened from time to time, nothing to indicate an organized onslaught. It was hard to know if that was true, or if in fact the war was coming, as they say, to a town near you.

Problem was, we had no real news to chew on. Every night, curfew drove people back into their homes, and us back to our dorms and dining hall, to pick over dinner and the day in private. The General or his sidekick made weekly telecasts about how great everything was going, and *City News* drip-fed us details now and then, but it was news-lite about the fighting. All we got from it were things like a day in the life of our boys/girls in the fray from first 'prayer and swear' through to supper in the mess with grinning thumbs-up from everyone. All of which was about as satisfying as candy at a carnival but it was seized on anyway, then people looked around, hungry for the next thing. We wanted to know. One of the great things about being in ISIS is that you would know.

I walked in the grounds, listened to the quiet, watched the moon rise above the walls, and kept an eye out for the security boys. I'd get a lecture if they saw me. There'd be paperwork and reporting and junk like that, so I did them a favor and stayed out of sight when their torch beams came waving around. Said hello to Hercules though – that's their giant wolfhound. He sniffed around and found me sitting on a bench but he knows me, so no problem.

When they'd all gone back into the dark, I talked to my mother for a while, told her that my life was pretty much sunk now that I was heading for the army with no get-out-of-jail card. But then I felt guilty about telling her that because it wasn't her fault that ISIS didn't want me. She'd probably had all kinds of grand plans for me and here I was trashing all her plans and she'd probably say to not give up, where there's life there's hope, and all those other cheery things that people like Mace are always saying, and maybe even believing.

The night was cold but clear, and there was no one around, which was a relief from always having someone in your face or your back pocket. So I stayed and watched the night go by and the morning come – the light coloring the old brick walls and the windows.

I was thinking about going back in and whether I'd

be seen, and if anyone had even noticed I hadn't been to bed, when a song came down the path. Fyffe on a morning walk, fair hair swinging side to side, happy, somehow, with the world.

'Hey, Nik,' she waved and came over, sat on the bench beside me and gave me her sunny smile. She smelled of soap and linen. 'You're up early,' she said. 'Usually it's just me. Isn't it wonderful?' She waved an arm at the sky, which was clear and blue, just losing the sunrise colors. No argument from me, but I mustn't have looked too impressed because she spared me the full-on 'praise be to God' speech and said, 'You shouldn't feel bad, you know. There must be a reason. There's always a reason.'

Yeah. Life Lesson No. 1. Hold your nerve when bad stuff happens because there's a plan and a reason for everything, you just don't know what it is yet, but you'll find out one day even if you're on your death bed when you do.

Well, maybe.

Fyffe hugged her knees and studied me. I didn't even try to look back. People think Fyffe's not very sharp because she's all 'wow! look at the trees!' and 'smell those flowers!' and arms flung wide at the morning sky. But they're wrong. She's smart in ways that are completely out of my league. She can read you with a glance, and you don't even know you're being read. So you don't go near her if you're trying to pretend things are great when they're not, because she'll know.

I rubbed my hands over my face and she said, 'You look awful.'

'Yeah… thanks.'

'So, what now, for you?'

'Breakfast?'

'You know what I mean.'

'The army, Fy. The army is what now for me.' I smiled at her to try to show I didn't care.

She looked away. 'It swallows people before they've had a life,' she said.

All too true. We'd got as far as senior school because we were either very rich or very bright. Whichever way, no conscription for us. Until now. Now it was my turn to join everyone who'd been kicked out of school at fifteen and assigned to one of the three Fs: Farms, Factories, Fighting. It used to be that after three years you could opt out of the one you were first sent to. But now, they can keep you fighting as long as they want. Until you're killed or wounded or way too old to be useful. Which is why, if you don't get into ISIS, you're dead. Sometimes for real.

CHAPTER 03

'**Gorton knows,**' said Lou.

'Yeah? Why do you say that?'

'Did he act surprised? No.' Lou blew smoke carefully out the dorm window. 'Does he care? Probably not. But it makes no sense. And they took Jono. Go figure.' He tapped ash onto the window sill. 'Want one?'

I shook my head.

'You should ask him,' said Lou. 'Gorton, I mean.'

'I did.'

'And?'

'It's not for him to say, apparently.'

'Well, who the hell can say? Bastard.'

Sunlight poured through the high windows of our dorm room and lit twelve beds, mostly 'made,' desks swept clean of junk because it was Wednesday and inspection day, and mirrors stuck with photos of families, girlfriends, pets, and other hangers-on. I was supposed to be helping Lou with a programming assignment but we hadn't got very far.

'You need to know why,' he said. 'How're you going to find out?'

'No idea.'

'A little hacking into Records wouldn't hurt.'

I shook my head.

'Come on! If not you, then who?'

Over the tops of our trees, I could see across to the hump of Watch Hill where the General sat in his office plotting the city's next brilliant move. Or maybe not. What if he just paced and frowned as he looked out across Sentinel Square towards the river and didn't have a clue what to do?

I looked back at Lou. 'They'll be hunting for an excuse to chuck me out now. I've got no one breathing down their necks to say they have to keep me, and my scholarship is theirs to stop when they want. If they catch me hacking anything, I'm gone.' I was gone anyway, but I wanted to see out the year if I could.

'Do you want me to try?'

'Hacking? You?'

'Dreams are free. Not hacking, then. I could just nosy around. Ask some people.'

'Like who?'

'Like Dr Williams.'

'*No way!*'

'No, think about it – it can't be your grades, and you're too damn careful to have much of a conduct record. It's brutal! If you'd known they were going to dump you, you could've had a helluva lot more fun. So it's not grades, it's not discipline. What's left?'

I shrugged.

'Jeez. What d'you think?' Lou tapped his head.

'Oh, great. So I'm psychotic?'

'Well… you are sitting in a third-floor window in the middle of a city in the middle of a war. In full view of anyone with a telescopic sight.'

'Where?'

He pointed a finger, trailing smoke. 'There's snipers out there, remember?'

'Rumors of snipers.'

'And where will that attitude get you? Nowhere you want to be. They've got, what, twelve years of records on you?'

'So?'

'So, who knows what they've made of them?'

'Do I look psychotic to you?'

'Only sometimes.'

'Funny.'

'Course it would help if you weren't caught out and about all night.'

'I wasn't caught.'

'And that's down to me covering for you.'

'Maybe I was in the infirmary, being psychotic.'

'Fy said she saw you. She said you'd been out all night and you looked like shit.'

'Fy said that?'

He grinned. 'It's what she meant.' The lunch bell rang. 'Oh, great.' He picked up his assignment.

'Give it here,' I said. 'I'll do it.'

It was weird. One minute they're falling all over you and you've got extra assignments and one-on-one tutoring and all kinds of people checking that you're okay and worried that they're working you too hard but they want to push you because you've got 'such promise', and the next minute, nothing. Just nothing. I could've put my feet on a desk, lit a cigarette, and thumbed through a comic and they wouldn't have cared. The difference between me and Lou is he would've done all that just to see what would happen. But I'd been schooled in school too long. Lou called me careful, and he was right. I always had been.

Part of that was, while I wasn't the only brown face in school, I was the only one without back-up. The Hendrys, sure, they sent hampers and gave me a home in the holidays sometimes. But all I had keeping me there was my scholarship and a record that said 'not too much of a problem' or words to that effect. But now that I wasn't an asset, had I turned into a problem? I didn't know. I did my work and most of Lou's, and watched them ignore me.

Lou nosed around, like he promised, and came up with nothing. He reported this at lunch one day, a week or so after Victory Day. Bella smiled pouty lips at him and called him a novice, a rookie, and a greenhorn. 'Watch and learn,' she said. And off she went to do her own investigations, hips swinging, black ponytail bobbing. Lou groaned.

Fyffe rolled her eyes. 'Could you try not to drool in the soup there, Lou?'

We didn't see Dash, or Jono. They were in training with the two ISIS agents who were living in while they took a look at their new recruits. They all sat at a separate table in the dining hall, spent the days in the staff labs, and morning and evening were out on the assault course in the back fields. Dash seemed to be doing okay. She gave Fyffe the thumbs up when she thought I wasn't looking, and she looked high on it all.

I volunteered for library detail. Dr Bonn arched an eyebrow but spared me the knowing smile. 'You can tidy up Nanotech.' So I got to watch the recruits, because from the shelves of dusty old volumes on Nanotech, History of, Level Three, you could see the assault course.

Late one afternoon Sol Hendry came wandering by. I tried to look busy shelving books. How Lou had a brother like Sol was one of life's genuine mysteries. He was a serious little kid with fair hair, big brown eyes, and a flair for mathematics. He'd only been at school a few terms and he was shy, not much of a talker, but he often turned up quietly at my shoulder to ask if I could make a number puzzle for him, and could I make it harder than last time, please.

'Hi Sol,' I said. 'How's things?'

He shrugged, hauled *Nanobots: Fear and Fantasy in Classic Science Fiction* off the shelf and leafed through it. I gave up pretending to work and stared out the window. Dash looked like she was born to the training. Fit, fast, graceful. By the end of it she'd be better still. Lethal.

Sol spoke behind me. 'Why do you have to go away?'

'Who says I'm going away?'

'Everyone. Dr Stapleton. He said you'll be gone soon. Into the army.'

'Did he? Well, what would he know?'

'I don't see why you have to go. Fy said my dad will find you a job. But Lou said it's not as easy as that. Do you want to go in the army?'

'What else did Dr Stapleton say?'

Sol put *Nanobots* back on the shelf – in the right place. Sol, the perfectionist. 'That we should do our work and not talk to people who'll be going soon. That's mean, hey? I think it's mean.' This judgment delivered, he shrugged Stapleton off and said, 'Do you want to play football?'

'Sol, my friend, what a good idea.'

By the time the bell went for dinner he and I were

three goals up against Lou and Sol's mate, Izzy. We'd yelled ourselves hoarse and I almost didn't care about the ISIS woman standing under the oaks watching us.

CHAPTER 04

Just like she'd promised, Bella sailed into the girl-infested swamp that is school gossip, in which sharper guys than me have vanished without trace and maybe you'd find their bones years later cast up on some shore, still with an air of surprise that they'd been crazy enough to stray there in the first place. Bella moved through it untroubled, gathering whispers of this and rumors of that, and she might have stooped, now and then, to something as ungainly as an ear to the ground, but I think she had people for that.

She came back the next day with nothing. No news, not a rumor, not a whisper. Lou grinned through an entire afternoon of calculus on the back of that.

'Ha!' he said at dinner. 'See? Not so easy after all.'

'But there can't be *nothing*!' said Bella. 'Believe me – there can't be. Nothing is strange. It's much stranger than something.' Her horn-rims flashed at me and I felt like saying sorry for denting her reputation.

I'd had enough by the end of dinner and as soon as it was dark outside I made for the kitchen. But this time I wasn't quick enough to get out before anyone could say, *Where the hell do you think you're going, Stais?* because someone said exactly that as I opened the door. Dr Williams. He stood in the pantry doorway with bread in one hand and a plate of corned beef in the other. 'Well?'

All the halfway decent excuses I could have made evaporated from my brain and I was left with, 'Out, sir.'

'I can see that.' He made himself a sandwich while I squirmed. 'You know we're in lockdown?'

'Yes, sir.'

'You know why we're in lockdown?'

I looked out the door. The dark smelled smoky and damp, and I could hear dead leaves rattling in the wind.

'Stais! Where were you going?'

I considered bolting, but if I did that I wouldn't get back, and I wasn't ready to go yet. I closed the door. 'Not far, sir. Just want some air.'

I waited for a pronouncement of punishment or expulsion or doom or something, but he just stood there, eating his sandwich and eyeing me. When he'd finished, he said, 'Come with me.'

He led me through the dorm, past talk and laughter

in common rooms and silence in study rooms. He nodded to the occasional teacher and told off the occasional loiterer, unlocked the staff-only door into the library and marched across its deserted ground floor with me trekking behind him. In the foyer the spotlit flag looked as though it was floating in the darkness. We arrived at last in the staff wing and he stopped at the infirmary.

'But, sir,' I said, 'I'm not sick. Can't I just have a detention and –'

'In.' The place smelled of disinfectant and liniment. He opened some glass-panelled doors leading into a walled garden about ten paces square. 'Air,' he said. 'Such as it is.' I went through and he closed the doors and went to work at his desk.

I blew out a long breath, looked back to check that he wasn't watching and thought about scaling the wall. But it was quiet in the garden and whatever was planted there made the air fresh and clean.

I lay on a bench and looked up at the dust of stars and space going on and on forever. We went there once. Humanity, I mean. Well, not there exactly: we got to the moon, and to Mars, but got lost on our way to Jupiter's moons. As the oil ran out at home and the water wars began, we crept back to ourselves, to our squabbles and our sicknesses and our dying planet – like we'd pulled a blanket over our heads and not looked up ever again. I lay there and watched it – the stars and the space between – and wondered what it would be like to go there. How quiet would it be? And how dark?

Around me I could hear the school settling. When the bell clanged for Silence, I got up, kissed the talisman round my neck for luck, and went inside to ask Dr Williams a question.

He was working at a desk in a pool of lamplight. 'Better?'

'Thanks, sir.'

'Good. I'll call Security to take you back.' He reached for the phone.

'Sir? Can I ask you something?'

'Go ahead.'

'Do you know why they didn't pick me?'

He put the phone down and studied me with his bedside-manner frown: his official version that was friendly but reminded you of your lowly student status. 'I can't talk to you about that,' he said. 'I'm sorry. If it's any help, I can tell you that you are as stable and sensible as any other senior student here – more than many, in fact.'

'I must have done something, sir. To not be picked.'

'Not in my book. But, as I say, I can't talk to you about that.'

'Will I have to leave?'

He looked down and tapped a pen on his papers. My heart sank through my boots. He said, 'I'm sorry, Nik. I really am. You don't have anyone to go home to, do you?'

I shook my head.

'Remind me.'

'My parents died in the uprising in '87.'

'Do you remember them?'

'My mother. A bit.' I shrugged to show I was past that now and I didn't need him coming over all sympathetic and nosy about it.

'You were very young when you came here, weren't you. I could look, if you like, to see if she left anything for you to have when you came to leave. Do you want me to?'

That floored me. It had never even crossed my mind. He smiled because I was standing there gaping at him, then he disappeared into his file room. He came back leafing through a folder but shaking his head. 'I'm sorry. There's just an enrollment application, and entry test results, which are...' he peered at the page, 'spectacular. No surprise there.'

I said, 'Can I see the enrollment application?'

He closed the folder. 'Why?'

'I have this memory of a woman who brought me here when I first started; not my mother, but she must have known my mother, and maybe my father. I don't know who she was, or anything about her except that her name was Frieda. I thought it might say, on the application, who she was. If I could find her, I might find out about my parents.'

'Do you remember your mother's name?'

'Eleanor.'

'And your father?'

I ducked my head.

'Do you know your father's name, Nik?'

Shook my head. I could feel him looking at me, thinking how pathetic is it to not even know your own father's name? And maybe that means your mother didn't know it either.

'Nikolai, perhaps?' he said.

The way he said it made me look up. He was watching me like he was thinking hard. This wasn't the official version of Dr Williams anymore.

'Sir?'

He tapped the folder on his desk, still thinking. 'I can't let you see school files, I'm afraid.' He turned away towards the file room, but he stopped in the doorway and looked back at me.

'Kelleran,' he said. 'Her name was Frieda Kelleran.'

When he came back from putting my file away, he was back to being his formal, teacherly self. He picked up the phone, called Security, said, 'I wish you well. I really do. I'm sorry I can't help,' and directed me out of the infirmary when the security guy showed.

I walked back to my dorm, thinking. I had now run out of obvious reasons for ISIS to cross me off their list. If Dr Williams knew any less obvious reasons, he wasn't telling me. But he had pointed me in a new direction.

Frieda Kelleran. Who was she and how hard could it be to find her?

When Tornmoor threw me out, I knew what I would do.

CHAPTER 05

In the dark, a blast blew the bones of the building apart.

The flash rammed light into closed eyes, punched glass from windows, broke beams and doorways like fingers.

The stomp of a giant boot shook skin from bone and eyes from sockets.

For a heartbeat, silence.

Then screaming.

Someone was yelling, 'GET OUT! GET OUT! GET OUT!' We fell out of bed and staggered about. Fires lit up broken windows and splintered glass; the voice kept shouting, 'GET OUT! GET OUT!' We grabbed jeans and sweatshirts and boots and stumbled towards the fire escape. 'GET OUT! GET OUT!'

I was yelling too. I dropped from the last steps of the

fire escape shouting Lou's name. People pushed past me, charging down the walkway between the dorm and the outside walls. No sign of Lou. We raced onto the lawn. Figures were weaving like drunks across the grass. The library was ablaze, flames roaring through its windows, but the dorm wing was still standing; people were struggling out of it, streams of people through the doors and down the fire escapes.

I left the chaos on the library lawn and went through the trees and across the driveway to the staff quarters. What I saw there stopped me dead.

The upper storey of the staff wing was gone. Huge chunks of masonry had crashed onto the lawns and lay half-buried, casting shadows in the firelight.

People weren't milling about here. They were standing and staring.

And waiting. For sirens to come tearing up the driveway, for the paramedics and the police and the army. We waited for them to come.

But no one came.

No one came.

After I don't know how long, I started to walk through the crowd gathered outside the staff wing. I was looking for Lou and Bella and Dash and Fyffe, but I reached the edge of the crowd without finding any of them. Then, because no one had come to say 'do this, do that, go here, go there' and no one was going to come from the staff quarters to say anything ever again, I picked my way through the rubble towards the infirmary garden where I'd been just a few hours before. Its walls lay smashed under pieces of fallen building.

I went through the garden and stood outside what was left of the infirmary. I was breathing hard but trying not to because the air was thick with burning and it made me gag. In the firelight, I could see shapes tangled in the demolished walls. People. Three people. I clambered over the wreckage towards them. They were bloody, their clothes burned black into their skin. The burning smell was them.

Dr Lewis. Sprawled on his back, his left arm half blown off, bones sticking out of it, and his face bloody all over.

Dr Stapleton. Frowning. As if this was one more thing he disapproved of.

And Dr Williams.

They were dead.

I knelt beside Dr Williams and shook his shoulder, lightly, just in case. His head lolled towards me, one eye wide and staring. The other side of his face was burnt through to charred bone and his whole left side was a mess of blood and burnt cloth. I thought, stupidly, this is how they look, people who die in war. They look like this.

I knelt there and knelt there and couldn't get up.

I don't know how long for.

Somewhere, far off, hammer blows beat the earth. Someone was talking in my ear. Telling me to stand up and get out, pulling me away.

Mace.

He hauled me to my feet and pushed me out into the smoking, noisy dark. He made me sit down, wiped the blood off my hands, and put his jacket round my shoulders.

Nearby, Jono was trying to stop Fyffe and Sol racing off to look for Lou. 'He'll find us. Don't worry.' He fished a flattened packet of cigarettes out of a pocket and handed them round, but I was shaking too much. Mace lit one for me. Sol sat down beside me, his face pale in the firelight. He looked at me with huge eyes and said, 'Will they get us?'

Fyffe took his hands in hers. 'Sol. They won't get us. I'm here, and Nik's here and Jono and Macey. And Lou will be here soon. We're going to be all right. Aren't we, Nik?'

'Sure,' I said. 'Sure, we are.' I put Mace's jacket round Sol's shoulders. Calming a terrified eight-year-old has its advantages: by the time Dash found us I'd almost stopped shaking.

'It looks like a coordinated attack across the city,' she said. 'But it's taken out communications, so we're guessing at this stage.' ISIS, she meant. She said 'we' like it was second nature to her already. 'Nik, they want to see you.' She put a hand on my arm. A whole hand – not smashed up or burned black with bones sticking through. 'Nik?' She brushed the hair out of my eyes. 'God, you're freezing. The ISIS agents want you. Come with me.'

I started to hand Sol over to Fyffe and stand up, but Mace said, 'Wait.' He stubbed his cigarette out on the grass. 'They say why?'

'No,' said Dash. 'Of course not.'

Mace lit another cigarette and watched me through the smoke. 'Did you wonder, maybe, why they didn't want him the first time?'

'Sure,' said Dash. 'But –'

'Anybody lost tonight from your new recruits?'

Dash looked at Jono. 'No. We were lucky.' She glanced up towards the smoking ruin that was the staff wing. Inside, I thought, if you go inside…they're all still there. The unlucky ones.

'They don't want him to make up numbers, then, do they,' said Mace.

Jono said, 'Say what you mean, Macey.'

'It's for Nik to say, not me. But I wouldn't be taking him to ISIS just now if I were you. Try this. Go and tell them he's lost, or gone or dead. See what they say.'

They all looked at me. I started to say, 'What are you talking about?' to Mace, but another explosion hammered the city down near the river and we all jumped. Sol leaned on my arm, breathing in little gasps.

Dash said, 'They must need extra recruits. That must be what it is.' She hurried away. The rest of us sat in that firelit dark under the smoke and the stars, with the clamor rolling on around us. I put an arm around Sol and he went to sleep on my shoulder. I needed to ask Mace what he meant, but I didn't want Jono listening in. At last Fyffe took him off to look for Lou, leaving Sol asleep with me.

I turned to Mace. 'What the hell?'

'Listen to me.' He was talking fast. 'You steer clear of ISIS. Don't talk to them. Don't let them find you.'

'Why? Is this about you teaching me some Breken?'

'Come and find me when all this is over –'

Dash was back.

Mace grabbed my shoulder and spoke in my ear. 'Find me!' Then he was gone.

Dash crouched in front of me. Her face was smoke-streaked. She took my free hand in hers. Her lips moved. 'Bella,' is what she said. Bella. She gripped my fingers hard. 'And Lou.'

Cold. So cold the breath stopped in my mouth, and the blood in my body. Dash's face blurred. She spoke again but my heart roared and I couldn't hear. I tried to say, 'Are you sure?' but no sound came out. I cleared my throat and tried again and she said, 'Yes. I'm sure.'

Sol's sleeping weight was heavy against my shoulder.

I said, 'Hey, buddy, wake up.' He opened groggy eyes and frowned at me. 'We have to move,' I said. 'We have to find Fyffe.'

Dash took him gently under the arms. 'Come on, kiddo, up you get.'

I climbed to my feet. Seemed to take forever to get there. 'Where?' I asked.

'I'll show you,' she said.

CHAPTER 06

Someone had laid Lou and Bella together. Which was right. On the grass at the far end of the library lawn, away from the building itself because the wall where the bay windows looked out on the lawn was blown out and part of the upper storey had collapsed. The wind from the flames blew bits of paper and ash into the darkness.

Fyffe was there, sobs wrenching her body. She reached out and enfolded Sol.

I looked down at Lou and Bella, still hoping there was some mistake. They were bloody and broken. Clothes burnt and shredded, hair matted with blood, faces... It was them, though. No way to pretend it wasn't.

I sat down beside Lou. 'Careful,' said Dash. 'There's glass everywhere.'

We stayed there. We didn't know what to do, who to go to for help. Nobody moved us on. Nobody noticed us. A security jeep arrived and parked in the driveway, orange lights flashing. And with it, two ambulances. Not enough, though. Not nearly enough. The line of people who were dead or injured stretched down the driveway, bleeding into the grass. People bent over them, wailing.

After I don't know how long – a long time maybe – someone touched my shoulder. Dash. 'I… I need to tell you…' She wiped her face with her sleeve, smearing tears and ash. 'When Macey sent me to tell the agents about you – before I saw Lou and Bella,' she reached out and touched Lou's hand like she was apologizing for not attending to him, 'I told the agents I'd found you, that you were looking after Sol. They got angry and said to go and bring you back to them. And do it straight away. *Without delay,* they said.' She sniffed back tears and cleared her throat. 'I don't know why. It makes no sense. Do you know why?'

Mace knew. Dr Williams knew – had known. I had to find Mace and quiz him about ISIS. I had to find that woman, Frieda, and ask her about my parents. But for now, all that could wait. I looked back to where I needed to be looking, which was at Lou and Bella.

Jono stirred. 'There must be something. Something you've done, something you know.'

'Christ, Jono,' I said. 'Like it matters now?'

Time passed. The ground shook – more explosions some-where away west. Dash stood up. 'We have to get Sol and Fy home. I'm going to ask permission to take them.' She put a hand on my head. 'Back soon.'

Fyffe had exhausted her weeping and knelt beside me, with her arm around Sol, now and then reaching out to touch Lou. Tears came and went.

I stayed. Like standing guard. In case Lou suddenly sat up, winked at Fy and said, *Ha! Joke's over.* It's his kind of thing. Scare the hell out of you and come out laughing at the end of it: *Your face! Shoulda seen your face!*

To which the standard response was *Jesus, Lou. Grow up.*

'Mr Stais.' I looked up. The ISIS woman. The one who'd been training the recruits. 'Friends of yours?' she asked.

I nodded.

'I'm so sorry. It's a terrible thing.' She put a hand on my shoulder and I shivered. 'Can I talk with you, please.' Not a question.

I nodded again.

'Now,' she said.

I touched Lou's arm and whispered, 'Gotta go.'

She took me down the driveway, away from the chaos. Two soldiers stood guard at the school gates, guns slung over their shoulders. The woman knocked on the door of the gatehouse. It opened and a fierce white light spilled out. 'Stais,' she said to the man inside – her ISIS partner. She pushed me through the door.

The man said, 'Turn out your pockets,' and he searched me. He found a few coins, an ID card, a phone – not working now – all of which he pocketed, but no guns, knives, grenades or anything else that he might have been looking for. He pointed me into a chair and I sat, staring at the floor, feeling sick in the too-bright glare.

'You're Nikolai Stais.' Calm, flat, like he was ticking off the school roll.

I nodded.

'Where were you tonight after supper?'

Tonight. Supper. Dr Williams.

'Nikolai? Where were you?'

'I was… I was in the infirmary garden.'

'Why were you there?'

'I needed to get out. Dr Williams –'

'Dr Williams?'

God. Dr Williams. I sucked in a breath. 'He let me sit in the garden.' I squinted up at the agent. He was dressed as he had been on Victory Day, in black, still neat as a bullet waiting to fire. 'I don't understand,' I said. At the back of my mind Mace's alarm bells were ringing louder by the minute. *Don't talk to ISIS.*

'What don't you understand?'

The world swam. I dug the heels of my hands into

my eyes and pushed my fingers through my hair. They came away black and gritty. 'I don't understand what you want.'

'What do you mean you needed to get out?'

'Just – for some air. Some space. You know.'

'I see. And Dr Williams will confirm this?'

I looked up at him. He looked back, waiting.

'Dr Williams is dead,' I said.

His eyebrows rose a fraction. 'How do you know?'

'I saw him. In the infirmary, with Dr Stapleton and Dr Lewis.' I gripped my hands together to stop them shaking.

'You went to the staff wing. Why?'

'I don't know. Everyone was… there was chaos, and I'd just been there, and… I don't know. To see if Dr Williams was all right, I guess.'

'Did Dr Williams talk to you when you sat in his garden earlier?'

'No. I mean, not really, just hello and good-bye.' I was lying to an ISIS agent. I could feel the sweat creep on my scalp. 'He let me sit in the garden and then he sent me back to the dorm.'

Silence. My heart thumped.

He changed tack. 'Nikolai, this carnage had inside help.'

'You don't mean Dr Williams?'

I think he almost smiled. 'No. Dr Williams, God

rest his soul, does not interest us.' He folded his arms and studied me with polite blankness. 'You, however, do.'

'Why?'

'Your name, Nikolai Stais.'

Not what I was expecting but I'd got tired of saying *I don't understand,* so I just sat and looked at him.

'Why did you keep it?' he said.

'Why did I keep my *name*? *My name*?'

'Just answer the question.'

'I don't understand the question.' I tried changing tack myself. 'Am I supposed to come up with something clever here? And then you recruit me because I've passed some kind of test? I don't have a clever answer for my name. So I fail your test. Can I go now? My friend is lying out there on the grass and he's dead. Do you get that? He's dead. And I can't do a thing to change that. So right now I don't give a… I don't care about my name, or your tests or whatever the hell else you're doing. I want to go back to him and sit with him and make sure they do right by him.' I stood up.

'Sit down.'

'No. I –'

He hit me – one sharp punch that pushed me back in the chair with my head on my knees, gasping.

'You will sit when I tell you to sit. And stand when I tell you to stand. Is that clear?'

I nodded, still too winded to say shit. And scared.

'Now,' he said. 'You will tell me everything you did tonight. Minute by minute.'

This was a minefield; I had no idea what would blow up in my face. He picked up the talisman round my neck and turned it to catch the light. I grabbed at it and he jerked it away from me, snapping the chain.

'Hey!' I dived after it but he stepped to one side and kneed me in the gut. I hit the floor. Someone knocked on the door while I lay there retching. I heard the agent open it and hold a murmured conversation, then his battle boots disappeared outside. The lock clicked. When I could move, I crept to the window and peered out. He was striding up the driveway with one of the soldiers who'd been guarding the gate. The other one stood at the gatehouse door.

I made myself breathe. Tried to think. My name. What didn't they like about my name? I had to find Mace, and Frieda Kelleran, and ask them about my parents. But the immediate question was, should I wait for the agent to come back so I could get my talisman, or should I get out while I could? I knew the right answer. That didn't make it any easier.

I crawled into the tiny back room of the gatehouse where Mace used to make me hot cocoa when I came to sit with him on winter afternoons. The guards fought off boredom by letting us sneak in and out – those of us prepared to pass the time of day with them. They'd made a trapdoor for us at the back of a cupboard, behind the cocoa and sugar and tea bags.

I hadn't been through it in years and maybe it wasn't still there. I took the shelf out and felt for the latch. The door opened easily. At the back of my mind, busy with getting out of there, came a thought that turned the sweat cold on my skin. The guards had played at those visits like a game, a prank for us to feel like we were fooling our teachers. But suppose you wanted to let someone slip into the grounds without going through the ID scan at the gate? Anyone could come and go at will through this little door. Anyone at all. Inside help, the man had said. From who?

I squeezed through, tumbled into the bushes outside and lay still, listening, wondering what to do next.

CHAPTER 07

Choices. I had some, and none of them looked inviting.

I could find the ISIS agents, and say 'Hey, give me back my talisman and I'll show you a secret door in the gatehouse.' And from what I'd seen already, how likely was it that they'd pat me on the back and induct me straight into their inner core? Yeah, very.

But running… escaping through this door was as close as I could think to standing on the rooftops, waving my arms and shouting 'Guilty!' of whatever it was they were accusing me of doing. I leaned inside and put back the shelf with the cocoa and sugar and tea bags best I could and closed the doors on both sides. Then I crept to the corner of the gatehouse and peered out. People were wandering about, still with a dazed how-can-this-be-happening look, but they were walking now, not running; the school was still burning, but not fiercely. The sun was rising red through the smoke.

I crouched there, searching the grounds for the ISIS agent, then I saw Sol. Someone had gathered the little kids together under a tree by the outer walls, away from the action. The school nurse was checking they were all right.

I watched them a while. Sol just stood there, pale-faced, and every now and then he'd do this little jitterbug, hopping up and down, and looking around. Just like you'd do if you were eight years old and your big sister had told you to stay put until she came back, and you were desperate for her to come and terrified that she might not.

I crept around the walls and crouched in the garden behind him. When the nurse was busy calming a hysterical kid, I whispered, 'Hey, buddy.'

'Nik!'

'Shh. Where are the others?'

'Looking for you!'

'Did Dash get permission to take you home?'

'Uh-huh. That's why they've gone to look for you. We're going to Ron David's place. And we can go from there to home.' He smiled a wan smile, pleased with himself for remembering.

'Ron David? Who's that?'

'I don't know. We're gonna meet up and the people there'll take us home. Dash said.'

It took a moment for the lights to go on. A rendezvous. Okay. We'd had drills for this, in case everything went haywire. The nearest rendezvous was the church at St John's Square.

'That's a good plan,' I said. 'Have you seen Macey?'

'No. Jono's looking for him too.'

'Jono? Why?'

He shrugged. But I could guess. Now that the immediate panic was over, the ISIS agents would be rounding up Southsiders, and maybe people who associated with Southsiders as well.

'Listen,' I said, 'When the others come back –'

'Aren't you gonna wait?'

'No. I've got something to do first. When they come back can you tell them I've gone ahead and will meet you at the rendezvous?'

'Sure.'

I wanted to find Mace, and I wanted to go back to Lou and Bella to say goodbye. But Mace had vanished, and Lou and Bella had been taken away. In the end all I managed was getting out without being seen. It didn't feel right, just to go like that. I knew Lou would understand. But it didn't feel right.

There's this blind skiddy in St John's Square. He used to sit on the steps of the church, or on benches, or in doorways, rattling his cup, humming to himself, always being moved on, always coming back. We called him Lev, because he was forever quoting Leviticus at us: *thou shalt* and *shalt not* do all kinds of weird stuff. Verse after verse of what to eat, what to wear, who not to have sex with.

It must've been noon by the time I came to the square, and when I arrived Lev was the first person I saw. In fact, I fell over him. He was wrapped up in his big old coat, and propped beside the rubbish bins on the corner of Skinners Lane and the square, legs sticking out. Which is how I came to fall over him, because I was all eyes for the church across the square to see what the action was at the rendezvous point.

I'd taken a roundabout way there, partly to pull myself together and partly because I wanted to come at the place sideways in case ISIS was waiting – though I hoped they had more important things to worry about by now than a runaway school kid with a name they didn't like.

That run through the streets made me wish I had eyes in the back of my head. The city was suddenly a ghost town. I ran through Sentian, in the shadow of Watch Hill. Its alleyways were deserted. A pall of smoke lay over the Hill, as though it had a storm cloud all its own. The bakers' shelves on Bridge Street were empty and the tiny cafes were locked and dark; around the corner, the window of the antique jewelry shop was smashed and its alarm sirened into the morning. All the banks were battened down, but their security guards were nowhere. Twice I heard glass shattering a few streets over – whether looters or hostiles, I didn't know. Either way, I didn't want to meet them.

I could imagine them though – hostiles going house to house through riverside homes and shops. Maybe they'd got further into the city by now, and maybe the streets were empty because the casualty count was high: people shot or their throats cut, or bound up inside their homes ready to be trafficked over the river.

By the time I got to Skinners Lane and tripped over old Lev I was pretty freaked out and I was glad to see a familiar face. I picked myself up and crouched down to say sorry. The words dried up in my mouth.

Lev was dead.

I don't even know how – caught by a flying piece of building in the night maybe, or knocked about by looters or hostiles, or trampled by people escaping north, or he might've just keeled over with a heart attack. But, the thing is, no one had noticed. It was the middle of the day, and no one had noticed a dead guy propped up on the edge of the square.

That's when I let myself hear what I'd been thinking all morning. No one is coming. No troops in their jeeps. No police. No emergency services. No one.

CHAPTER 08

St John's was teeming with people, all of them arguing. They crowded the steps and the wide-open doors, eyeing me as I went through. Inside they'd reorganized pews and occupied side chapels; piles of belongings were strewn everywhere. Downstairs in the crypt, I found Dash with Fy and Sol, and, unfortunately, Jono.

Dash stormed over to me as I came down the stairs. *'Where have you been? We thought they'd got you.'* She grabbed me in an almighty hug and I figured I was forgiven, temporarily anyway. Jono and Fy were sitting together on a bench. Fy looked exhausted. Sol was roaming around the crypt. He arrived at my elbow and said, 'Hi, Nik. Did you find Macey?'

Jono looked up. 'Macey? Why were you looking for him?'

What would I have given to have Lou there instead

of Jono? Anything at all, that's what. 'No reason,' I said. 'Just to say good-bye.'

'Is that so? How friendly of you.'

'What does that mean?'

'Nothing. Just you and your secret squirrel ways. Anything you'd like to tell us?'

'Sure. I know where there's a secret lunch stash with bread and cheese and pickles...'

Sol's eyes lit up. 'You do?'

'No. Sorry. Kidding.'

'But I'm starving.'

Dash put an arm around him. 'Me too. If these guys can just lay down their weapons for a minute, we might be able to think about food and how to get it. What d'you say?'

'Yeah,' I said. 'Good idea.'

But Jono pushed on. 'Did you find out what ISIS wanted you for?'

'Nope. Do you want lunch or what?'

He gave me a narrow stare then turned to Dash. 'What can I do?'

Dash had become team captain, which was fine by me. She was easily the best at it.

'We'll go and look,' she said. 'You and me and Nik. Fy, you stay here with Sol.'

Sol grabbed my arm. 'No! I'm going with Nik.'

He was wound up tight as a top. I could feel him

trembling. I looked at Fy. She was sitting on the edge of a bench staring through us. I said, 'You know, I think I'll stay. You ISIS-types don't need me.'

Jono turned for the stairs, muttering, 'That's for real. C'mon, I'm tired of doing childcare.' Dash looked from Fy to Sol, said, 'Yes, that makes sense,' and followed Jono up the stairs.

'Dash?' I called after her. 'Careful, yeah?' She gave me the thumbs up, and was gone.

We found some blankets and cushions in the minister's room at the back of the crypt and made a pile of bedding under an icon that glowed gold and blood-red in the dusty light that spilled down the stairs. The blankets were coarse and hairy and the cushions were hard but better than nothing on the flagstone floor. I played number games with Sol. Fy watched us and after a while she started to sing under her breath. Sol curled up and went to sleep.

I went upstairs then, to look about. It was chaotic. Some people had come because their homes were damaged, but mainly the place was full of people who were too afraid to go home in case more mayhem hit. They'd dug in to wait for help to arrive, and the way they did that was to have endless meetings, mainly entitled (as far as I could hear) 'Who Should Be In Charge Here?' and 'Why Hasn't the Army Arrived Yet?' I told one or two people about old Lev, and said shouldn't we move him because even beggars deserved some respect and anyway, the dogs would be out tonight and did they want him chewed on, and bits of him dragged around the square? I didn't actually say that last part, but I hoped their imaginations would get to work on the problem. That prompted yet another meeting.

Mid-afternoon, Jono and Dash got back. They'd scored three sticks of day-old bread, a jar of meat paste, some tins of corn, and four bottles of water. Also a lot of stories about hostiles rampaging across St Clare and Sentinel. 'Word is,' Dash said, 'they've taken the riverside between Torrens Hill and Moldam North. Someone said they've got Watch Hill and the Central Comms building, but that can't be right. I'd say they've taken some pockets here and there along the riverbank and that's it. They must know they can't win. They'll be back over the bridges by morning with the gates locked behind them. Count on it.'

Around sundown, the minister of St John's, who was looking very hassled and beleaguered by now, took Jono and me across the square with some sheeting and we hauled Lev back into the churchyard. The minister said that when the Services arrived Lev would be dealt with properly, and in the meantime did we want to say a few prayers for the old guy?

We said okay, and we all went back into the crypt and lit a couple of candles on the small altar there and sat on the benches. Jono said some words, and then Fyffe said some better ones, tears streaming down her face.

Because, of course, Lev wasn't the only dead person we were thinking of. Dash nudged me to say something, but I shook my head. The lump was too big in my throat and, anyway, I couldn't see the plan or the reason behind this one at all. Lev – well, maybe Lev's time had come, I don't know. But for the rest... as far as I could tell it was a futile, stupid, meaningless waste. And that's all it was.

The minister said we could sleep down there if we wanted though it wasn't exactly the Ritz, and we said that's okay, we were too tired to notice. When the lights went off for black-out we left the candles burning. I sat with Sol and played a memory game with him until he went to sleep. Then Dash said to me, 'Where did you go? This morning. You scared me, disappearing like that.'

'I wanted to look around, see what was happening.'

'Why not come with us?'

'Tell you later.'

She was silent then, which was a bad sign, but the truth is, I didn't want to tell her about my encounter with her ISIS buddies. I lay down and watched the candlelight flicker across the ceiling and thought about Lou and Bella, and Dr Williams. I heard Fyffe crying, muffled against Jono's shoulder, and I guess I cried too.

I thought about the people who'd done this. The Breken on Southside – also known as Soulside and Suicide on account of what happened to city folk who strayed over there. Southsiders, Shantysiders, Shadowsiders – they had lots of names, most of them unrepeatable.

What did we know about them? They were barbaric, we knew that – they kidnapped children for spare parts and fed aid workers to the river. They'd started coming here from Oversea, and from out of the Dry, four, maybe five, generations ago, and by all accounts they were still coming. They were running from their own wars, and from lands made unliveable by the breaching of the mega-dams in the South, the power-station meltdowns in the East, and everywhere, the desert, the spreading Dry. They wanted our land and our water and they'd take whatever else they could. In the early days they'd overrun the whole south side of the city and only ISIS and our troops prevented them from teeming over the bridges and taking the north as well. The vids from the unmanned drones that ISIS put in the air showed us two cities now: ours – the real city – and its shadow, a crowded, dark, derelict place where savage twins of each one of us watched over the river and made plans to replace us.

Over the years, quiet times had come, both sides drawing breath, but then the fighting would surge again as our troops went over to try to establish some order, or the Breken regrouped for an assault on one of the bridges.

But they'd never taken a bridge. They'd never crossed the river in numbers.

Until now.

CHAPTER 09

Help did arrive, but it took three days, and consisted of a single harassed-looking officer from Information Services on foot with a message. The message was this: Things will soon be under control. Could people please go home, or if they had friends in the north, now might be a good time to visit. Thank you and God bless you all. And now, he had a list of rendezvous centers to visit, so please could he just get on with it?

In the uproar that followed, a woman at the back called out what everyone was thinking: Wasn't the Breken strategy to rip out the center – Watch Hill and the core of the major services – scare the population north, and walk on in? After all, comms were down, and we hadn't seen anyone from the army, police or emergency services for three days. So wasn't this message an admission of defeat?

The yelling went on for some time after that, but

the officer was ready for it: Did this woman not understand that the Breken were a rabble with no chance against our own superb fighting machine? Did she not have confidence in the General? And would she like to give her name, because a reply from the General could certainly be arranged.

That shut everyone up. The man gathered up his case, slapped on his Services cap and stalked out. Then people went crazy. Dash led us back to the crypt where we held a council of war. We decided to find our own way north to deliver Sol and Fyffe home to Ettyn Hills, then Dash and Jono were coming back to be what help they could. They were still ISIS cadets, after all, and proud of it. And me? First things first, I said. Let's get out of the city.

But how were we gonna do that? The trains weren't running. Dash could drive and so could Jono but what were the chances of just happening on a car? Slim to nonexistent, or so we thought. But then we came to Fettlers Lane and the beetle. And that seemed to convince Fyffe and Jono that God was On Our Side. Which, if true, would've been helpful four days before, but there didn't seem much point in saying so.

So that's how we came to be driving up Fettlers Lane in a broken down taxi-cab looking for a road north.

What we found was a roadblock. A barricade of old furniture had been thrown across Drummond St, and five people stood in front of it. Three men, two women. They had assault rifles slung over their shoulders, and faded red bandanas over their faces. Breken.

Dash gripped the wheel. 'O God… ogod, ogod, ogod… I could run them down. I will – will I? *WILL I?*' But the beetle had zero acceleration and the rest of us were yelling, 'They've got guns!' She braked.

A boy – dark like me, and maybe my age – came towards us and peered at Dash. Lucky for us, we could've been theirs. We looked like looters. We were ragged and filthy. I could pass for a southerner and the others were fair enough for easterners. The boy shouted over his shoulder at his band, and then let loose at us with a stream of Breken. Beside me, Dash stared straight ahead, her eyes on the hostiles and maybe her thoughts on how easily she could gun the engine and do them damage. Sol leaned over my shoulder to get a better look. Fyffe pulled him back.

I looked at Sol and put a finger on my lips. Then I leaned out the empty doorway on my side and stood up so the Breken boy would have to look at me over the top of the cab and not at the others inside. He spoke again, another stream of Breken. I sent up a silent prayer to my mother and to Lou and to whoever else might listen, and answered him, in Breken. He didn't even blink, just carried on. 'What're you doing here?'

'Looking round,' I said. 'Why not?'

'Because you're not front line, are you? Just scaven-gers, yeah? What's your bridge?'

I tried, 'St Clare,' the closest one to school, and he seemed to buy it.

'Found anything?'

'Just this,' I slapped the beetle's roof, amazed and relieved that this was working.

He shook his head. 'You should never have been let through. You better get back by dark or we might mistake you for them.'

Then, miraculously, he waved us away. Dash reversed down the street at speed, and took the first corner she could find. She pulled up outside a smashed-up cinema with red curtains waving through broken glass doors. Somewhere nearby a kid was wailing, or maybe it was a cat, but the street was deserted.

Dash leaned on the steering wheel. Nobody spoke. Then she hit the wheel with the palms of her hands and looked daggers at me. 'How? How did you do that?'

Sol started to whimper. Fyffe hushed him and said, 'Macey taught you, I guess?'

'Was it Macey?' said Dash.

'Course it was,' I said. 'Who d'you think?'

'Why did he?'

'Why? He's from over the river. It's his language. So what?'

Jono chimed in helpfully from the back seat. 'So,

everything. Jeez. For all we know you're one of them. A plant. A sleeper!'

'Shut up, Jono,' said Dash.

'Hey!' he said. 'I'm not hanging round with any Breken-speaking –'

'Stop!' said Fyffe.

'Any Breken-speaking what?' I said.

'No, *stop*!' Fyffe took Jono's hand. 'We're in trouble here – and maybe Nik is the answer to our prayers. I mean, we prayed to be looked after, didn't we, and here's Nik, able to get us through.'

'You never told me,' said Dash, still boring holes with her eyeballs.

'What's to tell? I speak some Breken because Mace does, and he practically brought me up. You maybe noticed that it's not the most popular language in school, so I guess I didn't speak it aloud. All right?'

No. Not all right.

'What else haven't you told me?'

'Dash…'

'What else?'

'Nothing! Dammit!'

'What about ISIS?' said Jono. 'They must know. That must be why –'

'Listen,' I said to Dash. 'We're taking Sol and Fyffe home, remember? Can we try and do that? Because, I'm just guessing here, but it might not be as easy as we thought.'

She looked straight ahead out the windscreen and didn't speak. I rubbed my hands over my face and stared out the window too. Rubbish gusted across the wreckage of shopfronts and the sky was lowering to gray; maybe it would rain soon.

'Nik?' Sol.

'Yeah, buddy?'

'Can we go home now?'

'Yep. Just as soon as we sort something out.'

'Okay…When?'

I looked at Dash.

'You should have told me,' she said. She gunned the engine and we took off.

We met more roadblocks through the afternoon. And the same story at every one: men, sometimes women, with guns and questions.

'What do they say?' asked Dash after we'd been waved away by another one.

'Nothing much. They ask what we're doing.'

'And what do you say back?'

'I tell them we're scavenging, exploring, that kind of thing.'

'I don't get it. They always wave us east, never north. I thought they wanted to scare us north and leave the city to them.'

Jono stirred. 'Hey, yeah. That's right. We've been

going east all this time. Can't you ask your *brethren* to let us through?'

In a fight with Jono, I'd be the one surfacing with fewer teeth than I took in and fewer bones in working order, but there's times, I swear, there's times it'd be worth it, just to see how far I could get. I bit my tongue and shut up.

But Dash pulled the beetle chugging to the gutter. 'It's true, Nik. We're in Moldam North already. We're gonna end up at Port at this rate.'

'There must be a way through,' said Jono. 'They can't be holding the whole bank – that'd mean they had all the bridges. No way could they have all the bridges. They'd need firepower and organization way beyond what they've got.'

'We don't know what they've got,' I said.

'You might,' said Jono.

'Jono,' said Dash. 'Leave it!'

I said, 'If they're so disorganized, how in the hell are their roadblocks so well armed? And where the hell is our freakin' army?'

'Go and ask them,' said Dash.

'Yeah,' I said. 'Sure.'

'I'm not kidding. We need to go north and we're not going north. I don't know how much longer this fuel cell will hold up. You can talk to them – you could be one of them. Go, ask.'

'I'm not one of them!'

'Okay, okay, but you could be. If the cell gives out while we're still here, we're stuck. We could be there by tomorrow night if we can just get through. Ask them how far they've got, that's all.'

'Got my vote,' said Jono.

Fyffe stopped praying in that whispering way of hers and said, 'We'll make it. I know we will.'

Silence from everyone. I listened to my heart hammering.

Dash said, 'I'll keep the engine running – if they sense you're a city kid just take off back here and we'll run for it.'

'Dash, if they sense I'm a city kid, they'll shoot me.'

Jono said, 'Scared, are we?'

'Jono –' said Dash.

I got out of the car and looked back at their faces – wide eyed and pale under the dirt. I must've looked as bad. 'Yeah,' I said to Jono. 'I think we are.' I looked at Sol. 'Back soon.'

'No,' he said. 'Don't go.'

I went to look for a roadblock.

CHAPTER 10

I headed back to the corner we'd just come around and stopped in the doorway of a tiny shop that a week ago had been a friendly little lunch bar. A whitewash scrawl on its broken window announced cheese rolls and meat pasties, which, in different circumstances, might have depressed me – we hadn't eaten anything for a whole day. A street sign on the wall said Moldam Road. Behind me, the road ran down to the river through terraced houses hung with signs about rooms to rent, money to lend, old gear to buy and sell. A couch, a table and chairs, and a flatscreen sat on the pavement outside one of them, and I wondered whether that was looters busy looting, or some brave soul thinking, why should business stop for war? In the distance Moldam Bridge, the Mol, arched against the afternoon sky.

Ahead of me the road climbed a hill through more

of the same. About twenty houses up was the roadblock we'd just been turned back from – four people were sitting on the pavement smoking. They were Breken, and they had guns.

Taking armed hostiles by surprise seemed like a bad idea so I walked into the middle of the road. Of course, walking up a hill with hostiles training guns on you isn't such a great idea either. I made myself put one foot in front of the other while my brain was spinning in panic about how was I going to ask anything without them thinking there was something odd about this scruffy kid – like, why does he look so terrified and why is his Breken so bad?

They watched me climb. One of the men stood up, but the others just kept on smoking and talking. I was hoping one of them would come down towards me, so I wouldn't have to deal with the pack, but they waited until I'd almost arrived, then the one on his feet motioned me over.

I was still wearing what I'd hauled on in the dark on Tuesday night: sweatshirt, jeans, and boots, all stinking of smoke, thick with dust, and ragged from the rubble of smashed-up buildings I'd crawled through looking for food. Dried blood too – Lou's blood, and Dr Williams'. The Breken man, on the other hand, looked clean and deadly. He was a southerner – dark, and head to foot in dark clothes, with the assault rifle slung on his shoulder like it was part of him, a cherished part at that.

He was years older than the others and looked like he knew how to be in charge. He said, 'Where are you going? And where's the car you were in?'

I looked out east across Morstone Flats, mainly so I didn't have to look at any of them, and nodded towards the sea. 'They sent me to ask – how far is it safe to go? Can we get to the sea?'

He was watching me, narrow and suspicious. 'How old are you?'

Not a direction the conversation was supposed to take. The others stopped talking to watch. 'Seventeen.'

'Why aren't you in a squad?'

What the hell was a squad? Assorted answers sprang to mind: no squad would have me; my mother wouldn't let me; I'm on leave from one. I settled for the shrug. Not surprisingly, he wasn't happy with that.

'What's your bridge?'

Worse and worse. I said, 'St Clare,' hoping I'd get the same reaction as at the first roadblock.

But he raised an eyebrow. 'St Clare? That so? Why do you sound like you're fresh out of the Gilgate sewers then?' The rest of them laughed.

That would be because Mace, who I talked this barbaric bloody language with, came from the Breken township at Gilgate, which I couldn't exactly say, so I pulled out the shrug again. He said, 'Which is it, then?

'Gilgate,' I said.

'Thought so. You should be in a squad –'

A crack of rifle-fire sent everyone diving. My inter-rogator moved so fast I didn't see how he did it – I had barely hit the ground and he was sending off a barrage of shots and yelling instructions to his band. Two of them ran towards the houses under his covering fire. The other one, a woman, lay on the street in a spreading pool of blood.

I took off.

Down the street, round the corner, fast, with the gunfire close and loud. I skidded to a halt by the beetle and swung inside, yelling at Dash to *get moving – get moving now!*

It was empty.

The beetle was empty.

They weren't in it, they weren't under it. They were nowhere. I stared up the street. Maybe they'd heard the gunfire and run for cover. Maybe Jono had convinced them to leave me behind.

The firefight in Moldam Road stopped as suddenly as it had started. Up ahead I saw a figure in an army uniform running across the street. If that was the sniper, the Breken would be close on his heels. I watched for a while, but none of them appeared, so I headed after him, shaky with relief. We'd found the army at last.

CHAPTER 11

They were down an alleyway among overflowing bins of stinking rubbish – Dash, Fyffe and Jono, and two soldiers. One of the men swung his gun up at me and I skidded to a halt, but Fyffe called out, 'No! No! He's ours!' She came running and grabbed my arms.

'They took him! They took Sol!'

I was looking over her head at the others and saying, 'Where's Sol?' when I realized what she'd said. It punched the breath out of me and everything went slow and distant: the soldier kicking through the rubbish; the other one pacing at the far end of the alleyway, gun at the ready; Dash sitting propped up against a wall, pale as sin and Jono next to her with his head on his knees.

I looked down at Fyffe's dirty, tear-streaked face. She had a graze swelling purple and bloody on her forehead. She tightened her grip on my arm. 'The Breken took Sol.

Jono hit one of them but they hit him with a gun and they stomped on Dash's leg and knocked me down and they took… they took Sol and we have to go after them.'

'Ah!' The man in the rubbish waved a stick of wood. 'Splint.' He knelt beside Dash who was breathing real deep and shaky. The man took out a knife and started to cut through her jeans at the knee. 'Hold on to something, this is going to hurt.'

'Wait!' said Dash. 'I have to talk to Nik.'

Jono looked up, seriously groggy, groaned, and put his head back on his knees.

The other soldier, much older, came back down the alley. 'Lucky for you we were around.'

I was struggling to get a grip. 'You're the army. We can – can't we go after them? We can get reinforcements and go looking. Where are the others?' I looked around, half expecting a combat team to leap into existence, weapons at the ready.

'The others?'

'The rest of the army,' I said.

'What army would that be, son? If you mean the great and glorious Army of the People, the Righteous Army, the Army of God and the General – or should that be the General and God? – well now, that army's broken, isn't it? Split clean open last summer. Half of 'em scarpered up north, or Oversea, even over the fucking river. And the other half – here's the joke – the other half was sent to bring 'em back. And that left a skeleton crew,' he bowed, 'to hold the line here. So what happens? The South gets wind of this, and takes its chance. And here we are. Screwed.'

'But, no, but, the General…' I stammered.

'Dead. In the mutiny. Don't go pinning your hopes on any General. This place is finished. By month's end it'll be running with hostiles.'

'No! This makes no sense. What about ISIS?'

'ISIS? They're not gonna help the likes of us. No way. We're on our own.' He patted his gun. 'We're gonna have a Breken-hunt before we head north.'

'Nik!' Dash was staring at me hard. 'You have to go after Sol.'

The older man shook his head. 'You'd be a fool to do that. A dead one.'

I looked at Dash. 'What about you?'

The guy waiting to splint her leg said, 'We can look after them.'

Dash looked at me, bleary-eyed. 'You have to –'

'Yes,' I said. 'Course. I'll… Jesus.' I looked up at the older man. 'They'll have gone back over Mol Bridge, yeah?'

'I'd say.'

Jono stirred again. 'I'm coming.'

'No,' I said. 'You're not.'

The one with the splint shook his head. 'You're crazy.

If they catch you, d'you know what they do to people, our kind, over there?'

Not what I needed to hear. 'Where will you take these three?'

He squinted up at me and shook his head again. 'If you're going over there, I'm not telling you.'

'Why?'

'Aren't you listening? This place is going to be overrun. I don't want hostiles dragging information out of you about where we are.'

Great. That boded well for my future. I crouched by Dash and kissed her. 'I'll find Sol. And then I'll find you. I promise.'

I stood up. So did Fyffe. She was shaky on her feet, and tears shone on her cheeks. She wiped her face with her sleeve, then fished a dirty yellow scarf out of her bag and tied it round her head, tucking her hair into it and covering the bruise on her forehead. She pulled on Jono's big denim jacket, which made her look tiny. 'What are you doing?' I asked.

'Going with you.'

Over the general outcry I said, 'No way are you coming with me. No. Way.'

'He's *my* brother! Don't argue. Anyway, you don't know what they look like, the ones that took him.'

'So tell me.'

'Not the same.'

'Fyffe. Look at you – you won't last two minutes over there.'

'We don't have time to argue. I'm not afraid.' She grasped the little cross that hung round her neck. 'If I can't go with you, Nik, I'll go alone.' She looked at Dash and Jono and said, 'We'll be back, with Sol.' She marched off down the alleyway. I followed, protesting.

We weren't what you'd call well prepared for a foray into enemy territory. We had no weapons, no protective gear, no food, no water, and we were dead on our feet. Also, we had no idea where they'd gone, except Over The Bridge.

We sat on some steps in the doorway of one of the old terrace houses right on the riverbank and watched the foot traffic on Moldam Bridge. We told ourselves we were planning, waiting for nightfall, but we didn't have much to plan. I guess we were taking a deep breath.

Away west the sun was setting, but that was in a different country where life went on like it was meant to. Sunlight gleamed gold on the arch of the Mol but under that, the night rose up from the river. Bands of armed Breken were crossing back and forth, and alongside them rag-tag crowds came and went, like crossing the bridge was the most normal thing in the world. Like killing Lou and Bella and Dr Williams was normal too. And kidnapping Sol. All in a day's war.

I had tried and tried to convince Fyffe to go back.

Nothing doing. Now we sat there, argument exhausted, and watched the bridge. Fyffe took my hand. 'Remember that rhyme?'

'Yeah, I do.'

She chanted softly:

Over the Bridge, it's dark not day
Over the Bridge, the devils play
Over the Bridge their souls are BLACK
Go over the Bridge and you won't come BACK.

I thought of Fyffe and Lou and me, hunting each other through the sunlit upstairs hallways and rooms of the Hendry mansion. But the game always came to an end, usually with their smiling mother calling us downstairs to new-baked bread and honey, or biscuits and glasses of milk.

Fyffe peered at me. 'Are you scared?'

'Of course I'm scared. Aren't you? I wish you'd go back. You don't speak Breken – how are you going to get by?'

'I speak enough.'

'Since when?'

'Since a long time back.' She bent her head and studied her hand in mine, white against brown. 'How do you think I talked to the servants? Besides, you do. You speak it well.' She looked up at me. 'You kept that quiet.'

'Yeah, I did. Because, you know, I thought playing the "brown and Breken" card at school would be unfair. I mean, everyone wants to be mistaken for one of the barbarians at the gate, right?'

'Ouch. I'm sorry. Why should it bug you? It saved our lives today. Just because Jono baits you doesn't mean you have to bite.'

'I wish you'd go back.'

'I'm not going back. You'll look far less threatening to people if you've got a girl. And,' as if this was the clincher, 'Lou would've gone with you.'

'Is that what you're doing? Standing in for Lou? You're not Lou, Fy. What about your parents? Maybe they don't even know about him yet. Shouldn't you go home and tell them?'

'I can't get home, though, can I? And even if I could, how could I tell them we've lost Sol as well?' She wiped her eyes with the end of her scarf, took a breath and studied the activity on the bridge. 'Look down there, something's happening. Come on, they might be closing it for the night. We better go.'

So it was Fyffe who dragged me to my feet, then stood with her arms outstretched to the city behind us, saying good-bye to the day, and to the world we knew. Then she took my hand and we went together.

Over the bridge.

CHAPTER 12

Fyffe and I walked through the Cityside gate of
the Mol, trying to look like we belonged: two scavengers
heading home for the night. A man guarding the gate
stepped in front of us. 'Hold it! What did you find over
there? Come on, cough up!'

I nodded back towards the roadblock up Moldam
Road. 'Nothing we were allowed to keep.'

Every time I opened my mouth I expected someone
to yell 'Look! A Citysider!' but he just laughed. 'Doesn't
like scavengers, the Commander. On your way, then.'

So we went on, not what you'd call keen, but awed all
the same by the scale of the bridge. The gate at the other
end was lost in the murky late afternoon and the lattice of
ironwork towered over us like a gigantic, empty ribcage.
A cold wind blustered through it, trying to push us back
to the city.

Everyone was hurrying, heads down, battling the wind and we were dragged along in the jostle and rush. When we got about halfway, we stopped as if we'd both decided that we were getting there too fast. We worked our way to the side of the bridge and leaned over it so no one could hear us.

'There are so many people,' said Fyffe. 'I didn't think there'd be so many.'

They looked like the people we'd met all day at the roadblocks – their faces set at grim, their step a mix of military march and civilian scurry. I tried the 'You should go back' line again, but no joy, so I gave that up and peered over the side. It was a long way down. I'd never looked down onto the river before – not from so high up, not from right in the middle of a bridge. The water was black and tumbling, rushing towards Port. And wide. Hostiles had been known to swim it, but I couldn't see how, it looked too fast. But maybe swimming it would be better than heading over it into Southside armed with nothing but desperation and a few stumbling phrases of Breken. I needed Lou standing next to me saying, *Come on! What are you waiting for? They won't know what's hit them.* And laughing like a maniac.

'Well, well. It's the Gilgate sewer rat.' Not Lou. The commander from Moldam Road. He grabbed my sweat-shirt and hauled me round to face him. 'You know,' he said, 'I lost a good person today. If you were in a squad,

I'd have you for desertion. And if you were on my bridge, you'd be in a squad. So I might have you for desertion anyway, since here you are.' He looked me up and down. 'You don't have much to show for your scavenging. Who's this?'

'Just – just – she's with me.'

'Is she. And you're joining us. How fortunate for us.' He gave me a push. 'Move!' So we had no choice in the end. We walked down the Mol, past the guards at the Southside gate and into enemy territory, Breken militia breathing down our necks the whole way.

CHAPTER 13

As soon as we stepped through the bridge gate into Southside, I knew that what we were trying to do was insane. You forget, sitting back home behind the high walls and the locked bridges – you forget that Southside is nearly half of a whole city, and the dark half at that. We gripped hands and I glanced at Fyffe. She looked filthy and fierce, every bit the hardened scavenger she wasn't.

We stepped off the bridge onto what must have been a major trucking route once. Maybe it used to be busy with warehouses and truckstop cafes and markets and storage halls. None of that was left. Now a packed dirt road stretched ahead of us, lined with a jumble of low shacks crammed together, rigged from fragments of the original Southside. They'd used chunks of concrete for foundations and sheets of iron for walls and roofs; planks of wood leaned over doorways, and ramshackle brick chimneys leaked smoke.

For all that it looked like a dump, though, it was humming. Different from the stony silence of the city after dark. This place was alive and peopled: dogs barked and kids yelled and charged about, and people criss-crossed the road ahead of us, talking, calling to each other, laughing, and arguing. Some of them were lighting lamps and hanging them from the roofs of their makeshift shelters; others were building fires on grates by the roadside and huddling round them, warming themselves and cooking. Yes, cooking. The air just about knocked me over with the smell of spices and cooking oil and frying food.

Fish is what I could smell mainly. Fish done in spices and fried up sharp and hot. I'd gone about three steps and taken two breaths of that air before the world started to spin from how light my head was, on account of how empty my stomach was. Fyffe stopped beside me and breathed deep as though filling her lungs would fill her stomach as well. I wondered how hard would it be to filch some fish from a frying pan – pretty hard, because there were a lot of people crowded round each fire, a lot more than you'd think a pan of fish could feed.

'Sir!' A voice shouted through the crowd. The commander stopped and stuck an arm out to stop us too. A tall guy, a few years older than me, shouldered his way forward and gave a salute of eye-watering precision. He was darker than me, and sharply dressed, as though he'd just stepped off the pages of some zine – *Hostyle: For the Fighting Man*.

'Jeitan.' The commander returned a salute.

Jeitan said, 'They're ready with Tam now, sir. Just waiting on the others.'

'Right. On my way.'

'I should have been there, sir.'

The commander shook his head. 'There's nothing you could have done. We thought we'd secured the area. However, there is something you can do here.'

'Sir?'

The commander flicked my shoulder with the back of his hand. 'I want these two at the Crossing. They're scavengers from upriver and they think they're scavenging for free.' He glared at us. 'None of this is free. It's time your kind understood that. Watch and learn.' He turned back to Jeitan. 'Take them up the hill and get them cleaned up first. I don't want them polluting the Crossing.'

'Sir!'

Jeitan gave a sigh, like, why do I get all the rubbish jobs, and said, 'Names?'

I blurted out 'Nik' before I'd thought better of it, which, two seconds later, I had, but it was out, and too late now. Fyffe, smarter than me, said, 'Sina.' No idea where that came from – servants, I guess.

Jeitan said, 'That's Commander Vega. You address

him as Sir. Clear?' We nodded. 'Right,' he said. 'This way!'

'Where are we going?' I asked.

'Headquarters,' he said. 'Shut up and move!'

We pushed through the crowds and down another road lined with shacks – more bits of concrete and sheet-iron stuck together on a whim and a prayer – if they prayed over here, which we were told they did, but who to and how was always a matter of dispute back home. A mess of people from all over had brought with them a crowd of gods; how they'd negotiated religion in the generations they'd been here kept the strategists back home awake nights, mainly with how to set them one group against another.

I kept a lookout for a way to step sideways into the crowd and lose Jeitan, but he stuck to us like shit on a shoe. We passed families sitting in front of their shacks talking and eating. Little kids screamed around waving strips of red cloth, the same color as the bandanas the gangs on the roadblocks had worn, the color we made all the Breken wear as armbands when they got permits to come Cityside.

Lots of people waved to Jeitan and greeted him by name. But there weren't any victory dances. I thought they'd all be high because they'd done it – they'd broken out, they'd crossed the river, and this time there was no army to push them back and slam the gates. But they were quieter than that, sitting around, talking, hushing the kids. It wasn't over yet.

We passed a concrete wall where someone had scrawled *We Are Not Cattle* in jagged white paint. Another wall was stuck with posters listing all the city bridges in black chunky letters: Port, Mol, Bethun, Sentinel, Clare, Torrens, Westwall. With lines struck through each name. Jono was wrong. They'd taken the bridges. Every one.

We were climbing by then. Not a steep hill, but from it we could look back towards the Mol. Hundreds of tiny lights were blinking into life across the patchwork of iron roofing that spread out from the bridge. No blackout here. They must've been confident that they'd hit the city hard. We passed other walls stuck with posters – *Unlock the Mol* and *Free Movement for All* – marked with the logo of a globe with an arrow circling it. That was the CFM logo, the Campaign for Free Movement. I remembered Stapleton drawing it on the wall-screen in class one day and saying, 'This is all you need to know about CFM: it's a militant coalition pushing for a unified city, north and south of the river. According to their propaganda, they want a Breken voice in the governance of such a city. That's a lie, of course. What they intend is a unified city under Breken command.'

The **R** of Remnant was also plastered everywhere – another faction. 'Fanatics,' Stapleton had said. 'Committed to building "a renewed and holy paradise" on both banks of the river.'

CFM were godless heathens; Remnant were heretics. Take your pick who you'd rather be blown up by.

'Hey!' Jeitan snapped his fingers at us. 'In here.' He pointed us past two guards on a gate set in a high wire fence. Fyffe and I stopped in our tracks. Breken headquarters, in Moldam at least, was a rambling monster of a building that looked, oh so familiar: we'd come back to school. Some architect must have done a two-for-one deal: two storeys high, three wings, stone steps leading up to a huge wooden door, and a clock tower rising above that. The clock face was smashed and a lot of windows were boarded up and the brick walls were pockmarked all over; someone – or someone's army – had shot it up and the war had run over it a few times. But it was unmistakeable. Except that instead of the green lawns and trees of school, it was surrounded by ranks of modular, box-like buildings that must have been barracks for their squads from the look of the people coming and going.

'Hurry up!' said Jeitan. Fyffe gripped my hand and we walked inside. Floodlights, powered down to maybe thirty per cent, lit the grounds in a dim, patchy way: enough that we could see that the place was churning with people with a purpose. They all seemed to be looking miles ahead of themselves and in a hurry to get there. We were nearly bowled on the steps by a great hulk of a guy lugging a bundle of newspapers under each arm, then by a kid with a box brimful of those red armbands. When we finally got in the door, the foyer was full of people crowding around a desk. The woman behind the desk was trying to organize some of them into task groups and give map directions to others, while answering questions and a phone.

When we got to the front of the crowd, she looked up at Jeitan and sighed. 'Things are happening at last, so everyone wants to help. It's chaos. Still, we mustn't complain.'

'Make way!' Behind us, two boys pushed through carrying boards stacked high with flatbreads and sausages. 'You're late,' she said to them. 'Get a move on! Now, Jeitan. What do you need?'

I stared after the sausages until they disappeared around a corner, while Jeitan recounted his sad story about landing this babysitting job because Commander Vega was consciousness-raising again, so could he please access the stores to find us some clothes? The woman looked me over like I was an insect. She looked at Fyffe with a slightly more kindly eye, then fished keys from a drawer. She summoned a female equivalent of Jeitan to take Fyffe away and called, 'Right. Who's next?'

I opened my mouth to protest, but Fyffe went without a backward glance, head high, undaunted. Jeitan called after them, 'Back here in ten!' Then he marched me along a high-ceilinged corridor stacked with chairs and mattresses and folded-up trestle tables; the air was thick with the smell of cigarettes and unwashed bodies. We went past a lot of shut doors and stairways and boarded-up passageways, all eerily familiar. I tried not to look like I was curious, but I was looking all around and trying to feel if Sol could be there. He'd be terrified. I wondered if they had anyone primed to calm him down, maybe try and talk to him. Not that he'd say anything, even in Anglo. When he arrived at school he spent his whole first term sitting on the sidelines watching Lou from behind that thick fringe of fair hair and saying nothing. If you caught him looking and winked at him, he'd look away as if he hadn't seen you. Then one day he gave this half a smile before he looked away, and by half-year he was grinning right back. They wouldn't wait for that here, though. Would they even ask his name? Would he tell them?

We came to a storeroom where Jeitan grabbed some clothes and some boots, and then to a washroom fitted with decrepit showerheads stuck high in cracked-tile walls. I took the chunk of soap he gave me, turned on the tapful of stone-cold water, and I washed away four days of smoke and grime and dust and blood. Four days. That's how long it had taken for everything to go up in flames. When I'd finished, my old clothes were gone.

The new clothes were just what I'd seen on all of them – not a strict uniform where everyone's the same, but a dark shirt, trousers, jacket, and boots. They weren't new either; they were threadbare and patched and not what you'd call warm. I could feel every bump in the ground through the soles of the boots. It didn't take much imagination to work out that whoever had worn these before probably wasn't walking around anymore.

But for all the drama of standing up in a dead guy's clothes and trying to sense where Sol might be and worrying about Fyffe, what I was thinking about was food, because the world was spinning again. I crouched down just as Jeitan looked in to see why I wasn't hurrying up like he'd ordered. 'Now what?' he said.

I shook my head. 'Just hungry.'

'Everyone's hungry. Come on!'

'Okay, okay.'

'How long since you ate?'

'Um. Yesterday morning.'

'Not much of a scavenger, are you.' Which was perceptive of him but, since he wasn't fronting up with any actual food, not very helpful.

Fyffe and her minder arrived back in the foyer just after we did. They'd given her some black squad clothes that were too big for her and made her look more fragile than ever. Her hair, pulled back hard with a tie, shone gold in the dim generator light. The graze on her forehead was patched. She smiled and gave me a nod.

'Come on!' said Jeitan. So we followed him out of the compound and back through the crowds towards the Mol.

CHAPTER 14

Tamsin was her name. The one I saw shot on Moldam Road. They brought her back over the Mol that night in a procession they called a Crossing. A slow march, her body carried on the shoulders of six others. The Mol was lined with militia and one of them led the way, carrying a light.

Down off the bridge where we were, it was like the whole of Moldam township had turned out, holding any kind of light they could find. Everywhere I looked, faces flickered, watchful, waiting. There was no hum from Cityside. You could hear the river lapping and, above it, the boots of the people on the bridge. Around us people shuffled now and then, and occasionally a kid squawked and was shushed. But mostly the crowd held still.

When the procession reached the Southside gateway it stopped. The crowd parted and a woman came forward. She was tall and dark – black skin, black tunic, and baggy trousers. She stood in front of the ones carrying the body and everyone seemed to hold their breath. Then she sang. Just her, alone, calling out to the night, calling home the dead. And, I swear, the Mol sang back, because I was standing close and I heard the ironwork ring. When she stopped there was deep silence. Then the whole mass of them sang back. It just about knocked me off my feet.

The bearers of the body stepped off the Mol; that's when I saw there wasn't one body, there were five. We turned to follow them, me and Fyffe and Jeitan and about ten thousand other people. I held Fyffe's hand and stood still, letting an old man and woman go ahead of us, and a guy with a toddler on his shoulders, and a woman with a small girl. By then I couldn't see Jeitan anymore. We'd worked our way to the edge of the procession and now it flowed on without us, carrying its song and its dead away to whatever end they made for militants killed in war. I nudged Fyffe, and we slipped into a narrow space between two shacks and wound our way upriver.

After about half an hour of threading through crooked alleys that had no pattern to them we'd traveled beyond the shantytown into a more ordered set-up of streets. The houses were two- or three-storey terrace blocks, like haunted versions of houses over the river: walls were cracked and growing moss and ivy; windows were shattered and boarded up; balconies were rotted through, trailing greenery, and clotted with rubbish.

We tried listening at doorways and peering in windows but everything was dark and quiet. After about an hour flitting from house to house like a couple of ghosts, we sat down in a doorway. 'How will we find him in this?' said Fyffe.

There was silence all around us as though the whole of Southside had clamped its mouth shut on the secret of where Sol was. As we sat there, I got to thinking the place really was haunted, that everyone had gone over the bridge and into the city and left us behind with the dead. The dead were here because they'd been brought over in a Crossing, so here is where they had to stay. And as we walked we'd meet them round a corner or see them opening a door or watching from a broken window. And maybe we'd see our own dead too: Lou with his face half burned away and Bella, pale and bloody, wandering the streets.

I woke up with a jolt. The streets were still dark and empty; I was still sitting in a doorway. Fyffe was asleep on my arm. We were still famished. Still beat. And now I was seriously spooked as well; the cold crept like a spider between my shoulder blades. When raised voices came from somewhere nearby, it was almost a relief. I woke Fyffe. 'Stay here. I'm going to check it out.'

'No – but –'

'I'll be back in two minutes, promise. Don't move.'

I edged down an alley between two houses and came out into a lamplit patch of broken, weedy pavement – and a fight. A guy and a girl, both about my age, were swinging at each other, feet and hands flying. My fault, then, that when I stumbled in he took his eye off the ball – off her foot, in fact. It swung through the air and smashed into his temple. He grunted and folded onto the ground. She spun around with the momentum of her kick and landed in a crouch.

She was black, like the singer at the bridge. Her hair was wound in a million braids and her clothes were the same as the singer's – black tunic, baggy trousers. She flicked out a knife and glared at me. 'I didn't need your help.'

I backed away. She stood up, swayed, and waved the knife at me. She had a cut lip and a bruise rising on her cheekbone. The hand that wasn't holding the knife was dripping blood. She said, 'I am Lanya. I am a Pathmaker.'

I dredged my memory for Breken: Law and Lore – Dr Mercer (RIP, probably) – and found something about a pan-religious ritual for the dead. She stepped closer and I was about to turn and bolt when I spotted a board on the ground behind her with food on it: two strips of what looked like fish, flatbread, and a jug of something. A feast, in other words. The girl saw where I was looking and jerked her head at the boy. 'Coly brought it. He wanted me to eat and dishonor the fast. But I am a Maker. He will not stop me. You will not either.' She pointed the knife at me and came a step closer.

I held up both hands and said, 'You're bleeding.' Which worked, because bleeding clearly wasn't in her plan. She looked at her arm and swore. She swore the way Bella used to swear, in a sing-song voice that was as much for her audience as for herself.

Then she breathed deep and said, 'Have you been at the Crossing? Has it begun?'

'Hours ago.'

She swore again.

I said, 'I'll fix your arm, for the food.'

'Who are you?'

'No one. Arm. Food. What d'you say?'

The boy moaned. She glanced back at him. 'Yes. Hurry!'

'Put the knife away first.'

She grinned. White teeth. Shrugged a where's-your-sense-of-adventure? kind of shrug, but she folded the knife and pocketed it. She sat on the ground near the light and the food and held out her arm. 'Hurry!'

I hefted the jug, sniffed at it – water with a splash of wine. I took hold of her wrist, lightly, watching her. She was trembling, adrenaline still running. I said, 'Hold still,' and poured the water over her arm. She hissed. On her forearm below the elbow was a cut as long as a finger, not deep – the blood was already thick and slowing.

'Fight with knives often, do you?' I said.

'Never. It's forbidden.'

'Oh. Okay. And this is?'

'A scratch. That no one will see.'

'Does he still have a knife?'

'No.' She smiled and nodded towards a pile of rubble and rubbish at the back of one of the houses. A groan came from the boy. He was hauling himself to his knees, swearing. He stared in our direction and seemed to have trouble focusing. I hoped he could see four of us at least. He snarled something like 'You shit,' to me, and 'Whore,' to her, then staggered upright.

We were on our feet. She had her knife in hand and he was groping for his, but he couldn't find it. He pointed a finger at her, then at me, but whatever he wanted to say was lost in a mixture of concussion and fury. He wandered a drunken path over to the rubbish pile, kicked through it for a few minutes muttering, but soon gave up and staggered away.

She sank down again and I went back to fixing her arm.

She watched me. 'Are you an outcast?'

'What?'

'You said you were no one, so I thought you had been cast out.'

'Oh. Uh… no.' I filed that. Being 'cast out' must be some kind of official punishment. Outcasts became nobodies – forfeited their identity, maybe.

'Where are you from?' she said.

'Gilgate.'

'Why are you here?'

'Looking for someone.'

'Who?'

'Do you have something I can bind this with?'

She untied the red bandana from her neck. 'Who are you looking for?'

'No one you know. Is that too tight?'

She shook her head. 'You can know this – that I wouldn't know this person?'

'I have a pretty fair idea, yeah.'

'If you're not an outcast, what are you called?'

I ripped the end of the bandana in two with my teeth and tied it off. 'Done,' I said. 'Someone should look at it though. It might need more than a bandage.'

She shook her head, braids flying. 'You looked at it.'

'Yeah, but I'm no one, remember.' She smiled with more curiosity than was healthy. 'Can I eat?' I asked. She stood up, bowed, murmured something in Breken that I didn't understand, and took off back down the alley. I don't know if she noticed Fyffe peering round the corner.

We fell on the food: white, flaky fish and new-baked flatbread. It was gone pretty quick; I could have eaten the same again, twice. It was good to have ballast again – feet on the ground and head connected to the rest of me. I grinned at Fyffe. 'Better?'

She smiled back. 'Much. But what now? This place is so big.'

'What we need is some intel on local traffickers,' I said. And our own private army would be handy.

'What if they've sent him south already? Nik, what if they've…'

'Stop. Listen – best case is they find out who he is. He'll be worth a fortune to them to ransom. Once they know he's a Hendry they'll look after him better than their own kids. There's no way they'll send him south.'

'You think?'

'Sure. Of course.' Maybe. Ransoms were bound to be risky. If traffickers could get the same money by selling him south, that's probably what they'd do.

'I know!' She grasped my arm. 'What if I tell them

who I am? That I'm a Hendry and he is too and then they can ransom us both?'

'Whoa! Fy! Are you crazy?'

'No, it makes sense.'

'No it doesn't! They're traffickers. You can't know what they'll do to you. Don't even think that.'

'We'd better find him quick then.'

'Promise me, *promise me*, you won't do anything crazy?'

She hesitated for too long, but she said, 'I promise.'

I didn't believe her. If I'd been scared before, I was plain terrified now. She said, 'All right, then. What now?'

I stood up. 'Now, I think, I look for a knife.' I raked around in the rubbish where Coly had been searching and, being neither concussed nor in a fury, I found it straight away. It was a flick knife like the girl's – small, for hiding, and sharp, for hurting. I'd never had a knife before and, to be honest, pocketing one now didn't make me feel as safe as I'd hoped it would.

Fyffe stood up. 'That boy might come back. Where shall we go?'

'Their HQ. Let's see what they know about traffickers there.'

So we headed back downriver, through the darkened streets, towards the bridge. Before long we heard the crowd, and then we found it, still carrying the chant but no more than a low rumble now. The people swayed as though they'd sung themselves into a trance. We made our way towards the space that seemed to be the focus of the Crossing. It might have been a park once but now it was bare ground edged with the skeletons of trees. Even the kids crowding the branches of those trees were quiet.

In the middle was a mound, with a raised platform where they'd laid the bodies. Seven people stood around it, facing out to the crowd. They held orb-lights high in cupped hands. The sun was long gone and the orbs glowed.

As we watched, an old man leaning on a walking stick lurched through the crowd and climbed the rise to the platform. He was flanked by two younger men – one was Commander Vega from Moldam Road. The old man turned to the crowd and held up a hand. The chant rolled down to a murmur.

'My friends!' Silence all round. 'This is the first Crossing of the Great Uprising – the *last* Uprising!' Ten thousand voices roared – the sound of it thundered off the clouds and leaped over the river and I wondered if Dash could hear it in the city.

The man went on. 'There will be more Crossings. Perhaps there will be many more, before we taste freedom. But hear this! Reports are in from every district. We have taken every bridge!' The roar crashed around us again and I felt cold to my bones. 'Blackbyre has Watch Hill.' Wild cheering. 'Curswall has Central Communications.'

More cheering. 'Gulls Fort has the flood gates.' And more cheering. 'Moldam has the Marsh!' An almighty roar. Pitkerrin Marsh, they meant. The Mad Marsh we'd called it, back in school. It was a psychiatric hospital. I couldn't think why the hostiles would want it.

'We have been patient. *We are patient no longer.* We have been caged. *We are caged no longer!*' I felt sick and looked away, straight into the faces of two kids, little brown versions of Sol, with red bandanas round their heads and huge black eyes staring at us. I realized that Fyffe and I hadn't yelled or punched the air with the rest of them. I started to move us sideways, but Fyffe saw the kids and stuck her tongue out. They did the same, then grinned and looked back to the old man.

He was going on about the glorious dead and freedom waiting on the other side of the river. Glory and freedom and death. Glory and freedom and death… It pounded in my head and if he said more, I didn't hear it because all I could hear was glory and freedom and death beating like a drum, over and over. Then I realized there was, in fact, a drumbeat; the bearers of the orb-lights had marched back to the crowd, and out from the crowd came fire, leaping and spinning, flaming across the shadows, tossed high in the air, caught and tossed again. The crowd was silent and seven dancers, all arms and legs and sticks of flame, crept towards the platform like giant spiders weaving a fiery web across the dark. And yes, Lanya of the million braids was there. And no, you'd never guess the bandana on her arm hid the results of an illegal knife fight. She crept, spun and leaped, tossed flame and caught it with the rest of them.

They reached the platform and the drumbeat stopped. We held a collective breath. The dancers lifted their firesticks high and plunged them into the platform, then whirled cartwheeling away.

The pyre lit the night.

CHAPTER 16

I woke up on cold, clammy earth with a tree root sticking in my ribs and two boots in my face. One of them took a swing at me; I grabbed at it, missed, and it connected with my shoulder. But it only gave me a nudge. I pushed it away and scrambled up, trying to get my eyes open and my tongue round the right language. 'I'm awake! I'm awake! What d'you want?' The boots belonged to Jeitan, who looked like he'd slept all night in a warm bed, showered in hot water, and breakfasted on coffee and hot buttered toast and… that was a dangerous line of thought so I stopped it.

He almost screwed up his nose at me, but that would have wrecked the effect he was trying for. 'Thought you'd scarpered back to Gilgate.'

I rubbed the tree root bruise on my ribs, shivered, then remembered Fyffe and looked round in a panic. She was still there, uncurling and stretching. She started to say something, thought better of it and gave Jeitan a winning smile instead.

Over Jeitan's shoulder, the pyre smoldered. Beside it, Commander Vega was talking to one of the dancers. As I watched, they bowed to each other, a short curt bow like the one Lanya, the Pathmaker, had given me the night before. The dancer turned away and Vega summoned us. He looked us over. 'You watched the Crossing, then.'

'Yeah.' I said. 'And learned, like you ordered.'

'*Sir*,' said Jeitan, glaring at me.

'We watched and learned, sir,' I said.

The commander's eyes narrowed. 'They teach you to read in Gilgate?'

'Me, yes. Her, no.'

'I see. And write?'

'Sort of.'

'Sort of will do. If you're staying here, you're going in a squad. Is that clear?'

I nodded.

'Full of conversation, aren't we? IS THAT CLEAR?'

'Yes… sir.'

'Better.' He turned to Jeitan. 'I'm assigning him to CommSec. Her to the infirmary.'

'But, sir!' said Jeitan. 'Should you do that? I mean – is that…'

'Is that wise? Are you asking?'

'No, sir.'

'We need someone non-aligned who can read. Someone from outside Moldam, even better.'

'We don't know he's non-aligned, sir,' said Jeitan.

'Does he look like a Remnant devotee to you?'

'No, sir,' said Jeitan.

'And he's certainly not one of ours.' Vega turned a cold stare on me. 'You. Who do you pray to?'

Now that was a dangerous question. I tried, 'Why?'

'Never mind why.'

So I told the truth, as of last Wednesday. 'No one.'

'No one, *sir*,' muttered Jeitan.

'See?' said Vega. 'Gilgate breeds heathens. He'll do.'

'He won't stay non-aligned for long. Remnant will make him an offer.'

'First offer he takes, he and his young lady are going back to Gilgate. And I don't think they're keen on that, or they would have gone last night when you lost them.' Cue Jeitan looking crushed. 'Besides,' Vega went on, 'he won't understand what he's reading, and you'll be checking with CommSec on a daily basis to make sure he's following orders. Clear?'

'Sir.' The smart shoulders slumped. Not the guns and glory he was hoping for.

But we got the breakfast we were hoping for. Or at least *a* breakfast. A sludge of porridge slapped in a bowl and a mug of black coffee. Not much, but it stuck to my ribs and was a whole lot better than the nothing we'd had the last couple of days.

We were back at HQ where Jeitan had taken us the day before. The big dining hall echoed with chatter and the scrape of chairs, its windows steamed up by a bitter brew of coffee. So, phase one of our plan – get back to HQ – turned out to be surprisingly easy. Phase two – actually finding useful intel – was quite likely impossible. I looked at my porridge and wondered what Sol was eating. *If* Sol was eating. That kid was skinny. I hoped they thought him prize enough to feed him.

At the back of the room, Commander Vega stood up and rapped on a table and everyone shut up. He waited for absolute hush, then said, 'Thank you. As you heard at the Crossing last night, our first foray has gone to plan.' He held up a hand to quiet the cheering. 'It's a beginning only. We hold strategic posts that we will use to bring the city to the negotiating table. However. The mutiny of their armed forces that has given us this chance poses problems for us. It will take time to organize talks with a credible city command. In the meantime, our plan must be to hold the posts we have taken. Do not assume this will be easy. City forces are fragmented but they still have more weapons, more ammunition, more fuel, and more vehicles than we do. At present, they appear to lack an organized command structure. That will not last. Overconfidence is an enemy – watch for it. Your squad leaders have your orders.'

I was looking at Fyffe to see how much of that she had understood when the chair opposite me banged down. Coly, the knife-boy, leaned across the table and stared at me like he couldn't quite place me. I could just about see the cogs ticking round in his head. I waited, thought about trying to distract him with a hot coffee in the face, decided that wasn't such a good idea and waited some more. Eventually the little cogs in his brain clicked and his mouth opened. 'You're in deep shit.'

Yeah, surprise me. 'You were in a knife fight with a girl,' I said.

'She started it.'

'Sure.'

'You stay away from her.'

I got up to move away but he was round the table and in my face before I'd taken a step. 'D'you get it? Stay. Away.' He was a head shorter than me, but a whole lot more solid. Something was burning inside him that I wasn't keen to stir up. I turned away but he grabbed my arm and sent my tray crashing to the ground.

About a hundred and fifty heads turned in our direction. Just what I needed. Jeitan came storming over. 'You are asking to be sent back to Gilgate. What's going on?'

Coly looked smug. 'I'm reporting a transgression.'

Jeitan's eyebrows shot up. He glanced over where Vega was talking – arguing, in fact, if you looked closely – with the man who'd stood on the other side of the old guy who'd given the speech the night before. 'Report to me,' said Jeitan. 'I'll decide if it goes further.'

Smug turned to sullen, but Coly pressed on. 'Him and a Maker. I saw them. Together. I saw him touch her. Last night.'

'*What?*' That was me, so appalled my voice cracked.

'You saw what, exactly?' said Jeitan.

'I'm not saying here,' said Coly. 'I'll say in a hearing.'

Jeitan swore. 'You want to call a Pathmaker to a hearing?'

A sharp nod from Coly.

'You'd better be sure about this.'

'This is mad!' I said.

They ignored me. 'He touched her. She's unclean,' said Coly. 'She danced unclean at the Crossing.' That fire of his was burning bright and ugly. Breakfast turned sour in my stomach.

Jeitan chewed his lip and looked at me with even more loathing than before. 'I'll talk to Commander Vega. You,' to me. 'Clean this up – and hurry. There's work to do.'

Fyffe had gone pale and was staring at us, but there was no chance to explain. A girl had arrived at Jeitan's elbow and was waiting for him to finish. When he turned to her she asked could she take the Gilgate girl, and he sent them both off with a dismissive wave of his hand.

Fyffe and I were on our own, two Citysiders among a horde of Breken. A slip from either of us would send us both crashing and burning. We were going to try and meet at the next meal, but weren't even sure if we'd have mealtimes in common. Fyffe had this crazy confidence that we'd be 'looked after.' It scared the shit out of me.

CHAPTER 17

CommSec was Communications Security – anything from ordering supplies that kept the squads in boots and bread to high-security memos winging their way between bridges, not that I was supposed to see any of those.

The ogre/expert at the center of all this was Sub-commander Tasia Levkova: from a distance, a sweet old granny with a limp and a walking stick; up close, sharp and hard as knives and nails together.

'Jeitan.' She tossed a document onto her desk as we came in. 'Good, I wanted to see you. I want a word.' She eyed me. 'Who's this?'

'Commander Vega found him.' Jeitan pointed me towards the far end of the room. 'Go sit.'

While he gave Levkova the info, such as it was, on me, I wandered around. We were upstairs, in a high-ceilinged room with tall, dusty windows that rattled in the wind. From that vantage point I could see down to the river. The shantytown, with its jigsaw of iron roofing lapped the hill where this old school was perched and ran west, up the river towards Curswall district. Further upriver, and away south down the other side of this hill, lay the remains of the original Southside. My guess: the shantytown marked a kind of blast radius – our army had flattened everything near the bridge, and maybe done it more than once. But people had come back, as people do, and now their washing flapped on lines strung between their shacks, and smoke from their cooking fires settled in a dirty haze above them.

Sol was out there somewhere, in a shack, or an attic or a basement. And here were we, in the middle of the enemy camp, Fyffe madly confident and me not at all. I wondered if they'd got fed up with him because he couldn't understand Breken. Thinking what they might do scared me sick. They didn't need much to keep him quiet – a number puzzle, a bowl of noodles, a book about animals from the old wild places or with pictures of star fields and planets from the space telescopes. Not much. A friendly face. A familiar face.

Behind me a strip light hung low over a couple of trestle tables spread with piles of paper. Against one wall were four of the oldest computers I'd ever seen. I tapped the keyboard of one of them and the monitor lit up. Something pinged the back of my head. I spun round – Grandma

Levkova was giving me the full flinty-eyed treatment and aiming another pen at me. '*Don't. Touch. Anything!*'

I stuck my hands in my pockets and wandered on, but my heart was beating fast. Would traffickers send progress reports to HQ? If trafficking was part of the overall Breken strategy, they just might. Maybe I'd come to the right place after all. Maybe it was all here at my fingertips – who the traffickers were, where they kept their captives, timetables for transporting them south, all that. I just had to get at it before Sol was gone beyond reach, and before Fyffe threw herself on the greed of the enemy.

Levkova crooked a finger at me. 'You. What's your name?'

'Nik.'

She raised an eyebrow, and Jeitan said, 'That's all I got out of him too.'

'Well, Nik,' she went behind her desk and opened a door to a cupboard-sized, windowless room. I could see a small table in there, an old-style light bulb swinging from the ceiling and stacks of paper on the table and the floor. 'We've got quite a backlog, as you can see, and you're going to look at all of it. Understood?'

My heart sank. I needed to be on the computers, not stuck in a cupboard processing old files.

'Starting now,' she said. 'Leave him with me.' When Jeitan looked doubtful she said, 'I know. It's risky. First sign of trouble, he's out. But it's also urgent. We make do with what we've got. Check in this afternoon and I'll give you a report for Sim.' She glanced at me. 'For Commander Vega, I should say.' Jeitan nodded. 'And don't look so aggrieved, lad,' she said to him. 'Your time will come. Anyone can charge off over the river to fight. Sim needs a deputy here who's loyal and level-headed. That's you. Be honored.'

He looked like he didn't want to be honored, he wanted to be fighting, but he said, 'Yes, ma'am,' gave his text-book salute and left.

'Now.' Levkova shooed me into the cramped little space behind her desk; it smelled of mice and mold. She stood over me with her beetle-bright eyes and said, 'How's your memory?'

Pretty damn near perfect is how my memory is, but I wasn't telling her that. She said, 'I'm not going to write down a list of instructions. Let's try you remembering some and we'll see how we go.'

She rattled off a bunch of letter and word combinations and showed me some places in documents where they appeared. 'Find those. Mark them. Bring them to me. That's all.'

I leafed through a pile of documents and found lines and lines of gibberish. Intercepted comms from our side of the river – that was my guess. My job was sifting, searching, marking. Levkova's job with what I found was much more fun. Code-breaking.

I looked up to see her hesitating in the doorway.

'Is there more?' I asked, hoping she was about to let me use the computers.

'One thing more. You will not talk about what you're doing here to anyone beyond myself and Jeitan. And Commander Vega, of course.' She gave me a tight smile that struggled onto her face from places unknown and looked like it was anxious to struggle away again. 'Should you be tempted, just remember Jeitan can find you, and your young lady, much more unpleasant work to do than this. Is that clear?'

I nodded and made an effort to look at her and not past her to the room beyond. None of this paper was getting me near to finding Sol. I needed to get at those computers.

CHAPTER 18

By the time I went downstairs that night to eat, I had a measly nothing to report to Fyffe except the tantalizing possibility that the computers at CommSec might store the information we needed. 'Well, you've done better than me,' she said. 'The infirmary's got two wards with about twenty people crammed into each one, but there aren't enough beds. Some people must have come from the fighting; they've got gunshot wounds and burns. There's a clinic for everyone else, whether it's fever or broken bones. And there's a medicine room, but most of the shelves are empty. They've put me on cleaning. I wish I understood more Breken; my eavesdropping is hopeless.'

We were walking in the grounds away from prying ears, looking for somewhere to shelter out of the rain. We found an empty doorway and watched the gray evening creep across the compound: lights came on, people hurried about, doors were slammed and curtains pulled shut as the rain got heavier. Dismal. It had rained all afternoon – long enough for us to discover that all the roofs leaked and so did our boots, that the bricks of peat they used for fires were contaminated with other stuff and wouldn't burn hot or for long, and that although we'd wrapped up in everything we had, it wasn't enough. We were cold.

Fyffe said, 'It's Sunday, isn't it? It seems like forever since last Sunday. D'you remember last Sunday?'

'Don't, Fy.'

'A woman came into the infirmary this afternoon with a little kid with a broken wrist and the doctor was so careful and gentle about setting it and I thought, how could you do that? How could you take such care with this child here and plant a bomb in a school over there!' She sniffed and wiped her arm across her face but the tears kept coming. 'I wish… I wish that Lou…'

I put an arm around her and she buried her face in my shoulder and cried, and I had no words to help. Fy was always the one with the comforting words.

She was quiet after a while, then stood back and dabbed at my shoulder. 'Sorry.'

'Don't be. I want him back too. He'd have talked his way into this place and out of it again with all the intel he needed and people falling over themselves to help him out.'

'Except he didn't have Breken, the way you do.'

'No, I guess not.'

'You don't like that, do you?' I shrugged and she said, 'I'm not about to accuse you of being in league with the enemy, you know.'

'I know it's stupid, but I can't help thinking how Jono would spin all kinds of conspiracy theories out of it.'

She almost smiled. 'Yeah. But he's away over the bridge. I hope they're safe. I wonder what they think we're doing.' She took a deep breath. 'What are we doing? Do we stay here or go down into the township?'

'Stay, I think. Let me see if I can get on the computers in CommSec.'

'There's always my plan.'

'Your plan? Oh, you mean your turn-yourself-in-and-get-us-both-shot plan? Can you just hold off on that for a day or two? Give me a chance to break into the computers. Tomorrow. I'll do it tomorrow.'

Problem was CommSec was never empty. Levkova seemed to live there. Jeitan came and went, keeping half an eye on me and thinking I was slow as a skiddy on 'shine. Which I was – because why should I help the hostiles break into our comms? I didn't want to finish working on them before I'd had a chance at the computers.

In the room beyond my cupboard, Levkova ran the place with steely precision. The old computers and their printers whirred and clicked and taunted me from a distance. People came, sorted stuff and were dispatched. If there were crises they were also sorted, I guess, though Levkova never raised her voice and I think no one else dared to.

Monday, there was a power cut. Levkova had warned me. 'Monday to Thursday this week, power will be down from fourteen hundred to seventeen hundred hours.' The place emptied but that was no use to me because the computers were dead for the duration. I stayed in my cupboard and sat on the floor in the dark; Levkova thought I was asleep and left me to it. For three hours I ran the texts I'd been working on across my mind's eye, looking at them again and again. I was looking for a key that would let me in. I played with algorithms, with old-style encryption devices, and with anything I could manage without a computer. I knew I was probably dreaming – city forces were unlikely to use anything so simple. But Levkova didn't seem to be using a computer, and I wondered if the city was in such chaos that its army had resorted to primitive forms of communication. I hoped so. I wanted to crack these codes in case someone somewhere was saying something about Sol. Surely by now the army would be looking for him? I guessed and guessed again. At one stage I thought I'd found some words that tallied with bridge names, but they led me nowhere. You need luck when you don't have anything solid to work with, and I had no luck at all that afternoon.

Later that night, when I was flagging and everyone else had gone, Levkova put her head round the door and waved a fistful of paper at me. 'Nik, you're a dedicated child. Work through these before you finish. They've just come in. I have to talk to Commander Vega. Don't go till I'm back. And don't let anyone in.'

I waited thirty seconds, checked the hallway – dark, deserted – and sat down in front of a monitor. Whole minutes dragged by as the thing groaned into life, but at last it showed me an ancient version of an operating system that – hallelujah – I knew: one that we'd learned to dismantle and rebuild until we could almost do it blindfolded. First blood to me.

But once I was in, what to look for? Follow the money, was my first thought, because trafficking had to be one of their big earners, so they'd keep track, wouldn't they, of money they got from it and who the main players were? I found enough to tell me that money for buying weapons, ammo, fuel, and food was coming in from lots of places: from Southside, from Oversea, though I couldn't tell what it was payment for, and – this stopped me in my tracks – from over the river. I filed that mentally under '*What…?*' and moved on.

I chased a lot of dead ends while the clock ticked in my head, and I tried not to think of Levkova climbing the stairs, walking down the hall, closing the distance between us. The part of my brain that was watching for her was also registering just how easy it was to sit there and read screen after screen of Breken, even though I'd only ever spoken it with Mace, and then only when there was no one else around, over the summer holidays or playing cards in the gatehouse. It was a useful trick, but it creeped me out too. Jono would love it: if he could see me now it would take him about two seconds to conclude that I was a Breken plant, a sleeper.

I tried all the possible names for 'trafficking' and 'children' that the hostiles might be hiding this business behind, assuming that they wouldn't call it what it actually was. It gave me nothing. Before I gave up I tapped in 'trafficking in children' because there was nothing else to try. The screen filled up: Trafficking in children – penalties for, convictions related to, blacklisted names of known and suspected traffickers and their associates, laws against trafficking and amendments to said laws.

Laws against trafficking. My brain did a flip. Trafficking in children was illegal here.

'What are you doing?'

I jumped about a foot. 'Jesus!' The wrong, wrong thing to say. Lanya of the million braids was looking over my shoulder. I said, 'What are you doing here?' and got busy covering my tracks and shutting everything down.

'Jeitan said you were here. Coly has his hearing. On Thursday. That means trouble for us.'

'What d'you mean *us*?'

'I mean,' she paced up and down behind me, 'Trouble for me if you tell the hearing about my knife.' She stopped directly behind me. 'And trouble for you if I tell them you swear like a Citysider.'

'I'm from Gilgate. What do you expect?' I switched off and stood up.

She followed me to my cupboard and stood in the doorway, peering at me through her braids. I started on Levkova's papers. 'Go,' I said. 'Please. How dangerous is this – you standing there and no one else here? If Levkova comes back –'

'Levkova won't mind.'

'Look, I won't tell them about the knife. I promise. And you can tell them what you like, I don't care, I just don't want trouble.' I put my head down and went to work, hoping she'd disappear before she dumped me in a whole heap more of it.

'Why?' she said.

'What?'

'Why don't you want trouble?'

'Who wants trouble?'

'Coly. He lives for it.'

'Well, I'm not him.'

'No. Who are you then?'

'No one. I'm no one. I won't tell the hearing about the fight. I promise. Now, will you just –'

'Don't you know what's at stake?' She sat down at the table. 'Remnant are strong here. And getting stronger. They already control the Bridge Councils at Gulls Fort, Curswall and Blackbyre.' I must have looked blank because she said, 'How can you not know this? CFM holds the Moldam Council by... by almost nothing – two independent councillors who've pledged to vote with them. If Remnant sways the independents, the Council will be theirs. Then they'll control all the districts east of Ohlerton.'

She leaned over and snatched the papers out of my hands. 'Are you listening? That's why they're trying to shame me. They've created a great panic about purity, and this latest so-called scandal will be enough to push the independents their way. Do you want that to happen?'

'I don't do politics. Can I have those back?'

'Everyone does politics. There's nothing here but politics.'

'I could be one of these Remnant people, for all you know, so shouldn't you give me back those papers now and *leave*?'

Her black eyes studied me, her long fingers destroyed the staple holding the papers together. 'You're not. I'd know.'

'You'd know. How would you know?'

'Jeitan says you're a heathen. And you wouldn't have fixed my arm. And you'd have reported me by now. And

Coly wouldn't hate you so much.'

That got my attention. 'How much?'

'Enough. You should watch your back.'

I stared at her. How had something as simple as food and a bandage turned into a full-blown freakin' circus?

The door to the main room closed.

Levkova. She stood in the doorway of my cupboard and glared. 'Don't let anyone in. Did I say that?' Lanya stood up and I scrambled to my feet. They bowed that short bow to each other, and Levkova said, 'My dear, you are surely in enough –'

'Yes. In enough trouble already. I know. I'm leaving now.' She headed for the door.

But Levkova put up a hand. 'Wait. Someone's in the corridor. Put out the light.' She closed the door on us and we heard the key turn in the lock. I pulled the string and killed the light. Darkness, but for a thin line under the door. And Lanya breathing an arm's length away. The door in the main room opened and closed, then Levkova's voice said, 'Councillor Terten, what brings you here?'

'Sub-commander Levkova.' A man's voice. 'Working late?'

'As you see.'

Boots clicked on the floor as someone paced and stopped outside our door, blocking the thin line of light. Lanya drew in a breath. The steps moved on. She let out a ragged sigh and the beads in her hair made tiny clacking sounds in the dark.

The voice outside said, 'How long have you worked here, Sub-commander?'

'Since before the last uprising, Councillor.'

'Many years of active service, then. You have a well-earned retirement awaiting you.'

'I have no intention of retiring.'

'Times change, dear lady, times change. But I forget myself. There is nothing dear or ladylike about you, is there?'

'I hope not, Councillor. Did you want anything in particular?'

'I came, Sub-commander, because I expect to remove you from here, very soon. With God's grace, by week's end. I came to ask that you go quietly and with dignity. CFM has lost its way and we intend to make that clear to the people.' More pacing.

Levkova said, 'You lay great store in the hearing.'

'I lay great store, Sub-commander, in common decency, which your continued presence here offends. You appear but rarely at prayer, you scorn the modesty of widows, you assume control of affairs that should concern no woman. It's time for you to return to what is properly yours.'

'Speak plainly, Councillor. I can take it.'

'You take this lightly.'

'On the contrary.'

'If that were so, Sub-commander, you would understand that as long as you and your like, as long as your
beloved CFM, offend against God in this way, we will
never be granted victory over the city.'

'The city is in disarray, Councillor. If we could present
a united front, we could force it to the negotiating table.'

'There will be no negotiation when we take the city.
There will be no peace but ours.'

'Then we have nothing more to say to each other.'

A pause. 'Until the hearing, then.'

'Good night, Councillor.'

We stood listening to silence for some time, then
the lock turned and light came flooding back. Levkova
limped to the table and sat down. 'Councillor Terten.' She
looked from Lanya to me. 'The hearing is set for Thursday
morning. You are both summoned. You will be asked to
explain how you came to be together on Saturday night.'

'We weren't *together*,' I said.

'No. We thought not. Commander Vega and I were
of the opinion that what Coly saw was a stranger, possibly
you, harassing a Pathmaker and detaining her from her
duties during a Crossing.'

I opened my mouth to protest but she held up a hand
and looked at Lanya. 'But now you come visiting. Late at
night and alone, breaking all the rules. One of you will
please explain.'

We looked at each other. Lanya sat down in my

chair; I sat on the floor and listened. She left out the knife fight, but said how they were arguing, her and Coly, about the food he had brought and wanted her to eat, and how she refused because it would break some kind of sacred fast she was on and that would stop her dancing at the Crossing, so she gave it to me instead.

Levkova was silent for quite a while after that. 'Who hit you? That bruise, and the cut on your lip – these came how?'

'Coly.'

'Not just a simple disagreement then.' Levkova looked at me like I was a puzzle and a pain. 'So much easier if it had been you.' She rubbed her forehead. 'I see. I do. But will the Council?'

'Why wouldn't they?' I said.

'Because Coly will swear otherwise, and he claims to have evidence to prove what he saw. They've been hunting a Maker's scalp for a long time now; they'll not let this one go. You fall so neatly into their hands. A scavenger from Gilgate. A stranger with no family, no friends and no allies.'

'What evidence?' I said.

'A digi-graph. I haven't seen it. Remnant will argue involvement and consent on both your parts, the Makers will argue harassment, and probably assault –'

'*What?*'

'That's why I am surprised you came here, child,'

she said to Lanya. 'I'm sure you have instructions – and accusing Nik must be the first of them?'

Lanya looked at me. 'You have a name.'

I put my head in my hands. 'This is insane. Are those your instructions?'

She nodded.

Levkova sighed with something like real regret. 'And you won't accuse him. I see that. Otherwise, what are we but the liars and cowards our enemies believe us to be? This will go hard against us though.' She struggled to her feet, sent Lanya on her way and summoned Jeitan. 'Which are your quarters?' she asked me.

'Shed 12.' A drafty bunkroom in one of the prefabs; it housed auxiliary staff – from kitchens, comms, printery and so on – in narrow bunks with thin mattresses, thinner blankets, and a concrete floor.

'Not this week, I'm afraid. We need you under lock and key when you're not here – for your own safety, until after the hearing. Jeitan will take you to a safe room. You can go by Shed 12 and collect your belongings on the way.'

'No, but…' I needed to find Sol, and I had a lead at last, and if I was locked up Fyffe was likely to go and do something terrible like turn herself in. Then Sol would be lost for good.

But Levkova was saying, 'I'm sorry, Nik. That's an order.'

CHAPTER 19

So there was good news and bad news. The good news was that I had memorized a list of known and suspected traffickers and their associates, which I wrote down and pressed into Fy's hand at breakfast next morning. The bad news was that I now had a shadow: Jeitan wasn't going to let me out of his sight until the hearing, except when he locked me into a cell-like room in Shed 3 at night 'for my own safety,' whatever that meant.

I told all this to Fy as we sat at the end of a long table in the dining room, dipping chunks of bread into bowls of thin, chocolaty milk. We spoke low and put our heads together; the rest of the room was loud with talk and laughter and people ignored us, the strangers from Gilgate.

'A hearing?' said Fy. Her Breken was slow and stammering but getting better fast. 'That's not good.'

'Yeah. I know. It's going to be hard to get out of here until it's over. But there's more I can do on the computers. I want to plug in those names and look for addresses to go with them.'

'What happens if they find you guilty? Nik, they flog people here. Can't we just get out? Go down into the town and search there?'

I looked up the table at Jeitan. 'Maybe. But what with? We've got nothing to go on except that list. How are you getting on in the infirmary?'

'They think I'm slow – it's my Breken, and I keep forgetting to answer to Sina. But they don't seem to mind too much. They've made me a supplies assistant. That means I get to go down to the township with a supplies officer and collect things from the main hospital. We're going tomorrow. I might be able to do something there: listen for the names on your list, I don't know. *I don't know*. We're not getting anywhere!'

'Give it one more day. If we've got nothing more by tomorrow night, we'll get out of here. Or try to. Okay?'

She nodded. 'I'm still wondering if we should just tell them who we are and ask for help. I mean, if trafficking is illegal, it'd be reporting a crime, wouldn't it? But then, what chance would you have at that hearing, if they knew?'

Vega rapped on a table and stood up to give the breakfast briefing.

'City forces are regrouping in Sentinel... their attempts to retake Watch Hill have been unsuccessful, but these are sustained attempts.... Overnight rocket attacks from city forces have been indescriminate. They've destroyed homes in Ohlerton, a church in Blackbyre and a clinic in Gilgate... civilian casualities are significant...'

'The city fights back,' murmured Fy. 'I guess we should be cheering them on.'

'You don't look like you're cheering,' I said.

'The people in the infirmary aren't. It's so over-crowded no one can move, and they've got almost nothing to treat people with. No wonder they hate us.'

That afternoon I sat at my desk wishing Levkova would find sudden, urgent business elsewhere. Jeitan was arguing with her about Remnant. He was impatient to go looking for some dirt on them to pre-empt their take-over of the Council after the hearing. He paced in front of her desk until she told him he made her dizzy and would he please sit down. I listened with half an ear to his complaints about how corrupt Remnant was, and then he said, 'Look, if the rumors are true and they've got a big windfall coming, then chances are they're planning some-thing major against us.'

I stopped work and paid attention.

'Rumors,' said Levkova. 'We need evidence. How big a windfall?'

'Big. That's all I heard.'

'From what?'

'No idea. Spoils of war. Their hangers-on have been over in the city. Who knows what they've grabbed.'

'And for what? What are they planning?'

Silence. I could just about hear Jeitan shrug. 'But it's not looking good, is it?' he said. 'They take Council and they're flush with funds: that gives them plenty of scope to undermine us. Can't you raise something about this windfall at the hearing? You'll have the Council together and –'

'Not without evidence, no.'

'With respect, ma'am, you and the Commander play this far too straight. We need a strategy against them.'

'What we need,' said Levkova, 'is to stabilize the situation over the river. That has to be our top priority. And I think the independents will see that and stay with us.'

I stopped listening. Remnant had Sol. I was sure of it. What else could a big windfall be but a small city boy worth millions? I wasn't entirely sure who Remnant were, though. All I knew about them were headlines from textbooks that I'd paid too little attention to, and one or two Stapleton sermons about them. According to Stapleton, they were dedicated to building a Holy City on both sides of the river, and they were even stricter in their Rule than we were, Cityside, when it came to sex and food and ritual. That being so, I wasn't surprised to hear that they liked to play dirty in secret.

That evening I waited for Fyffe in the dining hall, but she didn't show. The rain was bucketing down so I asked Jeitan if we could pack up some dinner and take it over to people in the infirmary to save them getting soaked coming over. He said that was a pretty transparent ploy on my part to see my girlfriend, but not a bad idea. So that's what we did.

The infirmary was an ugly gray modular building sprawling behind the main building. It looked like a kids' block game gone wrong: a wonky E shape with rooms from different model sets stuck on over the years so that one good temper tantrum might break the whole thing apart and scatter it across the hillside.

Inside, people sat crammed shoulder to shoulder in the waiting room, and staff in white coats zoomed about. Notices cluttered the walls with warnings in no-nonsense black-and-white, reminding everyone of 'The Three Minute Rule' (how long to boil water for), 'The 30-Second Rule' (how long to wash hands for), to NEVER buy meat or fish from unlicensed sellers, and to PLEASE be patient, staff were BUSY, your number would be called in due course.

The staff were pleased with the food we'd brought over, and it got me a white coat's attention, which I would have struggled for otherwise. 'Sina,' he said. 'Yes, she's here. She's with someone.'

The someone she was with was dead. One of the Moldam squad, they said. He'd been caught in sniper fire over the river a few days before and had died two hours ago. I knocked on the door and Fy let me in. There was enough space for a bed and two chairs. The room had green walls, a skylight that the rain thudded on, a small leafy tree in a pot in one corner and a lamp stuck on the wall above it. The place felt like a prayer room and the steady glow of the light on Fy's face and hair and white coat made her look like a thin, thoughtful angel. There was a body on the bed – a young guy, maybe twenty years old. He was dark and his eyes were closed. He was covered up to his chin by a white sheet. Fy was supposed to be praying for him, and I bet she was.

'He was sitting up and talking this morning,' she said. 'And his family were here and everyone thought he would get better. But he got an infection that ran hot through him. Now they've sent for the family again, and someone must sit with him and wait for them.'

I sat down beside her. 'You all right?'

She nodded.

'Do you want some food? There's some in the staff room.'

'No, thank you.' She looked at me, frowning. 'Nik? You know that thing you wear round your neck, from your mother – oh, you're not wearing it.'

'I lost it – that night at school.'

'Oh, no. I'm so sorry.'

I shrugged. It seemed wrong to feel gutted at losing a talisman when she had lost her brother, maybe both her brothers.

'This man,' she nodded towards the body, 'I think you should look; he's wearing one the same.' She gave me a little push. 'Have a look.'

I got up and peered at the body. He looked peaceful and young. I tweaked the sheet under his chin and there, round his neck, was my talisman. Not mine exactly – this one was copper or bronze rather than silver, and it was smaller. But it was the same shape as the one I'd worn my whole life until a few days ago – an elongated S with a long narrow hole in the middle of it.

'So?' I turned back to Fy. 'It'll be a trinket they make here and ship over to the city. My mother must have bought one at a market. There's probably thousands of them around.'

Fy said, 'Maybe. But when we washed the body I tried to take it off him and they wouldn't let me. They were shocked that I would do that. They said only his mother or his father or his wife can do that.'

I looked down at him. My mind was blank.

'I don't know why they said that,' Fy was saying. 'I was afraid to ask, in case,' she hesitated, 'in case it's something I should know. In case it's something everyone here knows.' She chewed her lip and watched me.

I looked away, back at the body, and tidied up the sheet corner that I'd moved. My heart beat hard. 'It doesn't mean anything,' I said. 'We're here to look for Sol, aren't we? This is a distraction. It's not important. Sol is important. We've got a list of traffickers. Plus I have some news about Remnant. We need a plan, a strategy, we need to –'

'Slow down, slow down. I can't follow.' Fyffe stood up and turned me round to face her. She spoke softly in Anglo. 'I might be wrong, but if your talisman is the same as his, then it means something here. I don't care what – as far as I'm concerned, you're Nik and I trust you with my life, but if you want, I'll help you find out what it means. If you want. And that might help us, you never know.' Her eyes were blue and earnest and I couldn't look at them. I couldn't go where that thought was taking her.

'I gotta get back,' I said. 'Don't worry about this, okay? Don't put yourself in danger over a trinket.'

'But –'

'I'll see you at breakfast. Keep safe.' I headed out the door.

I worked late that night, hoping that Levkova would be called away and I'd be able to get onto the computers. Also, let's face it, cowardice. I didn't want to be locked up in my cell in Shed 3 thinking about that talisman. I didn't want Fy's questions in my head, and I certainly didn't want to see her, every time I closed my eyes, reading me in that watchful, worried way of hers.

I was sure the wires would be buzzing with Sol's disappearance. The top brass at ISIS had to know about it by now and they'd be working on a strategy to get him back. I could help them, if I could just crack the code and work out what they were planning. So I buried myself in Levkova's piles of paper.

As the night ticked by, letters blurred in front of me. I put my head on the desk and closed my eyes. When the ground began to shake I sat up thinking I'd dreamed it – most nights I saw the school go up in flames. But no, this was real: thumping concussions deep in the earth. I went out to the main room. Levkova was still there, but Jeitan had gone. I stood at the window looking out towards the Mol. I couldn't see anything over that way but far to the west, towards St Clare, the sky glowed; the city was burning. St Clare was burning. I saw it in my mind's eye: flames and choking smoke; people staring at the blood on their hands and clothes, wondering if it's theirs or someone else's; people stumbling through the rubble, calling out, falling over the dead, wailing. That sound. It's strange what you remember: that noise people make when the sky falls in and they can't work it out, what they've lost.

I could see it: the bread burned cinder black on the bakery shelves in Kendon Street; the ashes of books swirling through the blown-out roofs of Brown's and The Bard, the little bookshops along Sentian; the glass cracked behind the bars in the banks' windows on St Clare Road; trees turned to torchwood across Pagnal Heath; and then the whole city falling in a cascade of glass and brick and concrete from the river to the hills.

'…nothing to worry about.'

I turned round to see Levkova talking to me. She sighed. 'I said, it's upriver, Cityside. Them, not us. I think it's the armory at Sentinel. We were aiming to take it to stop their rocket attacks. I'd say that's the sound of it being destroyed.' She studied me. 'It's not Gilgate, is what I'm trying to tell you.' I turned back to the window and hoped she wouldn't come near, because right then I couldn't pretend.

'Who's in Gilgate that you're afraid to lose?' she asked.

'No one. Everyone. Doesn't matter.' But it did, of course. It's my city, I thought. I'm afraid to lose it.

And I'm afraid for it to lose me.

CHAPTER 20

Fy backed off and didn't say a word about the talisman at breakfast the next morning. She was all business – hair tied back, brows straight, eyes focused. All her movements burned with contained energy. She was going down to the main hospital in the township with the supplies officer. 'A shipment of medicine has come in from somewhere,' she said. 'So I'm hoping it will draw some of their dealers and traffickers out into the daylight.'

I told her about the Jeitan–Levkova conversation the day before, and the rumor that Remnant had snatched something valuable Cityside.

'Oh!' she said. 'You have to ask Jeitan. Would he help? It sounds like he would.'

'Maybe. I don't know. I want to connect the names on our list with Remnant and follow that trail. Plus, I'll see their big names tomorrow at the hearing. Could be useful.

Especially if someone challenges them about what they're doing.'

We stopped to listen to the breakfast briefing, given by Jeitan this time: '...continue to hold the strategic posts we've taken, but we're coming under heavy pressure, especially at Torrens Hill, Sentinel, and Clare where forces loyal to the city are regrouping under ISIS... major disruption continues across the city... food distribution a shambles, fuel scarce, power out... the roads north clogged with refugees.' He finished with, 'The place has been looted from Westwall to Port – but not by us. Commander Vega reminds all squad members that There Will Be No Looting. Looters will be punished. Clear? Thank you, that's all.'

Fyffe watched him sit down and I could see she was desperate to go up to him and ask him point-blank about Sol. But she said, 'No looting. I can't get it straight in my head how they can be bombers and kidnappers and at the same time be saying that looting and trafficking are illegal.' She stood up to go.

I said, 'Be careful, okay?'

'Don't worry. I'll be all right.'

'Just don't imagine anything short of a small army will keep you safe from these people if they find out who you are.'

That afternoon, Levkova went off to talk to the two

independents on Council and left Jeitan to hold the fort at CommSec. I plonked a pile of documents on her desk in front of him and tried my luck. 'You know your suspicions about Remnant?'

He looked at me as though I was being nosy about his love life. 'What do you care?'

'Are you going to do anything about them? Run a check on their finances? For example? No?'

'I don't have clearance.'

'Why would that stop you?'

'I don't know how they keep order in Gilgate, but we have lines of command here. They stop us descending into anarchy.'

'I don't have clearance either. I'll do it if you like.'

He chewed a thumbnail and frowned at me. 'Why would you want to? Why would I let you?'

'You're looking for dirt on them, right? And you want to find it before the hearing, but you're running out of time.'

He sat back and folded his arms, but his frown was more calculating now. 'And, of course, breaking news about Remnant crimes would distract the Council from the actual purpose of the hearing. Is that what you're hoping?'

I shrugged. 'Okay, so I have an interest. Do you want to try or not?'

'You won't be able to get in.'

'Want a bet?'

He looked around the room, which was empty, and back at me. 'You know how much we trust you?'

'Yeah, I do. You can watch me every step of the way.'

He stood up. 'Go on, then. You've got,' he glanced at his watch, 'an hour, I'd say, before Levkova comes back.'

'Want to help?'

He watched over my shoulder as I got into the system, which I did in as clumsy a way as I could, hoping he wouldn't click that I'd been there before. 'Hmm,' he said when I got in. 'Okay. Help how?'

'Remnant finances – how do we find them?'

He had a few suggestions and we dived in.

'Suppose we find something,' I said. 'You think Vega or Levkova would use it?'

'I wish. Depends how solid it is. They're so focused on what's happening over the river, they're not guarding their backs. They think the independents are as focused as they are, but they're wrong. And they think that if they're found to be investigating Remnant it will undermine solidarity in the uprising. It'd have to be very, very solid before they'd use it. Which is why Levkova will not be impressed if she finds us doing this. Hour's nearly up.' We'd found nothing that looked like a windfall. Which we wouldn't if that windfall was sitting in a cellar or an attic somewhere, cold and hungry and terrified, and hadn't been translated into cash yet.

'But look,' I said, 'if they've stolen something from over the river, maybe they haven't sold it yet.'

'Maybe.'

'So what if we cross check Remnant names with records of known dealers and traffickers?'

'Later. Get off there before Levkova comes back.'

'When later?'

'After the hearing. Get off there now!'

When Fyffe came back from the township she was all fired up. At the evening meal, which that day wasn't half bad – a chunk of grainy bread and a bowl of thick potato-and-bacon soup – she led me to an empty table in the corner of the dining hall. Jeitan eyed us from the food queue but left us alone.

Fy spoke fast and soft in Anglo. 'The supplies officer here is a dealer. He spent the day organizing something, I'm sure. He thinks I'm slow – that's why I'm the one to go with him – but I'm sure he's creaming off medicines from the shipment and selling them.' She paused and tore her bread into pieces, then went on in Breken. 'It's terrible. People here need those supplies. That boy, last night – they ran out of medicine for him. If he was over the river he'd still be alive. And if they weren't dealing in their medicines here, he might still be alive too. His mother just cried and cried.' Fy scowled and ate her soup.

'Anyway,' she went on, 'One of the people the supplies

man talked to looked familiar. I'm sure he was one of the men who took Sol. Almost sure. So I followed him –'

'You what? Are you crazy?'

'– but I lost him. I'm going back tomorrow.'

'Jeez, Fy. D'you think he saw you?'

She shook her head. 'I was careful.'

'Can you wait for me before you go following people? I think Jeitan might help us, but we have to wait till after the hearing. Don't do anything drastic, okay?'

Near midnight Levkova told me to finish up and bring her the work I'd been doing. She said, 'You and Lanya – I have not heard the full story, I think?' I shuffled paper and didn't answer. 'I see,' she said. 'The hearing will be ugly. You will be on the wrong side no matter what you say.' Another pause. 'What will you say?'

That I'm out of here, is what I wanted to say. That if you people are so desperate to tear each other apart, couldn't you concentrate on doing that and leave those of us on the other side of the river alone?

'Well?' she asked.

I dropped the papers onto her desk. 'That I stumbled on an argument I knew nothing about. That I barely spoke to either of them. That this is so obviously a set-up I can't believe anyone is taking it seriously. That it has nothing *at all* to do with me. Will that work?'

'Of course. If you were talking to reasonable people.'

'No, then. So what happens next?'

'They will try to cast you out.' She looked at me. 'To you that might just seem like moving on. What can they take from you that you haven't already lost? Not a home. Or belongings. Even your name – you'd invent another one, wouldn't you? But the borderlands are deadly this time of year, for the weather as much as the bandits. I think the best we can hope is that Lanya won't accuse you and the Council sends you back to Gilgate.' She gave a grim smile. 'Some would say that's worse than being cast out. Anyway, then you can go and leave us to our madness.' She picked up the papers. 'Thank you, Nik. I am sorry. The misjudgment was Lanya's not yours.'

'She gave me some bread and fish. How can that be wrong?'

'She's a Maker. Surely even Gilgate has kept its Makers?'

When I didn't answer she shook her head. 'Have things become so degraded that even the dead are left to cross alone? Our Makers fast in all things in the hours before a Crossing – they take no food, submit to no touch, and should not even speak. Lanya most certainly should not have been arguing with Coly.'

The phone on her desk beeped. She pressed a button. 'Levkova.'

'You sent for Jeitan, ma'am?' A woman's voice.

'I did.'

'Not available, I'm afraid.'

Levkova took her finger off the button and frowned at me. 'Who can I trust?' She pressed the button again and said, 'All right. Send me Rémy or Joseph.'

She turned back to me. 'One last thing. They will ask you tomorrow what you've been doing here. What will you tell them?'

There are moments, now and then, when the world you thought you had sorted spins ninety degrees on its heel and when it stops you see everything slant. When Levkova asked me that, with an edge in her voice, I had one of those moments. From the start she'd told me not to talk to anyone about what I was doing in CommSec. And here she was, not wanting the Council to know. I heard Jeitan in my head talking about Levkova and Vega: *they think if they're found to be investigating Remnant it will undermine solidarity in the uprising.* And I knew. Those comms I'd spent the last few days trying, and failing, to break hadn't come from over the river at all. They weren't encrypted Anglo. They'd come from here. Encrypted Breken. These people were spying on their own.

Levkova looked up. 'Well?'

'Filing?' I said.

Her mouth twitched. 'Filing. Yes. What's your other name?'

'Why?'

'No reason. Curious. Your parents?'

'I didn't know them.'

She nodded. 'You're a good person, Nik. Who'd have guessed it?'

Remember that, I thought. Remember that if you ever find out where I'm from.

There was a knock on the door and my Jeitan substitute peered in. 'Joseph,' said Levkova. 'Take him straight to Shed 3. No detours.' She turned to me. 'Off you go. And watch your back.'

But it wasn't my back I needed to watch.

CHAPTER 21

Joseph led me out into the night and promptly disappeared. And I walked straight into somebody's fist. Yes, I should have seen it coming, but I thought they wouldn't bother. I'd already served Remnant's purposes by walking in on Lanya's fight on Saturday night. The hearing would get me banished and the Pathmakers branded as 'unclean.' There wasn't much else I could do for them.

I don't know how many there were. Four? Four hundred? The first punch knocked the breath out of me. Something soft dropped over my head, the lights went out and I gagged on a mouthful of cloth.

Couldn't see. Couldn't breathe.

Someone behind me grabbed my arms and a fist landed in my gut. I doubled over, gasping, then straightened up fast as I could, heaved my shoulder upwards and connected with something, a jaw maybe. Its owner grunted, twisted my arms up my back then hurled me forwards. I hit the ground hard, on knee and shoulder. Pain went ringing through me. Still couldn't breathe or see. I tore at the cloth around my head, but a boot rammed into my ribs, folding me up. Another one landed hard on my back. I ripped the cloth off my head in time to see a boot swinging towards my face.

I woke up in the dark with a thumping head.

Lay still and listened. Heard nothing. Tried to sit up and couldn't. Panicked. Realized after a moment that I wasn't tied up after all, just so cold and so sore that nothing wanted to move. I lay there and thought about going to sleep, but a vestige of sense in my brain told me I was cold and getting colder and colder, so *shift*. I managed to half sit up, and not to throw up – a triumph in its own way – and eventually got myself semi-upright. I crawled about, found a wall to lean on and inspected the damage.

I had a lump on my temple that was tight and sore but my face seemed to be in one piece. The rest of me, not great. Pain around ribs, shoulder, gut and back. And my shirt was wet. I sniffed at it, hoping it wasn't blood. It smelled like alcohol. Someone in my welcoming party had been drinking and had upended their cheap vodka all over me. At least they hadn't bashed my head in with the bottle – look on the bright side.

I struggled to my feet. Got there without throwing

up or falling over, and looked around – the sort of looking you do when you think you've suddenly gone blind.

Directly ahead of me was a single faint line of gray light, a crack in a door maybe: I wondered if it came from the floodlit compound, or a lit street down in the town. I made my way around the walls towards it, fell over a few things – tools, bags of something, cement, I think – swore a lot, but got there in the end. It was a door, locked. I tried shaking it but it didn't even creak on a hinge. I yelled a few times, or tried to, but it came out feeble as hell because my ribs objected to anything louder than breathing.

I sat on a sack of cement, leaned against the wall and hated everyone, individually and collectively, on this side of the stinking river. Including myself. I was a miserable failure at finding Sol. And at looking after Fy. I could see the thread between Sol and us stretching and thinning to breaking point as he moved further and further out of reach.

For a while I drifted in and out of sleep, but the cold and the nightmares kept waking me up. To take my mind off them, I went looking for a puzzle, a problem, an unfinished proof, anything that would occupy my brain until daylight, or someone in search of a wrench, arrived.

I found one ready-made: the pages I'd been staring at over the last week. I went back to the words I thought might be bridge names and tried decoding for Breken rather than Anglo. It was like a homework extension exercise: 'For those with no friends and no social life to speak of, decipher the following code. Conditions: you must do this in a language not your own while in a vaguely concussed state of mind. You may have all night. You may not ask for help.' But I was so cold and so angry those words took on a kind of desperate clarity that kept me occupied until – I don't know how many hours later – I heard the door being unlocked.

CHAPTER 22

I waited for someone to appear but no one did, so I stumbled over and gave the door a push. Daylight came crashing in. It hammered my eyes and I threw up, which left me gasping. I crawled outside and put my face to the sun. I sat there with my eyes closed, letting the warmth soak into me and unknit the knots in my bones. Mending. The air was warm; it was one of those autumn mornings that made you want to skip class and head up to the heath. A shadow fell on me. I opened an eye.

'Jeitan,' I croaked. My mouth felt like paper. 'Looking sharp, as always. Can you stand out of my sun?'

'What the hell are you doing here? The hearing has started. They sent me to get you and you've been bloody nowhere. Come on!'

I shook my head.

He crouched in front of me. 'Gods, you stink! You're

drunk! You're not fronting up like this.'

'Don't intend to. I'm not going.'

'Don't be funny. They'll drag you in there if they have to.' He looked furious. 'Alcohol's forbidden here. You must know that?'

Right. Like knives.

'And you know what's at stake!'

I closed my eyes. 'I don't care. It's your fight. Go away and fight it without me. Just get out of my sun.'

'Not a chance. You are going to that hearing.' The voice of conviction, unfortunately. 'Come on, you're getting cleaned up.'

I thought about just staying put, but I knew he really would drag me there if he had to. And I hurt too much for that. 'All right,' I said. 'I'll go if you do me a favor.'

'A what? You can't be serious.'

'I am, though.'

He sighed. 'What do you want?'

'Ask at the hearing about Remnant's windfall.'

'What? Why?'

'It'll take the heat off me.'

'Council doesn't work that way. Levkova might raise it. I asked her to. But I doubt she will.'

'You and your lines of command. How do you ever get anything done? Okay, let's go and see.'

He shadowed me to my shed, shoved a spare set of clothes at me and pushed me into the washroom. I peeled off my alcohol-sodden gear, winced a bit, craved a hot, or even a luke-warm shower, dragged on clean clothes and emerged to a watch-tapping Jeitan. 'You still look like shit,' he said.

'Yeah. Sorry.'

'And you're walking like someone stood on you.' When I didn't answer he said, 'Are you going to tell me this isn't just the after-effects of cheap juice?' I couldn't see the point in having this argument and besides I was trying to focus on why I'd ever thought turning up for the hearing was a good idea.

Remnant, of course. I had to find out what I could about them, and get a look at their leaders. And I had to hope that someone would challenge them on their rumored windfall. And I had to avoid getting either cast out or shipped off to Gilgate.

Jeitan was busy grumbling. 'Go on. Tell me. One of your drinking buddies take a swing at you? Who was it? What did you do to deserve it?'

But we'd arrived and I didn't need to answer.

We stopped at the end of a long corridor that was almost empty. We were at the end of the south wing of the main building and we seemed to have left behind all the people hurtling about clutching urgent memos or waving the latest incoming from over the bridge. A bored guard slouched in front of a heavy wooden door. He nodded to

Jeitan and frisked me. Felt like he hit every bruise. And he found Coly's knife.

'Ah,' said Jeitan, as if this confirmed his high opinion of me. 'Anything else?'

'No,' I said.

He gave me a what-are-you-hiding? sort of look.

'Nothing!' I said.

But he shook his head. 'I was right, wasn't I? Someone took a swing at you. Come on.' He pushed open the door. 'In.' He nodded for the guard to follow us.

Levkova was there. And Commander Vega. They were sitting at a long table with a motley collection of others – twelve in all. Lanya stood at the head of the table flanked by a tall, fine-boned woman, a Pathmaker for sure. When we came in everyone turned, like puppets on a single string, to stare at us.

This was their Council room, but in its doppelganger over the river I knew it as the staff library. And maybe it had been a library here too: empty shelves lined the walls and the air had that musty old-book smell. The room was all dark wood, real wood. Tall windows reached up to a high ceiling but all except two were boarded up. Sunlight poured through those two onto the table, casting the rest of the room into shadow. No rugs, pictures, or books in sight. The room was stripped, like the rest of that place, hunkered down without extras of any kind. Battle-ready.

One of the men, a bull of a guy – huge shoulders, no neck – beckoned me over and spoke to Vega.

'This him?'

'It is.'

'And you brought him across.'

'I put him in a squad. We lost five people on Saturday. Replacements are hard to find.'

'A question of judgment, Commander. Poor in this case.'

'With respect, Councillor, nothing has been proved.'

'We've seen the digi-graph –'

'Shadows.'

'And he was seen drunk last night.'

So the vodka wasn't just someone being clumsy. 'Who by?' I said.

They looked at me like I was from off-planet. No-neck said, 'Be quiet.'

'And at the Crossing?' said a man down the end of the table. 'Drunk then too, I suppose. And the girl?'

'She gave me food when I was hungry,' I said. 'That's all. And I wasn't drunk.'

No-neck barked, '*I said, be quiet!*'

I looked at Lanya. She was staring at the table. The woman beside her put an arm around her shoulders. 'We have no doubt where the blame lies, Councillor.'

Then, as if they'd rehearsed it, the door guard said, 'Sir, found this on him.' He tossed Coly's knife on the table. It spun and slowed to a stop, neatly folded and lethal, its tiny flick-switch glinting.

Twelve pairs of eyes accused me of crimes against decency and clean living.

No-neck sat back, folded his arms, and smirked.

Vega sighed. 'You've proved nothing. He's a scavenger. You may loathe that – I do – but it's no surprise he carries a knife. It doesn't mean he used it on the girl.' He glanced at Lanya. She gave a single shake of her head. Her keeper glared at me.

They launched into an argument about whether they could believe Coly's evidence, and whether scum from Gilgate should ever be allowed into Moldam. I moved three paces to the wall and leaned on it. It was either that or fall over.

When I looked up they were still in full cry, except Levkova, who was watching me. I looked away, back to the action and wondered how grim it could all get. Very grim, was my guess. And if they hauled Fyffe in and quizzed her, we were dead. Her Breken wasn't fluent enough and we hadn't put together any kind of backstory these people would believe.

I focused on No-neck; I recognized his voice. This was Terten, the guy who'd heavied Levkova in the CommSec office a few nights before. A Remnant bully-boy. I wondered if he had Sol hidden somewhere. And if he did, had he seen him or talked to him? Or would the actual living, breathing child that was Sol be so far down the line that this guy could profit from him and never even know who he was?

Terten was enjoying himself. He stood up and leaned over the table. 'This much is clear. You, Commander Vega, are not fit to head this Council.' He turned to the rest of the table, opened his arms wide and launched into full preacher mode. 'My friends, we must not stumble now.'

'We are not stumbling!' said Vega.

But Terten rolled on. 'Our victory lies in God's hands. But here is dishonor at our very heart. Sin of the most shameful kind has wormed its way into our core…'

He seemed to make an effort to look sad but, really, he looked gleeful. He walked around the table and paused behind Lanya. She hugged her arms tight and stared at the ground; she looked like she was trying to make herself as small as possible. He walked on. 'Do we stand by? No! We excise the rot. We cast it from us. We cauterize the wound.'

A depressing amount of nodding rippled round the table. I knew they flogged criminals on Southside – sometimes to death. Or they cast them out, exiled, without food or water, into the borderlands in the far south. I had no allies here, and no leverage at all. A lone scavenger from Gilgate would be insignificant collateral damage in the power game they were playing.

'Councillor!' Levkova broke into the monologue.

'Please sit down. You judge too quickly. We have no clear evidence.'

Terten arrived back at his chair. He leaned on it and his beady eyes scanned the rest of the Council. He ignored Levkova. She sighed and shot a look at Vega.

'Compromise!' bellowed Terten. 'Is that our banner now? Mealy mouthed compromise? The sub-commander would have it so. And if we compromise here, in safeguarding our own purity, what then in our dealings with the city? My friends, we have been led down the path of compromise for too long. Do you have courage, do you have faith enough, to strike out on a better path?' His stare shifted to pick out each person round the table. 'I say we vote. Now. For a strong path, a pure path, a righteous path, a path that will lead us to victory.'

Levkova tried again. 'Councillor, your sloganeering will cost lives. I make no apology for seeking to exercise judgment and pragmatism in this uprising. You glorify righteous confrontation, but you do it on the bodies of our children.' She looked at Vega again.

Vega spoke up. 'Returning to the matter at hand, Terten. Of course, the safety and honor of our Makers is vital. But we have no real evidence here. And we have other urgent matters before us. City forces are regrouping at Sentinel, Clare, and Torrens Hill –'

But Terten interrupted, 'For continued poor judgment, now evident in bringing dangerous elements to our district and failing to safeguard our Makers, I ask Council for a vote of no confidence in Commander Vega as its head.'

There it was. An ambush.

They went around the table. I didn't know who was who, but I could count. Seven 'ayes' and five 'nays'. The independents had caved to the threat of appearing weak and gone with Remnant.

Terten smiled, smug as all hell. 'As deputy, I will take the chair until we make a full appointment. Next: I seek sanction on those involved in this scandal – this boy, and this girl.'

'Aye, aye, aye…' Twelve 'ayes' and no 'nays'. Even Vega and Levkova voted in favor of punishing us. I sucked in a breath and willed Lanya to look at me, but she wasn't risking that.

'I seek this sanction,' said Terten. 'The boy to be flogged and cast out.'

My mouth went dry. The 'ayes' began again, one by one, round the table. Lanya looked at me.

Vega stood up. 'No. No one will be flogged over this.' He leaned over the table into Terten's face. 'The Council may be yours now, Terten, but the army is not. This was a Crossing – an army matter. *My* troops, not your fanatics. While I head the army, I control its discipline. Sanction, yes. But there will be no flogging.' He pointed at me. 'The boy goes back to Gilgate. The girl to her family.' He stood back and looked around the table. Not too many of them met his eye. 'This is not the end of this discussion. But I have better things to do than battle over polemics and preaching at this table.' He left. Stormed past us without even a glare. Jeitan watched him, mournful as a lost dog.

Levkova said, 'If the Council permits, I will ensure the boy returns to Gilgate.'

'By sunset,' said Terten and no one objected.

Victory to Remnant.

CHAPTER 23

Exiled. Banished. Cast out. Call it what you like. It amounted to abandoning Fy and Sol. I stood outside the Council room with Levkova and Jeitan. They held a murmured conversation and I concentrated on staying upright. A fog had come down between me and the world and the corridor ahead looked hazy and gray. Two things were depressingly clear, however. I was no closer to knowing whether the rumored Remnant windfall existed, let alone whether it pointed to Sol. And I was being sent away.

I was trying to put together a coherent sentence to ask Levkova if I could please take Fyffe with me, remembering that I had to call her Sina and wishing that my brain would unscramble, when Levkova turned to me. 'Nik. I'm sorry. This is not your fault. You were in the wrong place at the wrong time and they've seized their chance. Jeitan, we'll go to my quarters. We must feed him at least.'

'Feed him to what?' muttered Jeitan.

Levkova smiled. 'Come with me.'

We walked out of the building and across the grounds without speaking – slowly, at her pace, which I was grateful for because I was finding it harder and harder to walk at all. On the way, Levkova crooked a finger and collected a kid maybe ten years old. She berated him mildly for not being in the schoolhouse. He grinned and jigged along beside us, chattering at Jeitan. But Jeitan was stony faced and silent.

We went through an archway in the brick wall that ran along the river side of the compound. Down the slope in front of us, stone markers grew out of rough cut grass with a few spindly trees scattered among them. Levkova lived in an old brick house on the edge of that graveyard. The house must've been impressive once: the entrance opened into a high atrium with hallways leading into shadows but they were roped off and barricaded with wrecked furniture. The air smelled of damp and rot.

She took us through a small door off the atrium and into a room that was old like its owner but, unlike her, shabby and comfortable: there were armchairs, a couch, a table, shelves and shelves of books, and tall windows with the sun streaming in. She called, 'I'm back!' and someone answered from another room. She disappeared into it.

I sat on the floor in a patch of sunlight and closed my eyes. Breathing was hard work, sharply painful every time. Before long, Levkova came back. 'I did tell you to watch your back,' she said.

'Yeah. I remember.'

She turned to the kid she'd collected. 'Go and get Dr Mayur for me. Quick now.' So he scuttled off and I sat in the sun and concentrated on breathing. The next thing I knew the room was full of people. Commander Vega had arrived. He was being called Sim, and Levkova was Tasia, so I figured we were among friends. Jeitan was still there, and two others I didn't know. One was a young woman called Yuna. She was dressed in squad clothes and she paced up and down in that small space like a fuse burning down to its fuel, her arms crossed, her head bent as she listened to Levkova report on the Council meeting. And there was a man about Vega's age. He crouched in front of me. 'Nik, is it? Can you get up?'

'Why?'

'Because I need to take a look at you.'

'Why?'

He gave a half smile. 'Orders.'

Levkova looked up from her reporting and pointed to a door. 'Go in there.'

'See?' he said.

I didn't move. I'd done enough stupid stuff. I didn't feel like adding to the list.

He fished in a jacket pocket and held up a little container. Rattled it. 'Painkillers. Scarce and pricey. Why Tasia's wasting them on you I do not know. But I suggest you count yourself lucky and let me take a look at why you need them.'

Okay. That was convincing enough for me.

When we emerged a while later Levkova and the others were sitting round the table – except for Jeitan, who'd taken up a position at the door as though he'd decided that these people needed a permanent guard. Levkova said, 'Well?'

'He'll live,' said the doctor. 'Couple of cracked ribs. Bruising. Mild concussion. I think that's all. If there's anything internal it's not obvious right now.' He held up the painkillers. 'Are you sure you want to give him these?'

'Yes,' said Levkova. 'I am.'

'Why?' said Yuna.

'He stumbled into one of our fights. I feel responsible. You don't really think this was a drunken brawl?'

'Looks like it to me,' said the doctor.

Vega broke the pencil he was fiddling with, said 'Sorry' to Levkova and looked at me. 'Yes,' he said. 'It's supposed to.'

'Who, then?' said the doctor. 'And why?'

'Makers,' said Levkova.

'*What?*'

'I know. It won't go down well with anyone to say that. But they needed to absolve Lanya, and for that they needed a scapegoat. The girl wasn't making accusations, so they improvised.'

'You don't believe that?' he said.

She looked at me. I don't know what she could make of me from knowing me all of five days, but she said, 'Yes, I do.'

The doctor shook his head but he tossed me the pain-killers. I closed my hand on them and felt an odd, and no doubt misplaced, sense of relief.

'Let's eat,' said Levkova. 'Here. I don't think any of us wants to face the hall.'

Lunch was served by an old man called Max. He was badly bent and lame and he was treated with such respect by everyone that I guessed he must be a relative or a friend of Levkova. He served up a stack of warm flat-breads, a spiced bean mash, and some fresh green leaves. Someone exclaimed over the leaves and Levkova was off then talking about her vegetable garden like nothing else mattered. Like the shifting of a deadly political balance between enemy factions was something that happened every morning of the week and didn't deserve lunch-time comment. I picked at a piece of flatbread, thinking I should be famished. I wasn't, so I retreated to an armchair and left them to eat and talk.

When I woke up my ribs had stopped hurting, which

made me feel stupidly optimistic for the nanosecond it took before I remembered Fy and Sol. Round the table they were onto politics and strategy: how to tip the balance back their way, how to restore CFM influence on Council. I didn't listen too hard. I was doing my own strategizing – I had to stop them sending me upriver to Gilgate.

At the table, the doctor was saying, 'They're not so clean. We just need to catch them at something they shouldn't be doing. How hard can that be? They've got enough rules. Surely they've got people breaking some of them?'

'Of course they have,' said Vega. 'How else are they funded?' He lapsed into an angry silence. I thought he'd probably been doing that a lot during the conversation.

'The problem,' said Levkova, 'is making criminal connections at Council level.'

'You're the code-breaker, Tasia,' said Yuna. 'Surely you've found something useful?'

Levkova shook her head. 'Not yet. And if I lose CommSec, the backroom project goes as well.'

'Has nothing come through all those memos?' said Yuna.

I sent up a silent prayer to Lou that this wasn't a huge mistake and dived in. 'Smuggling,' I said.

They looked at me like, who the hell are you to be entering this discussion?

The doctor said, 'And you know this how?'

I looked at Levkova. She frowned. 'Well?'

'Your messages,' I said. 'The ones I've been sorting.'

'*Coded* messages,' said Yuna.

'Yeah,' I said. 'Those ones.'

'They're *in code*,' she said, like I was very slow. 'How many of those painkillers did you take?'

The doctor turned back to Levkova and Vega. 'So. What's the plan?'

'Wait,' said Vega. And to me, 'Explain.'

I said, 'Whoever's been sending the memos – Remnant? – they've organized to get their people guarding the bridge gates tomorrow because they want to bring something over without being noticed.'

'Oh, yes?' said the doctor. 'And what's that?'

'I don't know exactly. They've reduced their alphabet – doubling up on letters – some words are hard to pick if you don't know them already. They called it DFO.'

'DFO,' said Vega quietly, staring at me in a way that made me deeply nervous. 'Not it. Him.' He held out the stub of the pencil he'd snapped. 'Show me.'

So I did. Scrawling on the back of an old requisition form. They sat round the table, watching. Even Jeitan came and looked over my shoulder. When I was done, the doctor gave a low whistle. 'That's some party trick.'

'Where did you learn to do that?' asked Vega.

I shrugged. 'It's just patterns, and a good memory.'

My heart was thudding. Vega got up and walked away. He stood staring out the window. Everybody watched him. At last he said, 'Where did you say you came from?'

'Gilgate.'

'Where in Gilgate? And you're Nik who? What's the rest of your name?'

I held up the page. 'Do you want this, or not?' I put it back on the table because my hand was shaking.

'I want to know who you are.'

'I'm no one. Do you want this or don't you? Because if you don't, I'm going. I'm supposed to be gone by sunset.'

'What's in it for you?' said Yuna. 'Why would you help?'

Levkova stirred. 'How suspicious we've become. Does it matter?'

'But don't you think it's strange?' said Yuna. 'Is this even accurate?'

Levkova took the paper and studied it. 'Yes, it is. It's exactly right. I've done the same work myself, only much more slowly. But I haven't seen this yet.' She waved the paper at me. 'This is one you looked at yesterday? Why didn't you tell me?'

'I only worked it out last night in that shed.'

'In the dark?' said the doctor. 'Wearing the after-effects of a beating?'

'Dark is best.'

Levkova looked at Vega. 'It's your call, Sim.'

Vega shook his head. 'I don't like it. He arrives here out of nowhere, with no papers, and no name that he wants to tell us. Three days later we're outgunned on Council because of him, and now he's decoding Remnant messages as though he's written them himself.'

They all looked at me and I felt like I had *Remnant Spy* inscribed on my forehead.

But Levkova said, 'It's all we have. I think we take what we've been given, however unlikely. I'll watch him.'

Vega frowned, narrow-eyed, at me. 'All right, Nik whatever-your-name-is, you stay. Here, with the sub-commander. But remember your cracked ribs, because if we discover you're a spy, believe me, cracked ribs will be the least of your worries.'

CHAPTER 24

So, a reprieve. Of sorts.

But the moment I showed my face outside I'd be gone, sent upriver to Gilgate, or worse. Contacting Fyffe was now a big problem. And urgent, because if she had seen one of Sol's kidnappers down in the township we needed to get on that trail before it went cold. And if she heard I'd been sent up to Gilgate, she was likely to go it alone, or to act on that crazy plan of hers to hand herself in.

That evening the light turned pale and gray and snow began to fall. Watching it gust in flurries at the window, I hoped that it would keep Fyffe indoors for the time it would take me to reach her. Levkova pointed me to Max's room. 'You can sleep here. There's a mattress but not many blankets, I'm afraid.' She rummaged in a cupboard and handed me an old army coat. 'This will help. Don't worry about Max, he doesn't sleep much these days, so you won't bother him.'

She told me that he had been her assistant in active service years before, and a stalwart supporter of CFM since he was my age. Now he was dying – some kind of slow unpicking of his bones and muscles. 'He has a lot of pain and we do what we can to get medicine. It's not easy.' He was sitting in the main room, a book on his lap, but his eyes were clouded over, as if they'd seen enough of the world, more than enough, and didn't want to look anymore.

'Long stories,' Levkova said to me when he'd dozed off after a ramble about the Crossover – the mass expulsion of Breken workers from the city in '48. He'd been part of that. He was seventeen.

'I don't mind long stories,' I said. And that was no lie. I didn't know the stories every Breken kid had chewed on since they'd cut their teeth. What I did know was that Max's story didn't mesh at all with the history I'd been taught. The Crossover – the expulsion of workers and the closing of the bridges – yes, I knew about that. That's when the gates were built, Cityside and Southside, on every bridge. But, as Max told it, there was a general strike leading up to the Crossover – a strike for wages. Not higher wages, just wages, rather than food and rent vouchers. I knew nothing about that. Or about the demonstrations and rioting that followed. Or about a massacre by city forces that ended it all. The survivors carried their dead back over the river. Every Crossing since then – like the one for Tamsin that Fyffe and I had seen – was an echo of that first one. Max was old and rambly, but he didn't strike me as deluded or dishonest.

'Well,' Levkova was saying, 'you are more polite than many. What about your own?'

'My own what?'

'Story, Nik. Your own story.'

'Oh.' I shook my head. 'It's short and boring.'

'I wonder.'

After a while I said, 'Do you know any Citysiders? Did you ever meet a good one – an honorable one?'

She paused. 'Once or twice, long ago. But when it came to allowing us freedom across the river – even they struggled with that. They're born to privilege, Nik. They can't let it go. You must never trust one. But I'm sure you know that.'

I wanted to tell her. I was inching towards it. Inching got me as far as saying, 'My friend, the one I came here with – she's working in the infirmary. I need to tell her what's happened, where I am, otherwise she'll think I've been sent back to Gilgate.'

She shook her head. 'Wait a day or so – they'll be watching her.'

A day or so was impossibly long. I lay awake that night, counting minutes, and when I was sure that Levkova and Max were asleep I threw on all the clothes I had and went to look for Fyffe.

The snowstorm had passed, leaving a clear, freezing night. I breathed out white fog, and my boots crunched on frosted ground. I hid inside the coat's big collar and deep pockets and stuck to the shadows. There were still people about, heading back from patrol or venturing out for a smoke. They stood together in threes and fours stamping the ground and talking about the explosions upriver, the snow, rationing, and hungry kids; about who was sick and who needed medicines that weren't there, had never been there because of the city blockade; about the ones they'd buried and the ones they expected to bury before winter's end.

My head was full of those conversations by the time I got to the infirmary, and I thought how ordinary they sounded. So much about these people was ordinary. No one was dancing gleefully on the grave of the city, no one was eating children. But for all that, someone here had Sol, and I had to get him back.

I found a boarded-up doorway on the end of the riverside wing and crouched on the step, watching the infirmary. Now and then its door opened in a rectangle of yellow light, and figures hurried down the steps and away into the dark. I waited until the sky began to pale. I didn't see Fyffe.

Max was dozing in his armchair when I went back to

Levkova's. I put a brick of peat on the fire and sat in front of it wondering what to do. The flames struggled back to life and I decided that if I couldn't find Fy by the end of that day, I had to tell Levkova who we were and ask her for help. And hope she'd be so busy with her own troubles she wouldn't care where we came from.

'Long night, youngster,' said Max.

'Yes, sir. Sorry I woke you.'

'No, no. Way you creep around, you're not gonna wake anyone. Scare the life out of someone maybe, way you appear like that, outta nowhere. But you're not gonna wake anyone 'cept maybe the dead. But tell me now.' He sat up and put what looked like a prayer book aside. 'You're afire with something. Comes in the room with you. Follows you round. Is it a girl?'

'No, sir.'

'What then?'

'It's nothing.'

'No one's wound that tight over nothing.'

'I'm cold, that's all.'

'You don't want to tell, that's fine by me. But a secret like that, it weighs you down. Hollows you out.'

'Aren't you cold? Do you want this coat?'

'No. She gave it to you.' He sat back. 'Safan's, that was. A good man. They had a child – him and Tasia. Pia, they called her. She was a sweet thing.' I knew as soon as he said that, that I didn't want to hear what was coming.

But he told me. 'They came on a sweep one day. City boys. Guns and uniforms. Sky-high confident, like they always are. Said they was looking for bombs, like they always do. Tasia was away from home, but Safan was there, and the child.' He peered in my direction. 'Your age she was. And the city boys. Your age too. Her father fought, as any man would. Tasia found them when she came home. Long ago that was. Long ago. Where are you going?'

'Out.'

'You've just come in.'

'Yeah.'

'Cold out there, youngster. Wrap up.'

I stood in the archway to the graveyard and looked across the compound. There was movement here and there in the gray nearly-light – people coming out of prefabs pulling on boots and jackets and stomping off in clouds of breath to visit the washrooms before the rush to get ready for drill. I thought about how close I'd come to telling Levkova who I was. But now, I never could. Because who could forgive what we'd done to her family? Wouldn't you want revenge? If two city kids came asking for help, why would you show any mercy at all?

CHAPTER 25

I turned away from the buzz outside and went back into the house. I couldn't face Max or Levkova, so I scrambled over the barricade of broken furniture that lay across one of the hallways and groped my way in the dark to the end of it. There I found a door and, through it, a cavern of a room. It was empty except for a couple of benches along one wall. The leaking roof dripped into puddles and dribbled down the windows frames. But those windows. They hit me with a memory of home – of school – sharp as the pain in my ribs.

It must have been a chapel once. The windows were tall stained glass with figures just showing themselves against the early light outside. How they'd survived when so much else was rubble I don't know. But survived they had and, now, with the sun starting to light them up, they took me straight back to morning prayer at school.

Dash and Fyffe and Bella sitting in their pew, two rows in front of Lou and Sol and me. The sun shining through the golden windows, Fyffe's hair glowing like a halo. Stapleton droning on at the pulpit, bald head gleaming, big white hands gripping the red cover of the lectionary, and none of us paying him any attention. Too busy watching each other.

'Hey!' said a voice behind me. I jumped about a mile.

Lanya stood in the doorway. She lifted her chin and watched me, wary.

I said, 'You make a habit of creeping up on people and giving them heart failure?'

She gave half a smile and came two steps into the room. 'You didn't swear this time.'

Like a Citysider. No.

'I thought you'd gone,' she said. 'Been exiled.'

'I was. I'm like your knife wound. I don't exist.'

She began to walk around the edge of the room, still watching me. She had a dancer's walk, light on her feet. As she reached the far end the east window lit up with the rising sun. She stopped under that window, closed her eyes and lifted her face to the light. She glowed black-gold. For maybe a whole minute she stood motionless, her braids falling back, like she was soaking up the sun, recharging.

The east window was gold with three monks in brown robes holding red bibles and looking at rows and rows of black birds. Lanya opened her eyes and looked at it. 'Birds,' she said. 'In a holy window. Why?'

'It's St Francis,' I said. 'Preaching.'

She turned to me. 'To birds? How do you know that?'

I shrugged. 'Just do.'

'Well, why then?' she said. 'Why would he do that?'

'No idea. Maybe they've got some repenting to do. Maybe they've been pecking holes in the grapes before the harvest, or shitting on some laundrywoman's washing.'

She laughed. 'What's he saying?'

'He's saying it's all about bread. Which gets their attention. But then he says it's the bread of heaven that they need, and they're thinking, no, thanks very much but if it's all the same to him they'd rather have the bread left over from breakfast.'

She laughed again; then she stopped and said, 'That makes you sad. Why?'

'I knew a window like that once. It's gone now.'

'Bulldozed?'

'Blown up.'

She nodded and resumed her walk around the walls. The room was quiet except for the drip of water into puddles, and still, except for the clouds of our breathing. She arrived in front of me. 'You didn't tell,' she said.

'At the hearing? They weren't the sort of people I'd want to tell anything.'

'Does Levkova know you're still here?'

When I didn't answer, she said, 'If she's hiding you she must have a good reason.' She tilted her head and studied me. 'I didn't know you'd been ambushed. They told me after the hearing. I'm sorry. Are you hurt?'

'I'm okay.'

'What will you do now? Aren't you going back to Gilgate?'

'Maybe. I don't know. What about you?'

'I'm not a Maker anymore. Just a plain person. So I'm joining a squad.'

'To fight?'

'Of course, to fight.' She smiled and turned for the door. 'I have to go to drill.'

I watched her go, then I realized she might help me. I called, 'Wait! Will you do something for me?'

She came back into the sunlight. 'I might. I owe you. What is it?'

'My friend. Sina. She's working in the infirmary. She might have heard I've been sent away. I want to let her know I'm still here.'

She stood back and did that little bow. 'I'll find her and tell her.'

'Today?'

She nodded. 'Today.'

'Can you ask her to meet me here this time tomorrow? And can you not tell anyone else or Levkova will be sunk.

And so will I. It has to be a secret.'

Her eyes lit up. 'I'll play.'

'It's not a game!' But I was talking to her back. And then she was gone. I stood there a while longer wondering how much of a mistake I might have just made.

I was learning fast – if Levkova was caught hiding me, I wouldn't be the only one in trouble. I don't know if they'd cast her out into the snows, but I figured they might. Remnant were old-fashioned like that. She had told me that everything would be much stricter with Remnant running the Council. People who were caught stealing or fighting or trying to go over the bridge without permission – their whole family'd go to the back of the queue for medicines. Their rations could be cut to nothing for a week or a month so they'd have to beg from relatives and friends or people on the street. The worst offenders would be cast out and would have to leave with nothing to go to another bridge or south into the borderlands. And anyone caught helping, well, they got to go too.

I headed back to Levkova's rooms. She was making tea and she put a mug of it in front of me. 'Drink.'

When I'd finished, she said, 'Now, tell me.'

'Tell you what?'

'Why you've been out all night when you have concussion, two cracked ribs, and I don't know what other hurts.'

I shook my head. 'I'm worried about my friend. I

need to find her.'

'What you need is sleep.'

'No, but –'

'Which is why the tea you've just drunk had a sleeping pill in it. Now go into that room and sleep.'

Which couldn't really be argued with.

What happened next was maybe because the sleeping stuff made me kind of drunk. When I got to the door of Max's room I turned back and said, 'I'm sorry about your family.'

'Ah.' Her eyebrows rose and she smiled a sad smile. 'Max has been talking.' She touched something at her neck and that's when I saw that she was wearing a talisman like the one the dead boy in the infirmary had worn. Like I had worn, for most of my life.

I said, 'Can I ask you something?'

'Only if you put your head on a pillow straight afterwards.'

'That talisman –'

'This?' She held it up. It was silver, like mine.

'Why do you wear it?'

'Hopeless, utopian optimism. I gave this one to Pia. And took it back from her when she was killed. There are, you know, too many parents wearing these nowadays. Why do you ask?'

I sat down at the table because the sleeping stuff was making it hard to stand up. 'I had one once. My mother gave it to me.'

'Well, well. You are full of surprises. But I'm pleased to hear that. Your mother wanted good things for you. You don't have it anymore?'

I shook my head. 'Someone took it. What d'you think my mother wanted for me?'

She took hers off and held it in her palm. 'The South-side Charter: *Not crescent, not cross, but blessing for all.* They were utopian, our forebears. But look at us now, at each other's throats. *Each to their own god and their own Rule, but space at the heart of every Rule for mystery, for the unknown.* That's the Charter. I hope that's what your mother wanted for you – to know that no one's god, no one's Rule, can be the whole.'

What my mother wanted for me. My mother.

Levkova put the talisman back round her neck. 'Now go to bed. If you fall over here, you'll be sleeping where you lie.'

I dreamed my mother's voice, singing to me. When I woke up I couldn't remember the words. Only that they were Breken.

The light was fading and the room was full of shadows. I lay on that lumpy mattress, shivering under a coarse blanket and the army coat, and my first thought was that I'd dreamed the conversation with Levkova. And my second thought was that I knew I hadn't.

What do you do with that? With discovering your mother was Breken? Does that make you Breken too, even if you've grown up your whole life in the city? And what about her dying in the uprising in '87 – which side of the uprising was she on? And who was Frieda Kelleran, the woman who put me in Tornmoor? She must have had some clout to get me in. Or my father did. Whoever he was. Was he Breken too?

It was like finding a mistake at the beginning of a pages-long proof – a single mistake and the whole thing unravels and you're back to square one, knowing nothing.

Not quite nothing.

I got up and peered out the window. It was late afternoon. I wondered if Lanya had given Fyffe my message yet. I did know one thing. I'd come to find Sol and that's what I'd do. Everything else would have to wait.

Meanwhile, there was a night's work ahead.

Levkova had anticipated the Remnant takeover of CommSec; piles of paper from her backroom project crammed the wardrobes and kitchen cupboards in her home. Now that I knew how to read them, I went back over all the comms she'd kept since Saturday, looking for something about a windfall, a boy, and a plan to traffic or ransom him. But their secrets were tame: some declarations by the Remnant-controlled Councils about purging the army of CFM sympathizers, some crowing that victory over the city was imminent. Only one of them made me wonder.

When Levkova came home about midnight, I handed it to her. 'Take a look. This is about a meeting Cityside. On Pagnal Heath on Crossover Day.' Which I figured must be a commemoration of the Crossover that Max had talked about – the mass expulsion of Breken workers from the city years before.

'That's next Thursday,' said Levkova. 'It doesn't give us much time. Who does it say is meeting? If Remnant are making secret deals with the city and we can prove it, we've got them.'

'According to this, Commander Vega and the guy they smuggled over the bridge, the one they called DFO.'

'What?' She snatched the page from me.

'Look.' I showed her how it worked. 'Do you know Pagnal Heath?'

'This can't be right!'

'But look where they're meeting. Do you know Pagnal Heath?'

'I haven't been there in twenty years, but yes, I do. Why?'

'You could read this as meaning the Commander is dealing with the enemy. Both enemies even – the city and Remnant – if this DFO guy is working for them.'

'But – are you sure that's what it says?'

'That's what it says. That might not be what it means.'

'Explain.'

Easy to say. Risky to do. But I owed her so I dived on in. 'Pagnal Heath is also called Pagan Heath.'

'Go on.'

'The reason it's called Pagan Heath – so they say – is they used to execute pagans there. Centuries ago. They burned witches and –'

She was looking at me oddly. 'How do you know this?'

'I – I scavenge. I pick up stuff.'

'I see. Is that what passes for scavenging these days? It's not exactly scrabbling in the gutters for old gear and leftover food, then?'

'Yeah, well, maybe I've done that too. Do you want to hear this or not?'

'Yes. Go on.'

'This guy DFO, who is he?'

'DeFaux. He's a Citysider. Used to be a top ISIS agent. He and Sim worked together once on a peace process that went nowhere.' She shook her head. 'Now he's just a mercenary. Very good at what he does. Very expensive.'

'Okay. A hired gun. So, what if this is not a meeting at all? What if it's an assassination?'

How do you count down to a killing? Levkova and her crew did it the same way they did everything – with a ground-down determination that looked the world in the eye and refused to be surprised by what it saw.

By about 3am we'd gone through most of the memos, looking for evidence of an assassination plot and come up with a few that looked interesting. Levkova said, 'Good. That's enough for now. Sim needs to see these.'

Five hours later Max shook me awake. 'Up, youngster! Commander's here.'

He'd come straight from a night on patrol, Cityside. The cold came off him like the wind off the river, but he didn't stop beside the fire or wait for the mug of tea Levkova was brewing. 'Sit,' he said to me, and 'Show me.' So I showed him the one about him meeting with DeFaux. When I was done, he sat staring at what I'd written, then looked up at Levkova.

'They want you out of the way, Sim,' she said. 'They've brought in DeFaux to do it.'

He shook his head. 'I don't have time for this. How can they afford DeFaux?'

'According to Jeitan they've had a windfall: spoils of war. This is real. We must take it seriously. *You* must take it seriously.'

While they argued, I took off for the old chapel to meet Fy. We had two leads to follow. One was the man she'd seen down in the township. The other was the chance that Jeitan would help look for a connection between Remnant and the traffickers. If that connection might be financing an attempt on Vega's life, I figured even Jeitan would break some rules to help.

I heard feet on the floor before I reached the chapel, so I stopped short of the doorway and peered in. No sign of Fyffe, but Lanya was there. She was dancing. And had been for some time, I think – she'd discarded her boots, jacket and overshirt. Her feet were bare and her face and shoulders shone with sweat. Without music, the beat of her dance was her breath: sharp and rhythmic, punching the air, propelling her around the room. The sunlight glanced through the cracked stained glass, patterning the floorboards gold and blue and red. Lanya spun and leaped through the light; her braids whipped her face and the beads in her hair sparked in the sun. She reached the far side of the room, then turned back in a series of cartwheels that skipped over the puddles in the middle of the floor and stopped about a body length from me. She stayed there curled in a crouch, head bent, breathing deep for a minute or so. Then she said, 'How long have you been there?'

'Not – not long.' I wondered if I should say sorry, but I wasn't, so I didn't.

She stood up and gestured across the room. 'I don't get the chance anymore, except here, in secret. Don't tell.'

'Who am I going to tell?'

She pulled on her overshirt and stuck her feet in socks and boots. Sunlight filled the whole room now. I said, 'Where's Sina? Did you find her?'

'Is she your girl?'

'No. She's a friend.'

'Well, I asked at the infirmary.'

'And?'

'They said she went down to the township yesterday afternoon on a supplies trip.'

'And?' My heart hammered.

'And she met someone she knew and went off with him.'

'She what? *She what?*'

'That's what they told me. Yesterday afternoon. What's the matter? If she isn't your girl, you mustn't mind too much.'

Jesus. 'Where? Where did she go? Who did she meet?'

'I don't know. They didn't tell me. Why?'

'I have to find her. I have to find her *right now*. Who did you talk to? Who told you she'd gone?'

'Just someone at the infirmary.'

'Let's go there now. We have to ask.' I started out the door but she darted in front of me.

'You can't go. You'll get Levkova arrested for trying to hide you. I'll go.'

'Now?'

'Later. I'm supposed to be at drill. As soon as I can I'll go and ask.'

'When?'

'After drill. But you can't go out in the daylight. Everyone knows what's happened with you and me. Meet me in the graveyard tonight after roll call. I'll find out who she went away with, and we can go into town and look for her.'

Commander Vega was sitting at the table looking at coded memos. He glanced up when I came in. 'What's the matter with you? Sit down. I need to look at all the memos that allude to DeFaux.'

The only thing that kept me sitting at that table was the chance of uncovering something about the windfall that was paying for DeFaux, and even then I was only concentrating with half a brain; the other half was careering through the township, searching for Fyffe.

It was slow going. Vega wanted me to show him how I'd decoded each memo, and he wasn't a man much given to fine detail. After a couple of hours it occurred to me that while I couldn't lead him wildly astray – because Levkova would always be there to confirm or deny – I could lead him slightly astray, and she might not notice. So when we took a break for lunch I constructed a memo of my own. It meant embedding the question I wanted to ask in some inter-bridge chat and constructing the whole thing backwards, which gave me a headache, but in the end the heart of it went like this: *Moldam–Ohlerton: Query: revisiting Night One targets.*

Vega frowned at it. 'What does that mean? Why would they query that?'

'What were they, the Night One targets?'

He sat back. 'What you'd expect. Watch Hill, financial hubs, comms hubs, a training school for the security services –'

'A school?'

'Of sorts. Why?'

'I dunno. Kids, I guess.'

'Privileged kids. Fascists-in-training, getting ready to join the interrogation specialists at the Marsh or follow their fathers onto comfortable seats on Watch Hill.'

'Why not hit the security services directly?'

'Ah, but where? They're dispersed and mobile precisely for that reason. But they've got an elite training facility at Tornmoor. That's what we targeted. They called it a school, but we know what it was. And for all that, we didn't take down the dormitories with the trainees – just the admin center and the officer block.' He was watching me. I doodled studiously in a margin, afraid that I'd pushed too far.

'You know,' he said, 'for every one of those privileged little monsters up there at Tornmoor I could show you a thousand kids down here in schoolrooms with no computers and no books, writing on recycled scrap and no chance, *no chance*, of becoming more than the serving class their fascist peers up there expect them to be. They're not innocent up there, for all that they're kids.' He leaned over and took the pencil out of my hand. 'You of all people should understand that. Tell me you'd rather be a scavenger than put that brain of yours to use with a decent education.'

I stared at the paper in front of me and my heart thudded so loud on my ribs I was sure he would hear it. Then he'd want to know why my curiosity about a City-side school came charged with such panic.

'Look at me,' he said. I lifted my head and looked him in the eye. His stare went right through me; I could almost feel it bouncing off my bones, calculating the sum of me.

'Do you think that's what your father wanted for you? To spend your days raking through the rubbish of the city?'

'I didn't –' I cleared my throat and tried again, 'My father died in the uprising in '87. I don't remember him.'

He tossed the pencil back on the table and sighed. 'Then let me tell you. You deserve a decent education. Got that?'

'Yes, sir.'

He stood up and stretched his shoulders. 'How many more?'

'Oh,' I tried to keep the relief out of my voice. 'Six? Five, six, something like that.'

'Take a break.'

I looked at the memo I'd made. 'Are you done with this one?'

'I think so. I don't know why they're harking back to first night victories, but it's not telling us where DeFaux is, so it's not a lot of help.'

I put it on the fire and watched it burn.

'It bothers you,' he said. 'That bombing.'

'I guess.'

'Why?'

'How did you do it? It must've been well guarded, a place like that.'

'It was a Gilgate–Ohlerton collaboration, that one. Your people, not mine. They will have had moles in there a long time. Straightforward enough to move things in, set things up, if you're careful. Patient. People come to be trusted. You just have to watch that they're not discovered or turned. Always a risk if they're there too long.'

I wanted to ask who. Who was their insider? Who set us up for that night? I was almost relieved that I couldn't ask and that he wouldn't know.

I said, 'Would you have done it? If it had been on your patch?'

He gave me another long stare. 'I have a war to fight. I'm not going to win it with a bleeding heart.'

The daylight was almost gone by the time we'd finished. Levkova came home and the doctor called in to see how Max was doing. I watched the clock. We ate cabbage soup and flatbread just for a change, and assessed progress to date: we had Remnant memos that put DeFaux on this side of the river and hinted at an assassination plot with Commander Vega as its target – perhaps at the Cross-over commemoration ceremony, where the Commander would be speaking to the crowd. For all that, we had no idea where DeFaux was. It was Saturday. We had four days to find him. My own thought echoed back at me: we.

'I don't know,' the doctor was saying. 'Why are you so sure DeFaux is still alive?'

'Kasimir saw him,' said Vega. 'In the Marsh.' A little silence fell, then he went on, 'And now the Marsh has been liberated, the politicals are free, but so are the psychopaths. I think he's out, and I think he's here.'

Pitkerrin Marsh. There it was again. The hospital the Breken had taken in the first assault of this uprising. I remembered the old guy at the Crossing that Fyffe and I had watched, and the great roar of approval that greeted his announcement that 'Moldam has the Marsh'. The Mad Marsh. And here was Vega talking about psychopaths and political prisoners. At school we'd never given a second thought to who was locked up there; hostiles and the criminally insane were all the same to us. Just like fascists-in-training and Cityside school kids were all the same to them.

I needed to get out and find Fyffe.

CHAPTER 27

That night was standard issue winter: blustery, sleeting rain that hooded people inside their coat collars and sent them racing heads down for whatever fire-warmed room they could find. I crouched beside the archway into the graveyard, wishing Lanya would arrive. Lines of stone markers reared out of the scrubby grass in front of me. They weren't neat, sculpted monuments – just hunks of riverstone set in the earth at more or less regular intervals.

I thought of the troops I'd seen laid to rest Cityside: our own celebrated dead, wrapped in the flag and laid in familiar ground, the gunfire salute crackling across the gravestones in their manicured lawns. I put my hands on the cold earth. What if Sol was here? Or somewhere like here? Buried, nameless, in hostile ground. Would they even bury our dead? And with what prayers, I wondered.

Fyffe would want prayers for him, but I couldn't say them. Fyffe, who thought she was so well looked after that she'd launched herself right at the enemy. Fearless. Crazy.

Lanya arrived in front of me as quietly as ever. 'Hurry,' she said. 'Before we're seen.' We set off around the walls. 'Makers look after this place,' she told me. 'Or did. It's not used anymore. They're supposed to watch over it still, but I don't think they do.' She kicked at the rough grass. 'I don't think anyone does. There should be a key still hidden here somewhere.' We'd reached a wrought-iron gate. She counted bricks and prized one out of the wall. 'Here.' She flashed a smile at me and unlocked the gate. 'Lucky for us. Let's go.'

We hurried down the hill. The rain and wind had dropped and puddles were already sheeting with ice. 'We're looking for a man called Goran,' said Lanya. I scanned my mental list of traffickers, but there was no Goran on it. 'Bowman, that's the supplies officer at the infirmary, he took Sina down to the hospital yesterday afternoon to collect some medicines for the infirmary. This man Goran came in with a delivery. He's a courier. Sina told Bowman she knew him and she was going to visit him.' Lanya peered at me. 'Bowman said he was expecting her to come back, but she hasn't yet. Is that why you're worried?'

When I didn't answer, she said, 'Bowman said to try the coffeehouse on the corner of River Road and Gantry

Lane. We might find him there. That's this way.'

We cleared the shadows of the half-demolished buildings across the road, and the township spread out below us. A scatter of fires burned on street corners. Shacks hunched in dark alleyways; lines of light leaked through their walls and doors. The smoky haze that hung across all of it was thick and bitter in the back of my throat. Across the river, darkness – you'd never guess a city lay there.

On the flat, every corner we passed had people huddled around brazier fires. They called greetings to us and invited us to join them. I wanted to head straight for the coffeehouse, but Lanya grabbed my sleeve and said, 'Come this way! I want to show you something.'

'No –'

'Yes! It's too early for the coffeehouse. People won't be there yet.' Then she was speeding upriver past stacks of empty market stalls wrapped in patched tarpaulins. 'Quick, it's nearly time.' We came to a place in the river-wall where the barbed wire across it was cut and bent back. We leaned on the wall and looked across the water.

'Watch,' said Lanya.

'For?'

'You'll see. It can't be long now.'

We waited. The night got colder. Below us, the water lapped against the stones of the wall and behind us the township muttered into the darkness. The bridge towered above us, a shadowy monster presence. It never looked the same twice. The time of day, the weather, your mood – they all painted it differently. That night a mist lifted off the river and mingled with the peat smoke of ten thousand hearth fires. The moonlight and the mist turned it blue-black and silver. We could have been standing in an old photograph.

I said, 'What are we waiting for? I need to find this man.'

'Wait! Wait, wait, wait – look, there!'

Back west, across the river, a light blazed in the middle of the city, where everything else was black.

'I think it's their command center,' said Lanya. 'The Citysiders – Witch Hill, it's called. It's come on at this time the last three nights. What do you think it means? Does it mean they're back in charge? The Commander said there'd been a hard battle for it. Maybe they've retaken it.' She watched it like a drowning person watching the land. 'What's it like?'

'What?'

'The city. You were scavenging over there. What's it like?'

'It's a war zone.'

She turned and looked at me. 'It won't always be. When we've won it, things will be different. We're going to throw open the bridges and smash the prisons and bring home the prisoners. There'll be hospitals full of medicine, and markets full of food, and banks of fuel cells for the taking. And we won't make the Citysiders slaves, even though that's what they did to us. But we'll punish their army. We'll make them grovel and be sorry and they'll be shamed because, unlike them, we'll be just and honorable. And everyone will have enough to eat and children won't die in the winter, and old people will be warm and fed.' She smiled at me and her eyes blazed. 'When we've won it.'

'And you think that can happen?'

'Yes! Don't you?'

I turned back towards the township. 'I'm going to look for this coffeehouse.'

'Tell me what you did over there,' she said, catching up with me. 'Tell me what you saw.'

'Later. Another time. Can we find Goran first?'

'There you go, running away again.'

'What?'

'You run. Every time we get near you, away you go.' She jogged backwards in front of me. 'If you're only a stray, where did you learn to read and write? And why aren't you fighting in a squad in Gilgate?'

'Look out,' I said. A little knot of people was gathered around a fire across the road. Lanya turned round and walked beside me, still talking. 'And how do you know about that window with the saint and the birds? That marks you as an easterner, which I wouldn't have guessed to look at you because you're too dark. But your name does too, I suppose – if you're a Nikos or a Nikolai. Are you? All right, not telling. Tell me this though: why, in the name of all that is holy, do you swear like a City-sider?'

'How do you know what Citysiders swear like?'

'No one here would blaspheme like you do – even in someone else's Rule. Do that in some people's hearing and you'll be lying in a gutter with a knife in your back before you know what's happened. You should know that. Why don't you know that?'

'So it's different in Gilgate, so what?'

She turned in front of me and put her hands out to stop me. 'Don't do it here. Don't. Do you understand?'

'Yes, all right.'

But she didn't move. 'I don't know who you are, Nikos or Nikolai or whatever your name is. And I don't know why you're here. Or what you're hiding from – or who. Maybe you're just afraid to fight – you've come to the wrong place if you are. But I do know this. You should tread with care. People here like to know what side every-one's on. And no one can tell what side you're on, because no one knows who you are and you never say.'

'Maybe I'm just on my side.'

'Maybe you are. But at the hearing you didn't turn me in for my knife fight. Which you would have if you were looking out for you and no one else.'

I walked around her but she danced back in front

of me. 'One more thing!'

'What?'

'If a patrol comes by they'll ask for papers. Do you have papers?'

I did, as it happens, have papers. But they were a thousand miles away in whatever was left of the school safe. They'd be ash and atoms now.

'So I'll vanish if a patrol comes anywhere near,' I said. 'Is that all?'

She smiled. 'For now.'

'You're enjoying this.'

Her smile got wider. 'It is better than sitting in barracks listening to another lecture on basic words and phrases of the enemy.' She walked on. 'What are you going to say to Goran?'

'No idea.'

'You should have asked Levkova for help.'

'She has troubles of her own.'

'Shall I ask her for you?'

'No!'

'You don't look very keen. You're more a behind-the-desk person, I think – than in the field.'

'Thanks. You're a great help.'

'Look! There's Gantry Lane. That must be it.'

CHAPTER 28

The coffeehouse was a low, concrete building lit from inside by candles and noisy with laughter and music. We peered through a cracked window. The place was wall-to-wall people. 'What if we meet someone who knows about the hearing?' I said. 'I'm supposed to be in Gilgate by now.'

'Don't worry. You're not important enough for the Council to have notified anyone down here about you. And even if people know about the hearing, they'll only know that some Gilgate low-life has been sent packing. They won't know what you look like.'

'Okay,' I said. 'You ready?'

'I'm ready,' said Lanya. I pushed open the door. People grumbled at us as we shouldered our way in, and after about six steps we reached a waist-high slab of wood that was the counter. The air was thick with smoke from a fire smoldering in a grate, and from whatever dried weed people were sucking on. You could probably get high from just standing there breathing. And whatever it was they were drinking, it did not smell like coffee. In one corner a singer was crooning, *Freedom's hour is comin'; set your feet to walk her path; freedom's hour is comin'; set your face for her return...*

'Help you squaddies?' A heavy, gray-haired man pushed past us, fingers clutching empty mugs. He clattered the mugs into a sink and peered at us from under bushy eyebrows. 'Well?'

'I'm looking for Goran,' I said. 'Got a message for him from up the hill.'

'He's out the back.'

We followed the direction of his thumb into a yard. A fire burned in a brazier and three men and a woman stood around it. The woman checked out our squad clothes and made room for us. She was the first richly dressed person I'd seen in Southside. She had thick, black hair falling to folds of fabric around her shoulders. Gold in her scarf and on her fingers shone in the firelight. She swayed in my direction. 'You're a ways from barracks, soldier boy. Night on the town is it, before you march off all brave over the bridge?'

'Yeah,' I said. 'Something like that.'

Lanya said, 'We wanted to see the light come on, over the river. Have you seen it?'

One of the men, fortyish with a patchy gray beard, said, 'Who's lightin' it, that's what I'd like to know.' He raised a flask in the direction of the Hill. 'To the uprising! Long may it last. And let there be gold,' he took the woman's hand and kissed her rings, 'for the victors.'

The door opened behind us and two men stumbled out, laughing and shouting. 'Goran! Got any more? We need more, right now, this minute, this very, very minute.' Graybeard let go of the woman's hand, said, 'One minute,' to her, and moved quickly to the men.

So, this was Goran. I watched him shut the newcomers up. He was weedy, with a pale, lined face, thin, graying hair and beard, and long fingers. He made my skin crawl. He wrapped his arms around the men's shoulders. 'Boys, boys, boys. Warmer inside, yeah?' He steered them back inside.

One of the others by the fire, a square, solid younger man, watched them go and grunted. The third one, older, with a pinched look and an ingrained scowl, said to us, 'You been over there yet?'

'Soon,' I said. 'Next week, maybe.'

He looked me up and down like I was a disappointment but what could you expect, youth these days and all that. 'You're not from here.'

'Gilgate,' I said.

He held up a hand, the stump of a hand with just a thumb and an index finger, gnarled and twisted like a tree root. 'See this? City blew it off. I sat in one of their stinking prisons for two years. Lost my fingers. Damn near lost my fuckin' mind. You get the chance when you go over – you do the same to one of them, yeah? Anyone'll do.' He grabbed my wrist and stuck my hand out above the fire. 'You hold them down. You take your gun.' He pointed his stump, like he was taking aim. 'You blast it off. Fingers, everything. Tell 'em you're doing it for Sett Rorkin. Got that?' I pulled away from him. He stuck his stump back in his pocket and grinned at the fire.

The woman said, 'You pay no attention to old Sett here.' She put a hand on my shoulder and breathed 'shine in my face. 'I'm sure you got plans, don't you, love? Off to seek your fortune? Nice lad like you deserves a bit of fortune. What about your girl? Taking her with you?' She patted my shoulder and peered back towards the coffee-house where Goran had gone. 'Time for you kids to be on your way back up the hill. Off you go. Fight a good fight, now, won't you.'

The old guy, Sett, grabbed my arm as I turned to go and waved his stump in my face. 'Remember! A hand for a hand.'

We pushed our way back through the crowd inside and came out onto the road. A breeze came fresh off the river and we breathed deep. 'Horrible man,' said Lanya. 'Horrible people. Why would your friend know these people?'

'Let's get out of sight,' I said.

We crossed the road to where a mangled dredge had been abandoned and settled in to wait for Goran to head for home. Lanya leaned on the riverwall and looked across at the city, dreaming, I guess, of future glory. I sat on the ground and watched the coffeehouse.

'You might wait a long time,' said Lanya. She sat down beside me. I thought about suggesting she go back up the hill, but I was fairly sure what she'd say to that. She hugged her knees and laid her head on her arms. Her braids fell across her long dancer's neck. For all that she buzzed with energy, when she sat still, she sat still. She looked up at me with a smile, then fixed her eyes on the coffeehouse, watchful and intent, as if it might vanish at any moment.

I said, 'Can I ask you a question?'

'No. You didn't answer mine.'

'Sina fell in with some bad company, that's all.'

She smiled sideways at me. 'I'm sure that's not all. But ask away.'

'Who's Kasimir?'

Her smile vanished. 'Who's been talking about Kasimir?'

'Vega. Tonight at Levkova's. Everyone went quiet.'

She nodded. 'That's his son. Married to Yuna – did you meet her?'

'Yeah. What happened to him?'

'Kas was arrested in a raid two years ago. Their little girl wasn't long born and Yuna was sick. Kas was pulled off the street. They took him over the bridge and put him in the Marsh. Our people offered a suicide switch to get him back.'

'A suicide what?'

'Switch. Kasimir, in exchange for a city spy held over here.'

'Why's it called that?'

'They don't tell you anything in Gilgate, do they. We're not supposed to call it that, but everyone does. A suicide switch is when they wire up the ones being exchanged with belts of explosives and each side carries the other's trigger. So, with Kas, one of our men went over to verify that it really was Kas they were sending back, and he got to hold the trigger for the city spy being exchanged. The same for the city – they sent a triggerman here and he took the trigger for the explosives on Kas. So the triggermen go to the middle of the bridge and supervise the exchange.'

'That is barbaric.'

'It keeps everyone honest. You don't end up with squads from both sides on the bridge and there's no danger of snipers taking out one of the hostages because the other one would be blown sky high if that happened.'

'What happened with Kas?'

'They're supposed to deactivate the triggers once

the prisoners have been exchanged in the middle of the bridge, but the city spy got to the exchange point, grabbed his own trigger and blew himself up. I don't know why. Shame, perhaps. Or perhaps he knew what they'd do to him once he got back. Kas was caught in the blast. He didn't die straight away. Yuna and the Commander got to say good-bye, at least.'

Insane. Brutal. War. What did I expect?

We watched some people leave the coffeehouse, calling to friends inside, cursing at how cold it was outside.

'What about you?' said Lanya. 'Who've you lost?'

'Parents.' I said it without a second thought, without all the hesitations and reservations that came with that admission at school. Where's your mother? Who's your father? Why don't they come, call, visit, take you away for the summer? But here, the assumptions all ran the other way.

'Oh,' she said. 'I'm sorry.'

'You?'

'No. No one. Still have parents. Still have brothers. Also grandparents, aunts, and cousins. The aunts are not pleased with me. A disgraced Pathmaker brings dishonor on a family, as they keep reminding me. But my parents believe me, that Coly was playing Remnant's game.' She glanced at me. 'They don't know about the fight. Do you have aunts or cousins?'

I shook my head. 'Sina is as close to family as I get.'

We watched the coffee house for a while, and at last crowds of people started to spill out of it.

'There!' said Lanya. Goran and co. were leaving in a flurry of farewells. We fell in with the scattering of late-night folk and followed them east along the river road. They stopped at a crossroads where some cookshops were hoarded together and a crowd was waiting outside for kebabs and stuffed pocket-bread. The air was smoky from the frypans; the spice of it caught in my throat and made me hungry and sick together. But our quarry didn't stop for food. They worked their way through the crowd, greeting people as they went, and Sett – Stumphand – lifted a bag from some poor dupe waiting for his fry-up. They headed into an alley running down beside the cookshops. Once they'd turned a corner, we went after them.

We were walking on gag-inducing sludge through a tunnel of shack walls stuck together, badly, in a jigsaw of corregated iron and wooden slats held in place by nails half banged in and bent at crazy angles. If I put my hands out I could touch both sides at once. Our only light came from cracks in the walls where lamplight bled through, and from the moonlit strip of sky above us.

We followed Goran's group around a corner into another alley exactly the same. Then another. And another. As we made our way through a maze of twisting, narrow spaces we fell into a pattern of one of us going ahead and watching for where they turned next, then beckoning to the other. They weren't hard to follow – they were in high good humor, or maybe they were just high. They stopped at last beside a tall wire fence with a padlocked gate. Goran let them all in, glanced up and down the alley, then locked the gate and disappeared inside.

I started towards it, but Lanya grabbed my arm. 'No, no, no. Wait! What are you doing?'

'Taking a look.'

'Listen to me! They're dealers. And with a fence like that, they'll be traffickers as well. There are people in there they don't want to let out. If you try to get in, they will kill you. And you don't even know if Sina is there.'

'It's all I've got. I'm just gonna look. I won't go in.'

'Ask Levkova for help.'

'I'm just gonna look.' I shrugged off her hand and walked up to the fence. Inside it I could see three shacks and a larger, more solid building behind them. A lantern hung from the porch of one of the shacks and lit the groundspace in front; it was scratched and scuffed where someone had tried to grow something, or bury something. A washing line draggled rags between a rainwater barrel and a latrine. No signs of life.

Around me the alley was dark and quiet.

I figured that Goran and his team would be snoring by now; they'd been drunk enough. If the fence could hold my weight, I could get in and take a look around. I hated the thought that Fyffe might be in there. Was probably in there, since she'd followed this man, then disappeared. I couldn't leave without looking.

The fence was tall. I could've reached the top of it at full stretch if my ribs had been working properly. I put a hand on the wire lattice, gripped it, shook it lightly. It felt solid enough. I gripped a fence pole, pushed a boot into the lattice, and hauled myself up. The fence creaked. I froze. Looked around. Couldn't see anyone. Grasped the top of the fence pole. Pulled myself up another few feet. Nearly there.

A hand grabbed my ankle and someone hauled hard on my coat. I crashed onto the ground. Pain exploded in my ribs. A man dragged me upright and stuck his arm round my neck, just about lifting me off my feet. I gagged and tried to struggle but the pain had left me gasping.

A knife, sharp, cold and to the point, pressed my cheek. 'Well,' said a voice in my ear, 'Look what we have here! What are you doin', soldier boy?'

'Nothing! Just looking.'

'Nope. Don't believe you.' The knife pressed harder; I felt blood trickle down my face. 'We don't like to be spied on. It ain't good for our peace of mind. You could lose an ear or an eye at this point. *With* this point.'

He laughed at his joke. 'As a message to other snoopers. Hold still – or it'll be both.'

Stupid. Stupid to think that traffickers would leave

themselves unguarded. I tried to see the knife, afraid of what it would do next. I was thinking, hoping, that maybe he'd take me inside. It would make it worth getting caught if I could find Fyffe. But he sounded as if he'd rather carve me up there in the alley.

'Which is it to be?' he said. 'Ear?' He flicked the knife point at my ear lobe. I tried to slow my breathing. Tried to think. The blood was pounding in my head. 'Eye?' He drew the point from the corner of my eye across my temple. I tried not to flinch in case he slipped. 'Choose!' he said.

Then he grunted, his legs went from under him and we collapsed on the ground. Lanya was shouting, 'RUN!' I scrambled up and raced after her down the alley.

We ran, stumbling through sludge, pushing ourselves off walls and round corners, glancing over our shoulders for the lookout or his mates. At last Lanya stopped, hands on knees. I leaned on a wall, breathing hard. She grinned up at me. 'My boot, his knee. He won't follow in a hurry.'

I blew out a breath. 'Okay,' I said, 'I think it's fair to say that you don't owe me anything anymore.'

She stood up. 'I told you.'

'Not that they'd have a lookout.'

'No. We should have guessed. What now? You look a mess, by the way.'

I touched my temple. Blood. I was starting to shake. The adrenaline was wearing off and my ribs felt seriously bad. 'I don't know what now.' I looked back the way we'd come. 'I couldn't find it again if I tried.'

'I could.' She held up a hand to shut me up. 'On one condition.'

Her face blurred in front of me and my knees buckled. I crouched on the ground, thinking how useless I was at all this. 'Only one?' I said, and tried to smile at her. 'Name it.'

'You must ask Levkova for help.'

Pounding on the door jolted me upright. I was sitting on my mattress, still in yesterday's clothes. I grabbed a lantern and lit it with shaky fingers while Max struggled out of bed, swearing and shrugging on his coat. He took the light and went out into the living room, closing the door behind him. I opened it a crack and peered out.

'Easy there!' he called. 'Take it easy! I'm coming.' He opened the door to two young guys in battle gear. They gave him the half bow and one of them said, 'Morning, sir!'

'What in the name of all the known gods is going on!' That was Levkova. More saluting.

'Sub-commander Levkova?' said one of them.

'Don't be ridiculous, Rémy. It's the middle of the night! And freezing. Come in and close the door. What's happened?'

'It's 5.30am, ma'am. Wanted to give you a good start.'

'A what?'

'Time, madam.' A new voice. Queasily familiar. 'Time to pack.' No-neck from the hearing pushed his way inside.

'Councillor Terten,' said Levkova. 'How did I miss you there? What do you mean?'

'Time to *pack*, I said. We need these rooms. For people on active service.'

Levkova frowned at him. 'I see. I have some spare floor space for an extra —'

'No, no, no. *Listen*, woman!' No-neck waved a piece of paper at her. 'Your eviction notice.' He lumbered over to the table and slammed the paper down. Then he moved on around the room, ran a fat finger along the spines of books on the shelves, leafed through the book on Max's armchair and sat down. 'You are to be out by Wednesday.'

'I beg your pardon?' Levkova looked steely and furious together.

'You heard, madam. You have three days. If you use them wisely you can throw out a lifetime's rubbish.' He nodded towards the bookshelves. 'This furniture, though.' He patted the arm of the chair and looked around. 'Stays.'

'It's my furniture.'

'I doubt it. And you won't have room for it.'

'Don't doubt, Councillor. It is mine. Won't have room where? Where are we to go?'

'To whoever will have you.' He stood up. 'If any will.'

'And Suzannah Montier? She shares these rooms.'

'The Montier woman is not my concern. I understand she was not in the Marsh when it was liberated?'

'No. ISIS have taken her somewhere else. We don't know where.'

'You should take more care of your protégés, Sub-commander.' He turned on his heel and left. The two young guys shuffled behind him.

Levkova called one back. 'Rémy! Who does Councillor Terten intend to move in here?'

'Sub-commander Stell, ma'am.'

'Naturally. His latest woman. On very active service.'

The guy went bright red, bowed, and escaped.

Levkova watched him go, and closed the door. She looked at Max and me. 'Well, gentlemen. As an opening gambit, that's impressive. They want us busy in the lead-up to Crossover Day. And they're making all the running. We need something to hit back with. Any ideas?'

'I have one,' I said.

When Commander Vega arrived later that morning, Levkova had a stand-up row with him about being assassin-bait. 'You are not standing on that platform in full view of an assassin!'

'I am,' said Vega. 'DeFaux takes a pot-shot at me, we seize him, make the links to Remnant and they're exposed.

Simple. You're being sentimental.'

'Nonsense. I'm being entirely practical. If a pot-shot, as you so romantically call it, happens to kill you, CFM in Moldam is leaderless and Remnant have won for the foreseeable future.'

He sat down and rubbed a hand over his face. 'You lead them.'

She sat opposite him. 'Sim, you have a deathwish. If you give in to it, don't imagine Kas would forgive you.'

A small, dangerous silence fell.

'We need you,' she said.

He shook his head. 'What we need is vision, and belief, and someone the people will follow.'

'Yes. We need Suzannah back. But until that day, we muddle through. And not by losing you as well. Listen.'

She told him my idea. 'If Goran has moved into trafficking and we can prove it, that's all we need. I know we can show his links to Terten. Please, Sim. It has to be better than giving DeFaux the satisfaction of killing you.'

Vega looked at me. 'You're supposed to be in hiding. Not prowling the district after dark.' He stood up. 'All right. We'll raid Goran's outfit. But if we don't find anything there, Crossover Day goes ahead as planned.'

It wasn't exactly what I'd had in mind. I'd been hoping to find Sol, and now Fyffe, without drawing attention to any of us. Now here we were, going into a place where either or both of them might be, and doing it with all guns blazing, possibly, for real. What if Goran decided to fight his way out? What if it turned into a bloodbath?

The next day, around dusk, Lanya took a raiding party back to Goran's. She and I went ahead and were followed in the shadows by Vega, Jeitan and, they assured us, a bunch of others that we hadn't yet seen and wouldn't until crunch time. I couldn't tell if this set-up was the answer to my prayers, such as they were, or just plain fatal.

We got to the corner just before Goran's place and stopped. The plan was that I would knock on the front door and offer to run a ransom to the city for them, for anyone they had in there who might be worth one. Once they showed an interest, Vega's squad would step in.

Lanya looked at me. 'You're nervous,' she said. 'I'll do it.'

'I bet you would,' I said. 'But that's not the plan. And what about the guy you crippled last night? You probably shouldn't meet him any time soon. Wish me luck.'

'They'll have knives,' she said. 'You won't see them. Watch their knifework.'

I walked up to the padlocked gate and shook the wire fence. The hairs on the back of my neck stood up. I waited for a lookout to show – possibly an angry one with a stuffed-up knee. Instead, Goran came out of the building behind the shacks. He peered at me through the gate. 'Whaddya want? Where've I seen you before?'

I put on my best, roughest Gilgate accent. 'Talk some business? About Citysiders and ransoms.'

'Don't know what you're on about.' He turned away.

'I heard you had one here.' That stopped him. 'A Citysider. At least one,' I said. 'Thought you'd want someone to run the ransom. I got some Anglo. And I know the city, some. Been scavenging there.'

He considered me for a long, nerve-wracking moment.

'Or,' I said, 'I could go and talk to someone up the hill about it.'

'Ha! Kid, you wouldn't get to the end of this road. And even if you did, they wouldn't believe a word up there, filthy accent like that. But I could do with a bit of Anglo. Talk me some.'

So I repeated what I'd just said, in Anglo, with as much of a Gilgate accent as I could muster. He smirked. 'Horrible. But not bad. Know the city, do you?'

I nodded.

'Flat rate.'

'Sure.'

'All right, kid. Come in here. Let's talk.' He unlocked the gate, peered up and down the alley, and nodded me through. He locked the gate again.

There was a loud whistle, boots clanged on iron above us and suddenly there were figures with guns on the rooftops. Vega's squad. Goran pushed me towards the shacks, yelling, 'Sett! Sett!' I stumbled, heard Goran shout, 'Grab him!' and saw Stumphand charging towards me. I stuck out an arm to fend him off but he swung a knife at me and ripped open the palm of my hand. A blast of pain shot up my arm and then he was at my back, his stump round my throat and the point of his knife pressed through my coat. I clenched my bleeding hand and tried not to yell.

'Goran!' Vega stood outside the gate, Jeitan beside him. 'Open up.'

'Commander Vega,' said Goran. 'What's brought you here?'

'News,' said Vega. 'And how unsurprising that it turns out to be news of you.'

'What do you want?'

'I want in. Open this gate.'

'Well now, all in good time. This kid one of yours?' He peered at me. 'Too scruffy to be one of yours, isn't he? And recruited from Gilgate – you're scraping the barrel there. What line's he fed you about me? Bet he hasn't told you he's dealing. Tried to sell me some stuff a few days back. I threatened to turn him in, so he's turned on me instead.'

I watched Vega. He wouldn't buy that. Come on, I thought. Hurry up. Get in here before they smuggle their city kids out a back way.

Vega's gaze flicked to me and back to Goran. 'What've you done to him?'

'He tried to attack old Sett here. It's a scratch, is all. Better than he deserves.'

'Let me in. I want to talk to you.'

'Got a warrant?'

'I don't need a warrant to talk.'

'Come on in, then. Course, I'll have to tell Council you're doin' illegal searches. That all right with you?'

Vega outstared him. 'Open up.'

Goran looked at the guns above us and opened the gate. The knife dropped away from my back and Sett sped off into one of the shacks. I went after him in case he was planning to hide whatever, or whoever, was in there.

The room we went into was nearly dark, but the reek of it made me retch. When my eyes got used to the gloom I could see five kids sitting or lying on filthy blankets. They stared up at Sett, mouths open, eyes rolling. They looked drugged. None of them spoke. Sett walked round them, touched their heads, bent down, and whispered at them.

Fyffe wasn't there. And none of them looked like Sol. I was almost relieved.

'See?' Goran came in with Vega and Jeitan. 'Just my kids. They've been working all day, scraping a living, like all of us.'

'Yours?' said Vega. 'In what sense, yours?'

'I find 'em on the street. Give 'em a home – some shelter, some food. Without me they'd be street scum.'

'Did you find any of them over the river?'

Goran screwed up his face, pained at the accusation. 'Some of 'em might've drifted over the bridge from City. I don't notice. I just see hands to work and mouths to feed. What's wrong with that? It's a public service, that's what it is. We got a recycling business going here –'

'Scavenging.'

'Call it what you like –'

I pushed past them and went back outside. I peered into the second shack. It was almost completely dark in there. A woman lay on a camp bed near the door and beyond her in the shadows were piles of furniture. I couldn't see any kids. The woman moaned at me and shooed me out or beckoned me in, I couldn't tell which. She was deep in some disease or other – skeletal, haggard. I backed away and went to the third shack. I found kids there, four of them. Same deal as before: eyes staring, mouths open. Silent. Like they were spellbound. Vega and Jeitan arrived in the doorway behind me.

'They're drugged.' I said. 'Or drunk.'

'They're hungry,' said Goran, pushing through us. 'That a crime? Never seen hungry kids before? Look!' He walked up to one of them, a boy maybe eight or nine, skinny and filthy. Not Sol. Goran pulled him to his feet and gave him a little push. The kid stumbled forward and stood in front of the Commander, like he was waiting for inspection. Vega looked him over and said something to him and the kid replied in Breken, then turned away and sank back to the floor. 'See?' said Goran. 'Free to move around. You're a Campaign for Free Movement man, Commander – you should appreciate that.' He sniggered at his joke. 'Only thing they're not free to do is eat, 'cause we got no food. You could help us, Commander. What d'you say? A little charity'd feed a hungry tribe. Then maybe I wouldn't have to go to Council about your illegal search.'

Vega nodded at Jeitan. 'Talk to them. Find out where they're from. If they're here willingly. I'll start on the others.' He headed for the door.

Goran put a hand on Jeitan's arm. 'That's a big step without a warrant. Wouldn't you rather do some business?'

'What business?' said Vega.

'I hear you're looking for DeFaux.'

'Where do you hear that from?'

'Ah, well. Word's about.'

'You've seen him?'

'May have. May have. Can't help you though, if you destroy my little operation here.'

Vega hesitated in the doorway and I saw my chance slipping away – they'd take this deal, they had to. DeFaux was what they wanted, not some crook they might or might not be able to pin a trafficking charge on.

I went back into the yard. If Fyffe was here, I had to find her now. The Commander was going to leave at any moment and I was going to be left with nothing.

My hand dripped blood on the ground and hurt like a burn. What if she was here and hurt? Or drugged like those kids? I couldn't leave without knowing. And I'd run out of time.

I put my head back and yelled in Anglo. '*Fyffe! Are you here? Fyffe!*' The Commander turned in the doorway to stare at me and Sett came out of the first shack, knife in hand. I yelled again, turning a full circle. In the doorway of the middle shack where the sick woman was, a figure appeared on hands and knees, wearing ragged clothes and with a mess of fair hair. She pushed her hair out of her eyes and looked across the yard at me.

Goran strode over to her. 'That's my niece. She's sick. You can't come in here and harass my family.'

'She's not your niece,' I said. 'Get out of the way.'

'I got her papers.'

'You can't have her papers. She has no papers.'

'Then you can't prove she ain't mine.'

'Yes,' I said, 'I can.' I pushed him out of the way and knelt in front of her, brushed her hair back from her face. Her eyelids fluttered, almost opened, closed again. 'Fyffe,' I said, and in Anglo, 'Talk to me. Come on. Wake up.'

'Nik?'

'Yeah, it's me. Come on, wake up. You've been drugged. We need to get you out of here.'

'Where's Sol? I can't go without… I've lost…' She started to cry.

'Fyffe, please. Try to stand up. You can do it. Come on.'

'I saw him. I saw Sol. He was here, then they took him away. Nik…'

'Come on.' I helped her stand.

She put her arms round my neck and her head on my shoulder. 'He was here.'

'Good. Because you know what that means? That means you did it. You found him. And he's still alive and in Southside. We'll track him down. I promise.'

Commander Vega was staring at me, narrow-eyed. Then he turned to his rooftop gunmen and shouted, 'Round them up! Dig deep. They'll be hidden, most of 'em.'

The squad jumped down and began kicking in doors and herding out kids. Vega snapped his fingers at two of the squad. 'Stefan and Marena, work out who's local, who's city. Feed them all. Put them somewhere safe – and watch them. I want to talk to them once we're done here.' He looked round and saw Lanya standing by the gate. 'You! Go with Marena. Make sure this one gets to the infirmary.' He nodded at Fyffe, then he looked at me. 'Jeitan! Benit! Lock him up.' Jeitan and a pale, thin young guy stepped forward to stand on either side of me. Vega scanned his squad to make sure everyone knew what they were doing and said, 'Go!'

We went.

CHAPTER**30**

They took me back to HQ and stuck me in a cell below ground. It was windowless, concrete, and narrow, with a mat a thumbnail thick on the floor and a jug of water in the corner. Benit was enjoying himself. He snapped his fingers at me. 'Boots.'

'What?'

'You heard me. Take off your boots.'

'You're kidding.' I looked at Jeitan. Nope. Not kidding. They were going to do this by the book. I took off my boots. Felt the cold seep through the mat.

'Coat.'

'No.' I stepped back, hit a wall.

Benit marched up to me, stuck an arm against my throat and his face in mine. 'Everything you're wearing is ours. We could take all of it. We'll take the coat. Be grateful.'

Grateful, no, but I could do the sums. I took off the coat and he tossed it to Jeitan.

'Better,' said Benit. 'Right. Name? Full name.'

I'd given up pretending. 'Nikolai Stais.'

He hit me hard across the mouth. 'Real name!'

I licked blood. 'That is my real name, you shit.' That got me a punch in the stomach.

I heard Jeitan say, 'Go easy, Ben.'

The guy backed off, but he wasn't done. 'Think you can stuff us around? Think again.'

'Leave it,' said Jeitan. 'Not our job.'

He glanced at Jeitan. 'C'mon, J. We could find things out. Save Vega the trouble.'

'Leave it. Let's go.'

They slammed the door and left me in the dark.

The blood on my palm had dried and crusted. I thought about trying to wash it but I couldn't see, and anyway I didn't know how clean the water in the jug was.

Some time in the early hours, the door opened and a light came in. The doctor crouched in front of me. 'Show me your hand.' He cleaned it, stitched it, bandaged it, and left without another word. No painkillers this time.

I don't know how long they left me there. Long enough that Lou showed up in the corner and started talking to me. His face was bloody and so badly burnt I could see his teeth and tongue through his cheek. *I knew,* he kept saying. *I always knew you were Breken. We all did.*

Some time, a long time, later, when Lou had gone, the door scraped open. Jeitan tossed me my boots and coat.

'Out!' He led me blinking up the stairs to a wash-room, then to a tiny kitchen where he gave me a mug of something hot and bitter and a flatbread pocket stuffed with a cold slab of meat sub. Silent the whole way. I tried thanking him for getting the doctor. And I thought about asking if they'd come yet to evict Levkova and Max, but I'd forfeited any right to know.

Finally he took me up some stairs to a wood-panelled room and locked me in. The room was like the staff offices at school, but it was bare, like most of the rooms in HQ. There was a fireplace but no fire, shelves but no books, a table and a few chairs but none of the clutter people usually make when they live somewhere. A window looked down towards the graveyard and, beyond that, to the bridge. I tried to make out the city on the other bank, but the day was low and gray and all I could see were dull shapes in the mist. Dash was over there somewhere, waiting for us to bring Sol home. We'd been gone ten days. It felt like a year. I wondered if those two army guys had done as they'd promised and taken Dash and Jono somewhere safe to shelter and mend.

Talk outside the door pulled me back; I sat down at the table as Commander Vega and Benit came in. I didn't stand up. That seemed like too much of an invitation to get thumped again. I sat still and said, 'Where's Fyffe? Is she okay?'

Vega sat down opposite me. 'I need to know who you're spying for and what you were sent to find out. I don't want to use unpleasant methods to do that.' I looked at Benit standing by the door and wondered how 'unpleasant' things could get.

'I'm not a spy.' My voice came out quiet and shaky – real convincing.

'Indeed. You infiltrate us from the city, you disrupt the balance on Council in favor of Remnant, you get access to secret documents which you appear to decode with ease, you lie...'

'I told one lie. That I was from Gilgate. And you gave me that.'

'One lie? What about your name?'

'That's not a lie. That is my name. I came here with my friend to find her brother. When we find him, we're out of here. That's all.'

'Yes. The girl. She's told me where you're from.'

Oh. So, it was good that she was well enough to talk. Not good that that's what she was talking about. 'I know you think Tornmoor is a training ground for ISIS, and they do go there recruiting, but –'

'You fabricated that memo. What others did you fabricate?'

'None. That one. Only that one. I wanted to know why you'd bomb a school.'

'Where did you learn Breken? Is ISIS teaching Breken at Tornmoor?'

'No, they're not. I don't know where I learned it. Maybe from my mother. I don't remember.'

'From your mother. How did you get into Tornmoor if your mother was Breken?'

'How would I know? I was five years old. I did the entrance tests. They let me in.'

We went round and round in circles for quite a while. I tried to ask about Sol, but Vega was asking questions not answering them. Eventually he got sick of it and told Benit to take me back downstairs. I hated that cell already and I'd only been there one night. Benit took my boots again and I waited for him to demand the coat but he said, 'Keep the damn coat – J. will just whine at me if I take it.'

I sat in the dark and added things up. They didn't look great: being at Tornmoor, speaking Breken, working my way into one of the factions here, code-breaking, claiming a name they were sure I'd invented. I wouldn't trust me either.

Voices outside made me sit up. I heard Benit say, 'Hurry up, then. I'll be listening.' The room flooded with light and by the time I could see again Lanya was crouching in front of me. Benit lounged in the doorway.

Lanya was staring at me like I was some rare animal high on the soon-to-be extinct list. I tried, 'Hello.'

She stood up and walked away. Leaned on the far wall, arms folded. Studied me. 'You cut your lip,' she said.

'Yeah.'

'How?'

'Got careless.'

Her eyes narrowed. 'You're from the city.'

'Extra careless.'

She shook her head and began walking up and down the room. 'And I thought you couldn't play secret police. The things you told me – are any of them true?'

'It's all true. Except I'm not from Gilgate.'

'No. You're not. I was slow, wasn't I? You swear like a Citysider, you speak Anglo, you never talk about yourself. But you're the wrong color for one of them, and you talk like one of us.' She crouched in front of me. 'And I liked you.'

I had no answer to that.

She turned away.

'Wait!' I said. 'Is Sina okay?'

She was at the door already. Benit tapped the key on the palm of his hand.

'Please?' I said.

'Fyffe, you mean,' she said. 'Yes. She is.'

Then she was gone and the light went out.

Lou came back. He sat at the other end of the cell, talking at me. He'd taken up residence in the corner of my eye. I tried to ignore him and concentrate instead on working out how to convince them I was who I said I was.

The only evidence I had for not being with Remnant or ISIS was the memo about the assassination plot: if I was a spy I would have buried it and left Vega to DeFaux's bullet.

But what if I was wrong about the memo? What if no attempt was made on Vega's life? How would they read that except as me trying to sow chaos in their ranks? Then again, suppose I was right and Vega was killed? He was CFM's senior military figure in Moldam, and with him dead, opposition to Remnant would be crushed. What chance of rescuing Sol then?

I'd find out soon enough. There was one day left before Crossover.

CHAPTER 31

In the morning, Jeitan took me upstairs again. This time he gave me some clean clothes. I couldn't tell whether this was a good sign or a bad one. He took me back to the wood-panelled room. Levkova was waiting there. She stood by the window watching sleet hammer the glass. She didn't speak, didn't need to: a city boy standing there wearing her dead partner's coat said it all. I had nothing to say that could make it right.

The door opened behind me. Vega came in, followed by the doctor, and Benit with Fyffe. They'd let Fyffe get cleaned up and changed back into squad clothes. 'Nik!' She escaped from Benit's grasp and hugged me.

I looked over her head to the others. They were talking in low voices, except Benit and Jeitan who stood by the door watching us.

'Tell me about Sol,' I said. 'Tell me what you saw.'

'He was there, Nik. At Goran's place. But when I turned up, they sent him away.'

'He's alive, then. How was he? Was he okay?'

'I don't know. Sedated, I think. But he knew me. We have to make them find him.'

'Do you know why they brought you here?'

She shook her head. 'Maybe they're letting us go?'

I didn't think so.

Something had been decided. Benit came and grabbed Fyffe's arm. I pushed him away. 'Don't touch her!' But Jeitan dragged me into a corner. Benit sat Fyffe in a chair then stood behind her with his hands round her neck. I pushed hard against Jeitan. 'Don't touch her! What are you doing?'

The doctor put a case on the table and took out a vial and a syringe. Fyffe stared at it, and then at me.

I pushed harder. *'What are you doing?'*

The doctor glanced at me. He pushed the syringe into the vial. 'Something we got from the Marsh. A dose of this and we have people telling us all kinds of useful information.'

We looked at each other, Fyffe and me. I know my face was a mirror of hers, wide-eyed and stricken, and I know her heart was hammering as hard as mine. 'Use it on me!' I said. 'Why not use it on me?'

He shook his head. 'It's a little… unpredictable. I think we want you in one piece just now.'

'NO!' I struggled to break free, really sick now. 'Stop! I've told you everything. I'll tell you anything. Anything! Just don't hurt her. Don't!' Fyffe was breathing short and shallow. The doctor pushed the air out of the syringe. I yelled, 'DON'T!'

Jeitan pushed me back.

I shouted at Levkova, 'You know what this makes you?'

Jeitan punched me. 'Shut up!'

I gasped, 'It makes you… everything your enemies… believe you… to be.' He punched me again. I doubled over on my knees.

I heard Levkova say, 'Are you lecturing me?'

I had no breath. 'Re… minding… you.' I looked up at her, willing her to remember that night when she'd refused to throw me to the dogs.

She limped across to where I was kneeling, grabbed a handful of my hair and pulled my head back. 'Tell me your name, city boy. Your real name. Not a placeholder. Not a joke. What's your name?'

'Nikolai…' I gasped, '…Stais.'

She looked at me hard. Then she let me go. 'Why would they tell him to say that? Once, all right, it's a taunt. But to persist. It's suicide. I'd have thought they'd want him back.' She stuck a hand under my chin and lifted my head. 'Don't they want you back?'

'No one wants me back. I'm not *with* anyone.'

She turned to Fyffe and said, 'Enough' to the doctor and Benit. The doctor stepped away and Benit took his hands from Fyffe's neck. Fyffe blew out a breath. I blew out a breath. Levkova spoke to Fyffe in Anglo, 'His parents? Have you met them? Do you know them?'

Fyffe shook her head.

'Never?' said Levkova. 'They never came to Tornmoor?'

Fyffe spoke slow, careful Breken. 'They're dead. He used to talk about his mother sometimes. Not much. You had to push him for it. And I never heard him talk about his father. Everyone knew they were dead.'

'What did he say about his mother?'

'He remembered her, kind of, from before he came to school.'

'Did he tell you her name?'

Fyffe looked at me. 'Eleanor.'

'Eleanor,' said Levkova quietly, and walked away to the window. She stood staring at the wild day and at last turned back to Fyffe. 'Why would he take such a risk for you? Are you lovers?'

Fyffe went red. 'No. Friends. He'd do that for a friend. Wouldn't you?'

'And ISIS? Tell me about him and ISIS.'

'They didn't want him. We couldn't understand why. He's so smart, we thought they'd be sure to take him. We tried to find out, but no one would say. But then, after the school was bombed, they came looking for him.'

'Did they find him?'

'I don't know.'

Levkova turned to me. 'Yes, they found me,' I said. 'They didn't like my name either.'

'Do you know why?'

'No.'

She leaned on her walking stick and studied me. 'You really don't, do you.' She turned away to talk to Vega and the doctor. I couldn't make out what they were saying, so I sat on the floor and looked at Fyffe and she looked back at me and we didn't move; we just sat there looking, as though, if we stayed still and watched each other, we could somehow keep Benit and Jeitan and the whole pack of them at bay.

In the middle of all that the door burst open and a woman charged in. 'Sir, I'm sorry –' She looked around at us and stuttered to a halt.

'Go on,' said Vega.

'They got to Goran.'

'And?'

'He's dead. In his cell. We don't know how.' The doctor picked up his bag, but she said, 'They've got the body. You won't get a look at him now.'

'Faster than we thought,' said Vega. 'But it can't change our plans.'

'Sim, no,' said Levkova. 'You can't go ahead with this now.'

'I've got to. We call them out with what we've got.'

'What we've got is nothing. Except you, standing on that platform, waiting to be shot.'

'Then be ready.' He nodded to Benit and Jeitan. 'Lock these two up again. Then go with the sub-commander and make preparations to get out.'

'Sir, no!' said Jeitan. 'You need someone with you at the ceremony.'

'No,' said Vega. 'This is my call. Go. Now. That's an order.'

So they marched us away. At the door of my cell I said to Jeitan, 'I don't suppose you'll tell me what's going on?'

But all he said was, 'Keep your boots,' and he shut me back in the dark.

CHAPTER 32

My name is Nikolai Stais. It's just a name. No big deal. No one cares what school kids are called. But to the ISIS agents who came to Tornmoor it was a problem. Here on Southside, according to Levkova, it was a taunt. And then there was Dr Williams. I thought of Dr Williams as I sat, adding things up, in that underground cell at Breken headquarters in Moldam. I could see him with my file in his hand, standing behind his lamplit desk in the school infirmary, asking me, did I remember my mother, and did I know my father's name. 'Nikolai, perhaps?' he'd said. I thought he was guessing, to make me feel better. But then he broke the rules by giving me the name of the woman who'd enrolled me at Tornmoor – Frieda Kelleran – from a file I wasn't supposed to see. Now, I realized, he'd given me a lot more than that.

I knew my father's name.

That was all I knew about him. I thought that if I ever saw Levkova again I would ask her who he was. I was the enemy to her now. But maybe, for the sake of the ten days we worked together, she'd tell me.

The door opened and a torch shone in my eyes. Jeitan's voice said, 'Come with me.'

'Where? Is Fyffe okay?'

'With your Maker friend. Hurry up. And keep your mouth shut. We get heard, we're dead.'

I followed his torchlight along a twisting basement tunnel, through a series of doors. He fumbled with a bunch of keys to unlock each one, then locked them carefully after us. We went up some old stone steps to a ladder and a trapdoor, where he stopped. 'This takes us outside. I'll have to kill the torch and if you choose to run, I won't stop you.' He looked hard at me, the 'guns and glory' guise all gone.

'But?' I said.

'Commander Vega could be killed tonight. Levkova has a plan to stop that. She needs us to put it in play.'

'Us?'

'You and me. She doesn't know who Remnant has got to, so she can't trust anyone in the squads. She thinks she can trust you.' He shrugged in a God-knows-why sort of way. 'Up to you.'

That was it: no threats – no 'help us or we hurt you'

or, worse, 'help us or we hurt Fyffe,' just 'help us.'

'All right,' I said. 'Let's go.'

We'd come out on the west side of the hill, beyond the compound fence. The moon shone so bright that we cast shadows as we hurried down the slope. Jeitan broke into a jog once we reached the flat and after about twenty minutes we came into an unlit street where the houses all had tiny square patches of grass beside their steps, and broad pavements where bare-branched trees gleamed faintly in the moonlight. He unlocked the door of one of them and nodded me inside. 'Levkova's in the kitchen at the end. Go on.'

How do you front up to your enemy – that you've lied to and whose trust you've betrayed, and who has recently scared the living, breathing daylights out of you – how do you front up and ask them the most important question of your life?

I knocked and Max opened the door on a big old kitchen with a fire burning and a hefty table where Levkova was sitting. He patted my shoulder. 'Youngster. Here you are. Jeitan's lost his wager then.' He cackled to himself as he left. I watched him go. I couldn't look at Levkova.

'He's a good man,' she said as the door closed. 'A good man... I think I said that about you once. I was surprised, you see, that a scavenger from Gilgate should behave with such… humanity. And now I'm even more surprised.'

'I lied to you.'

'And you would again, if you needed to. And rightly. Perhaps I cannot entirely trust you – no one trusts the city – but I do now believe you came here to find your friend.' She studied me. 'I know fear when I see it. It's a great leveler. We use it when we must. We would do the same again.'

'I almost told you once, but then Max told me about your family.'

'Ah.' She nodded and fell silent. The fire crackled and spat. At last she said, 'It's time, isn't it, that someone told you about your family. Sit.' I sat across the table from her.

'Your mother's name was Elena,' she said.

'You knew her?'

'No. I never met her and – here's an admission – I didn't realize she was black. You're the wrong color, you see, for all my preconceptions. But now that I look at you, you are so like your father. I should never have missed that.'

'How do you know about her if you never met her?'

'Your father told us. But they lived in the city and she never came over the river.'

'You met my father?'

'Oh, yes.'

'What happened to them?'

'Elena was killed in an ISIS raid on what they thought was a Breken cell. Your father was in the Marsh at the time.'

'Is that where he died?'

She looked at me. 'Nikolai, child. Your father is not dead.'

CHAPTER 33

Who is he? Where is he? Why don't I know about him? Does he know about me? If he knows, why did he leave me in that school all those years? Can I meet him? All that, I wanted to know – and more.

Levkova told me some of it. 'He's a strategist. One of our best. He moves around – it's safer that way. We spread the rumor that he died getting out of the Marsh and, as far as we know, ISIS bought it and aren't hunting for him. We must keep it that way. Do you understand?'

'You mean I can't tell anyone.'

'I mean exactly that.'

'Can I meet him?'

'Yes, you can meet him, I promise, but right now I want to save Sim from a bullet. Oh, one more thing. Your friend is here. Sleeping upstairs. Safer, I thought, than leaving her in the infirmary.'

She called Jeitan in. 'Jeitan thinks I'm mad to ask you for help. Why would a Citysider save the life of one of the city's ablest enemies? But Sim is also one of its best chances for peace. Without him, CFM crumbles and the fanatics rule the day.'

'What do we do?' said Jeitan.

'Start a rumor. That DeFaux is back, that he intends to assassinate Commander Vega at the ceremony tonight. Say that there's a price on DeFaux's head: medicine for a year for the family of whoever finds him before sundown. Nik, you'll have to do this – you're not a known face in the township and people down here won't know or won't care that you've been banished. Jeitan, go back up the hill, and when the rumor gets there, do your best to confirm it as officially as you can. Say that you've heard that Council will guarantee the reward. They can hardly deny it.'

'What if we get to sundown and we've got nothing?' asked Jeitan.

'Then we escalate.'

'How?'

'We start a riot. Anything to stop the Crossover ceremony taking place. Are we clear? Good. Find some food and take an hour's sleep upstairs if you must. I've sent word to the CFM leadership in Ohlerton, Gilgate, and Ferry Junction.' She looked at me. 'Those are the bridge councils that CFM still holds, upriver. I hope some of their people will get here in time for tonight.'

I hesitated in the doorway and decided to push my luck. 'After this – if it all works out – will you help me find Fyffe's brother?'

She looked up from the fire. 'Yes, Nik. I will.'

Crossover morning dawned cold, with mist rising off the river. I spent it standing in the bread queues, wandering in the Crossover Day market, and hovering at street corner fires saying, 'Have you heard…' And thinking about my father: I had a father and I was going to meet him. Did it occur to me that he might not want to meet me? Not for a second. He was going to be overjoyed that I (a) existed, (b) had survived, and (c) had found him at last.

Before long I realized that I had a shadow. Lanya was watching me. She didn't come close enough to talk, but whenever I looked around, there she was, standing on a street corner or leaning on the side of a building. After three hours of me wandering about rumor-mongering, she was still there. I came out of the crowd in the market square and saw her sitting on the steps of an old theater. She looked up at me as I approached and I stopped in case she didn't want me near, but she nodded towards the steps and I sat beside her.

'How's Fyffe?' I asked.

'She's on the mend, but worried about her brother. What are you doing?'

'Something for Levkova.'

'Oh.' She nodded. 'Do you think she's forgiven you?'

'I don't know. Have you?'

She looked across at the crowds in the market. 'I can see why you did it. You couldn't leave a child to the traffickers. I asked the Commander about Fyffe's brother – they turned Goran's place into pieces, but he wasn't there.'

'No. They got wind we were looking and took him somewhere else. At least we know he's alive.'

We watched the crowds and Lanya said, 'What you're doing for Levkova. Is it so secret you can't tell me?'

'Probably,' I said, and told her.

She listened, frowning, then said, 'Remnant are on the attack. We can't lose Commander Vega. That would be disastrous. Levkova is right: if anything's going to unearth DeFaux, the promise of a year's medicine will do it. But there's not much time, is there.'

'We have to try.'

She held up a finger. 'Did you hear that?'

'What?'

'You said *we*. *We* have to try. What do you mean? Why would you help us? Don't you have loyalties?'

'To what? The city?'

'Of course.'

'I don't know what that is anymore. I thought I knew. I thought I knew what Southsiders were like as well.'

'I see. You're not a very good Citysider, are you?'

'My mother was Breken.'

'Your mother? Well, that explains a few things. But don't you have people over there? Fyffe's family? Your school?'

'My school is a bombsite. My best friend is dead. Fyffe's family – yeah, I'll do what I can to get her and Sol home.'

'You have a girl. Fyffe said so.'

'Sort of. At least… I don't know. I thought I did.'

She grinned. 'You *sort of* have a girl?'

'Well, you're finding it hard to forgive me and I've known you all of two minutes. I've known Dash most of my life and I've only just told her I speak Breken. She didn't take it all that well. She doesn't know about my mother yet.'

Lanya laughed.

'What's funny?' I said.

'You are. You're afraid to tell your girl – what's her name? Dash. You're afraid to tell Dash about your mother.'

'So?'

'You think she'll be upset because your mother was Breken?'

'Yes. No. All right – she'll be upset because I am.'

She twisted round to look at me, still smiling. The world brightened. 'There,' she said. 'You said it. It's not so bad! And for that – yes, I do forgive you. Can I help you spread the rumors?'

Early afternoon, we headed back to Levkova's. Fyffe was sitting at the kitchen table, talking to Vega and Levkova about Sol. 'Remnant have him, almost certainly,' said Vega. 'I'd say he's well cared for. He's worth a lot of money.'

'For you, too?' asked Fy. 'If you get him back, you'll have us both to ransom.'

Vega sat a while looking at her and I think he was angry, but when he spoke his voice was quiet. 'I know what they tell you over the river about us. Let me tell you this. Not all of us are prepared to barter the bodies of children for profit.'

Fyffe dropped her head and whispered an apology.

'No matter,' said Vega. 'If we can find your brother, we will.' He stood up, greeted Lanya, and nodded at me.

Before I could work out what that meant, Jeitan came in at a run, calling, 'News!' He pulled up when he saw Vega and remembered to salute. 'Sir!'

'Go ahead.'

'Sir, we have a lead on DeFaux's whereabouts.'

Vega glanced at Levkova. 'I see,' he said. 'Where?'

'The old art gallery in Newbourne Lane.'

'Is that so? Well, it's useful, certainly, but if we take him now, we've got no evidence.'

'We're not waiting until he shoots you, Sim,' said Levkova. 'I've sent word to the others. I think you'll find you're out-voted.'

'Outmaneuvered, you mean. I won't ask how you did it, but I assume you have a plan?'

'Take him now. I think he'll sing us a sweet little song about Terten. He has no loyalty. He'll do what's best for himself.'

'That may be so but I can't just walk in there with a squad and no proof.'

'So we send Jeitan and Nik. They watch. They send word when he makes a move. We'll have a squad ready once he reaches the square.'

Which is how I came to be doing an impression of a skiddy, lounging under a tree in the park – what used to be a park – in front of an ugly concrete block of a building that had once been an art gallery. They'd given me a lethal-smelling bottle of 'shine, and a description of an assassin: fortyish, short, thin – everyone was thin here – long face, straight nose, large ears, and close-clipped, fair hair.

I was sitting there wondering how Sol was, where Sol was, when I felt the press of cold metal on the back of my neck. The chill of it charged straight down my spine.

'Well, shit,' Benit's voice. 'Just look at this. An escaped prisoner. Should we shoot it?'

'I'm game.' Hell. Benit and friend. 'We'll ask questions later, yeah?' He laughed at his own amazing wit.

'Get up.' Benit again. The gun knocked at the top of my spine and I thought about the damage it could do even if he never fired it. 'Get. Up.' I stood up. 'What are you doing here?' he said. 'Why aren't you under lock and key up the hill?'

'Why don't you go up there and ask them?'

He spun me round and pushed me against the tree. 'That mouth of yours ever get you into trouble?'

'Now and then.'

Benit and Benit II were a match – same haircut, same sneer – but Benit II must have been junior because he didn't have a gun. Benit senior had an elderly assault rifle. He lifted it in my face. I looked at his eyes, narrow and stony above the barrel, and wondered how worn the trigger was and how itchy his finger. 'You should run,' he said. 'That's what your riot police say, isn't it? Run or we'll shoot – of course what they really mean is run *and* we'll shoot, but I guess you know that.' He smiled a cold tight smile. 'Go on, then. Run. We'll look after your whore.'

Benit II sniggered. 'You know what they say about city girls.'

'I SAID RUN!' yelled Benit.

'Ben!' Jeitan's voice, behind me. I didn't dare turn my head to look.

'J!' said Benit. 'Look what I found!'

Jeitan arrived in front of us. 'He's with me,' he said.

The gun wavered. 'He's what? He's supposed to be locked up.'

'Put the gun down. What're you two doing over this side of town? You're supposed to be drilling for parade tonight. *Put it down!*'

'Special detail,' said Benit and he lowered the gun. I practiced breathing.

'For what?' said Jeitan. 'Who authorized it?'

'Can't say.' Benit II was shooting agitated looks towards the gallery.

Jeitan watched him, frowning. 'Protection duty?'

Benit II said, 'A VIP for tonight.' His partner gave him a shut-the-hell-up look and he shrugged.

'DeFaux,' said Jeitan. 'You're protecting DeFaux. Who're your orders from?'

Benit stood up straighter. 'High up. Can't say. What are you doing letting City boy here walk around? Is this that old bag's idea? I bet it is. You spend too much time with her, J. You're turning into an old woman yourself. You're forgetting who the real enemy is.' He started to lift his gun again.

Jeitan hit him. And then it was on. Benit II piled into Jeitan, and I threw 'shine into Benit II's face and piled into him. Fists flew, boots swung – it wasn't exactly the ultimate in hand-to-hand combat, more like wrestling mixed with landing whatever punch or kick you could.

It was over fast. We beat them into the ground. Which surprised us both. We sat on them for a while, breathing deep: Jeitan on Benit and me on Benit II, twisting their arms behind their backs when they squawked or struggled. When he could speak, Jeitan said, 'You fight dirty. Where'd you learn that?'

'At a very religious school. But it's nothing to what Levkova will do to us if we've missed DeFaux.'

'I don't think we've missed him.' He twisted Benit's arm. 'Have we? What were your orders?'

There followed a lot of swearing and arm twisting. Finally, we got '16.15… Discreet escort… Crossover Square.'

Jeitan checked his watch. 'Eleven minutes. Good timing.' He nodded at me and we climbed off them. They scrambled up. Jeitan picked up Benit's gun and said to him, 'Do you know why DeFaux is here? You don't, do you? I hope you don't. There's a contract on Vega. He's here to close it. Tonight.'

'Shit. But… but… shit!' Benit stepped back.

'Well put,' said Jeitan. 'Now. The Commander will survive this. If you want to survive as well, I suggest you get back up the hill and practice being inconspicuous. Tell them you took your gun for servicing. Get lost!'

They took off.

Jeitan watched them go. He weighed Benit's gun in his hand. 'Want this?'

'Not really.' A Citysider on the streets of Southside had to be a target. An armed one might even be a legitimate target.

'Take it.' He handed it to me, then said, 'I can't believe I just did that.' He looked doubtful. 'Know how to use it?'

'Sort of.'

'Well, try and look like you do, because we're the new escort. You know you're bleeding?' The bandage on my hand was soaked bright red where the stitches ran across my palm. Better not to think about it.

'Look,' Jeitan nodded towards the gallery. A lone figure in a long dark coat hurried down some side steps and sped away across the park.

'That him?' I asked.

'That's him. Come on.'

Crossover Square. Cracked paving stones lifting at the corners. A twice-lifesize statue of a woman standing beside a child, one of her fists lifted to the sky, the other arm around her kid. Broken chains trailing from her wrists.

The buildings enclosing the square were three and four storeys high, built of gray stone with steep roofs, balconies, fancy cast-iron railings, and gargoyles. They'd been hotels once, maybe. I don't know who occupied them now, but one thing was clear: they were sniper heaven.

Already hundreds of people packed the square. DeFaux kept to the edges of the crowd so we were picking our way through traders' spreads of cheap shoes, jewelry, used clothes, and much thumbed books. The greasy smell of hot chips and cheap sauce was everywhere. The afternoon was fading fast.

A stage had been set up at one end of the square and a squad stood to attention around it. Old soldiers were organizing themselves in front of it, putting the disabled ones first, in chairs and on crutches. On one side a band was tuning up.

Lanya appeared at my elbow. She sauntered along, watching the crowd, not looking at Jeitan or me. 'Levkova sent me. When you've worked out where he's going, I'll take word back to her and the Commander. Is that him in the long coat?'

The band started practicing; a few trumpet blasts punched the air. Some people lifted fists, then voices, and an anthem rolled like a wave across the square. But from somewhere near us a voice yelled, 'Terten's a traitor!' Others picked it up in a ragged chant that swept back against the anthem and suddenly there was nothing musical about any of it. Levkova didn't need us to start her riot: primed by the rumor of Vega's imminent assassination, supporters of CFM squared off against the Remnant faithful, and the whole place erupted.

And DeFaux was gone. Jeitan dived through a doorway and Lanya and I raced after him. The doors closed behind us, muffling the noise outside. We were in a gloomy, high-ceilinged foyer. A wide set of stairs headed up into shadows. Jeitan put a finger to his lips, listening, waiting for our eyes to adjust. He nodded to me to follow him up the stairs and signaled to Lanya to stay put.

We crept towards the first floor and I wondered if Jeitan had any idea what we were supposed to do when we confronted an ISIS-trained assassin, with no hope of back up. I looked over my shoulder and stopped dead. 'Jeitan!'

He swore at me and kept going.

I turned around slowly and tried to sound calm. 'Jeitan! Look.'

'Will you shut up!' But then he turned around.

DeFaux stood at the foot of the stairs.

With Lanya.

He held an arm across her shoulders, and a gun to her temple. He opened his eyes wide at us, grinning. 'Bang!' he said, and laughed.

'Let her go!' I said, stupidly. Uselessly. Finding it hard to breathe. 'A squad's on its way.'

'I don't think so. Squads will be busy out there, won't they. Take the ammo out of your guns, boys. And put them down.'

I watched Jeitan unload his gun, and followed what he did.

'That's it,' said DeFaux. 'Now come down. Slowly. Good. Stand right there, and don't move. That's it. This girl and me, we're going upstairs, aren't we, sweetheart.'

He started moving backwards up the stairs, his arm still round her, the gun still on her temple, watching us all the way. Lanya fixed her eyes on me. Her mouth was set in a line, her face was still, but her hands clenched and opened. DeFaux moved her away from us, backwards, whispering in her ear. All I could think was, *If you hurt her, I will kill you.* DeFaux said, 'That so?' and I realized I'd said it aloud.

'I WILL!' I shouted.

They were halfway up, past where we'd laid down the guns. I edged forward to keep them in sight through the shadows. Jeitan put a hand on my arm. 'Better not.'

'Staaay!' demanded DeFaux. 'Stay, or your girl will be a mess. A real mess. I promise. Would you like to know how much of a mess I can make of her? No? First, I almost kill her, but not quite. More? No?'

My heart thumped. I'd never wanted anything as much as to charge up those stairs and throw him down them. But he would shoot her if I moved. I had no doubt about that.

Lanya stumbled. Jeitan gripped my arm and said, 'Wait.'

DeFaux took two steps sideways to steady himself. Lanya stood up straight and flung her arms out so that his hold around her shoulders loosened. Then she twisted away and turned an astonishing cartwheel up the stairs and out of his grip. He fired the gun, shattering the air in that huge, hard space.

I charged up the stairs. He'd shot her. I was sure he'd shot her.

But her foot came back at his head. He overbalanced and pitched down the stairs, yelling, arms and legs flailing.

Lanya had folded up. Her whole body was shaking. One side of her face was a mask of blood and her breath came fast. I knelt in front of her, held her shoulders, and tried to see the damage. 'Lanya?'

She opened her unbloodied eye and, miraculously, gave me half a smile. 'Good?' she whispered.

'Amazing. You are amazing.'

Jeitan shouted, 'She all right?'

'She's hit,' I called back. 'But not bad. Have you got him?'

'You'd think he was dying from all the moaning. Broken leg, maybe worse, if we're lucky. Can you come down? And find his gun!'

'In a sec.' The bullet had burned a graze above Lanya's temple. I undid the bandana from her neck; my fingers were shaking so bad it seemed to take forever. I pressed the bandana against the bleeding and she flinched. 'Sorry,' I said. 'I'm sorry. You hold it. Hold here. Press.'

She pressed, flinched again, half-smiled again. 'You keep patching me up.'

'You keep fighting people. Or dancing at people. One or the other.'

'I'm dizzy.'

'I'll get you home.'

I half-walked, half-carried her down the stairs.

Jeitan was sitting on DeFaux. He'd tied his belt around the man's hands and, yes, there was a lot of moaning going on. I sat Lanya on the bottom stair and wrapped her in my coat. I recovered our guns and DeFaux's small pistol, then crouched beside Jeitan and looked at our man. 'He wasn't going to shoot anyone at long range with this,' I said. 'Where's his real gun?'

'It'll be hidden upstairs,' said Jeitan. 'You're going to have to get help.'

'Will you be all right?'

'Give me his gun.' He took it and aimed it experimentally at DeFaux's head. 'With any luck, he'll try to escape.' He looked at me and grinned. 'Good work, City boy.'

Vega stood in the light of a huge bonfire in the middle of the square and conducted his squads as though they were an orchestra. They'd tamed the riot and now they were mopping up, helped by the dark and the cold – it was starting to snow. I remembered what Vega had said to Terten at the hearing: the army was his. He was right. If the rioters had been hoping for assassination and mutiny, they were twice out of luck.

He beckoned me over.

'We found him,' I said. 'Jeitan's got him.'

He was speechless for a moment, but he recovered soon enough. 'Damage?'

'Lanya's hurt, but not bad. DeFaux too, thanks to her, but not bad either.'

He motioned to one of his deputies to take charge. 'Custody for anyone who wants to be trouble. And get me a medic.' He called up two others to go with us. 'Now. Show me.'

I led him back through the swirling snow. Lanya, Jeitan, and DeFaux were all as I'd left them. The flash of enmity between DeFaux and Vega was impressive – history there, for sure. Lanya was a mess of blood, but she held out a hand to me and let the medic take a look. 'Not too bad,' was the verdict, 'but get her home.'

Pretty soon, Vega had us all heading in different directions: Jeitan to round up Benits I and II for questioning, DeFaux to custody, a squad to search the building, Lanya and the medic back to Levkova's lodging, where I was heading too.

'Stais!' No one had called me that since school. I turned back to Vega. He gave me that look – the calculating one that bounced off my bones – and said, 'I see it now. It's time you met your father.'

CHAPTER 35

My father was at Levkova's. He'd arrived early in the morning and gone straight into a meeting with others in the CFM leadership, the ones Levkova had called together from Ohlerton, Gilgate, and Ferry Junction. Max told me this when I came down to the kitchen. He put a big mug of tea in front of me and said, 'Stick around, youngster. There's someone here you want to meet.'

'Is he here? Where?'

But he put a hand on my shoulder. 'They're in the study, four of 'em got here. They're meeting with the Commander and Tasia. Patience. They'll be busy for a while yet. They don't get together too often, and Remnant's stepped up a gear. They've got a lot of talking to do.'

Which left me sitting, then standing, then pacing in the hallway. My stomach was churning, and the hall was too close and airless.

I went outside and sat on the steps. Across the road a man was trying to fix his wreck of a car, and three others stood around him, smoking, laughing, offering advice and friendly abuse. A couple of old women in black came out of a little church down the way. Its dome, which probably once shone gold or bronze, was stripped to a dull gray base.

At last the study door opened. Jeitan came out with two women and a man. They were deep in conversation as Jeitan ushered them into the kitchen and I heard him say, 'Max will look after you.' Then he came down the hall to me. 'Your turn. In the study. But wait in the hallway till you're called.'

Easier said than done. I leaned on the door Jeitan had come out of and listened. I heard a voice I didn't know. A man's voice. And Levkova's. The man was talking but I heard only fragments, as if he was pacing towards the door and then away. 'No, of course I didn't… what Elena wanted… a child grown fat on their lies… or a feint, it would be a potent weapon for them…'

The churn in my stomach climbed up my throat. I gripped the door handle hard. Levkova was saying, 'I don't think –'

'What don't you think?'

'He doesn't strike me as either of those.'

'Don't go soft on me, Tasia.'

'Will you see him?'

'I'll have to.'

Yes, I thought. Yes, you will. I opened the door. The man stopped pacing and looked at me. Levkova bowed to him and headed for the door, but he said, 'Stay, Tasia. Please.' Commander Vega was across the room by a tall window.

My father was white, an easterner for sure. His hair was gray, but his face wasn't old. It was strong and hard. Battle-hungry. He was lean, like all of them, and tall, and his stare was sharp and calculating.

'Sit down.' He nodded towards a chair in front of a wall of shelves crammed with books and watched me cross the room. I sat on the arm of the chair and dug my fists into my pockets.

My heart beat hard.

He went back to pacing. 'So, then, here's my dilemma,' he said, like I was part of the conversation he'd been having with the others. 'I'm telling you this because, if you're a soldier you'll understand. If you're not… well… My dilemma is this: even if you are who you say you are, I can't know *what* you are. Twelve years in an ISIS school is too long.' He glanced at me. 'In any case, I don't have time to find out. Regardless of who you are, if they've sent you, that means they've found me. That would be a useful thing for us to know.' He drew on his cigarette and breathed out a cloud of smoke. 'They say you speak Breken. Have you understood me?'

I nodded.

'What did they tell you, in the city, about me?'

'That you,' I cleared my throat and tried again, 'That you were dead… in the… in the uprising in '87.'

'Do you remember Frieda Kelleran?'

'A bit, not really.'

'She didn't visit you?'

I shook my head.

'Did anyone else?'

'Visit me? No.'

'It was not my wish to put a child in that school. When I got out of the Marsh, I was told what Frieda had done. Then it was too late.'

'Why too late?' I asked. He studied his cigarette as it burned down to his fingers and didn't answer. 'What was it too late for?' I said. 'To get me out? You had moles in there. You were planning to blow it up. How hard could it be to get one kid out?'

'Nik…' said Levkova.

He stared at the cigarette. 'That child is lost to us.'

My throat closed.

'Tasia tells me you claim to remember Elena?' He rolled another cigarette and lit it. Watched me. Waited. 'What do you remember?'

I watched him back.

'Well?' he said.

'This is a test, right?'

'I'm wondering what you remember, that's all.'

I headed for the door.

'Wait!' he said. 'It's a simple enough question. Why not answer it?'

I stopped in the doorway. 'What would that tell you? That they've briefed me well? She'd be a key piece of intelligence, wouldn't she? Looks. Quirks. Habits. Manners. There's bound to be an ISIS dossier about her for just this purpose.'

'So you don't remember –'

'Or I haven't read it. Which do you think?'

'Come back and sit –'

'I remember her voice in my ear saying my name. I remember her hair reaching down to her waist when she let it out. I remember her smell, like soap and linen. I remember the orange scarf she wore when she went to market and the gold pins in her ears. I remember her fear when men came pounding on the door and wrecked the place – for you? Was that? Looking for you. And I remember the sound she made after they'd gone. I remember *her*. I don't remember *you*.'

Enough. More than enough.

I left.

CHAPTER 36

If you climb the Southside riverwall at the western boundary of the Moldam district and work your way past the smashed-up signs telling you not to and through the barbed wire strung across the top, you can drop down onto a narrow stretch of bank where things wash up and get caught in the reed clumps that grow there. Bits of make-shift boats and rafts, bodies sometimes, and pieces of them, mines escaped from their moorings. The bodies get fished out when someone notices them, but the mines are left alone. There's too many, they're too dangerous to defuse, and detonating them could destroy the wall. To the right is the Mol, Moldam Bridge, in all its glory. And a way off west, to the left, hazy in the river spray, are the bridges at Bethun, Sentinel and, a long way lost in the distance, St Clare.

The riverbank was clear of boats and bodies that

day, picked over by scavengers who'd left nothing but gravel and clay and a few tufts of spiky grass. In among the reeds I could see the glint of a couple of small metallic disks untouched by any scavenger. Mines. I wondered if they really would take out the riverwall. I sat down and scooped up a handful of gravel and threw a pebble at the nearest one. I was pretty sure it would take more than a stone. Anyway, my aim was off.

Across the water the city shimmered in hazy afternoon light. I imagined I could see Bridge Street, a dark narrow strip going up from St Clare gate through Sentian. North-east of that was Watch Hill and, beyond that, Pagnal Heath. The trees would be bare now, and there'd be a blanket of snow except on the walkways where it would be shovelled sideways into muddy piles. Not many people would be out in all that wide, empty space. But well before the heath, if you turned left at Weston, and took the short cut through the alleys, Kemryn, Ry, Madan, you'd come out on Tornmoor Avenue. Walk up Tornmoor for about five minutes and you arrive at the school gates. I stood there once, with Frieda Kelleran – stood and looked up the tree-lined drive towards the library. Memory flickered. She wore black gloves and a long gray coat, and she held my hand as we walked up the driveway. At least I think she did. Maybe I'd made that up. Maybe she never existed and it was all a lie and ISIS was playing a very long game after all.

When I hauled myself back to the riverbank, Eleanor was there – Elena – my mother, whose right name I hadn't even known. I watched her out of the corner of my eye. Threw another stone. She didn't speak, just sat there and looked across the water.

'Nik! Hey! *Hey!*' Lanya's face peered over the wall above me. 'What in the holy name of God are you doing?' She rolled over the top of the wall and dropped beside me, hit the handful of gravel out of my grip and grabbed my hand with both of hers. 'What're you doing?'

'Nothing.'

'Those are river mines. Did you know that? You did know that.'

'It'd take more than a stone to set one off.'

'How do you know? You have no idea.'

'What d'you want?'

'To stop you making a horrible mess – that would be a good beginning.'

'Too late.'

'Come with me! We're going back up.'

'No.'

'Nik! This is no place for anyone.' She still had hold of my hand.

'I'm okay here.'

'No, you're not. You're really not. And I'm not either. This place is for ghosts and lost souls. It's not for us.'

'You're a Maker. Were. You should be used to them.'

'In their right place. That's what Makers are for. To help make the paths for them to go to the right place, so they don't come wandering in places like this.' She stood up and pulled on my hand. '*Please?*'

'You shouldn't even be up,' I said. 'And you're freezing. Do you want my coat?'

'I want you and me back over the wall.' She crouched down again. 'Right now. That's what I want.'

She was staring at me hard and gripping my hand. She had a white gauze patch across her temple that made her eyes look blacker than ever, and the beads in her hair were trembling like all the fire in her was about to burst alight.

She tried again. 'Levkova says, please will you come back. You got a "please" out of Levkova! Come and talk to her.'

'No.'

'At least come away from here. Look, she gave me this.' She handed me a scrap of paper with an address scrawled on it. 'She said it's a safe place to sleep tonight.'

I scrunched it up. 'I don't need her help.'

'You know, if once in a while you behaved like a normal person and took the help that's offered, you might be amazed at the result.'

'Meaning?'

'Meaning people would line up to help you.'

'I don't want help. I don't want a listening ear, I don't want people rallying round, I don't want sympathy or advice or rescue.' I pitched the paper into the river.

'Fyffe needs you.'

'No, she doesn't. You'll look after her.'

'So, this is you running again, is it? Levkova told me – about your father. But how bad could it be? He's your father! He's here and not dead or disappeared. That makes you one of the lucky ones.'

When I didn't answer, she stood up. 'Come on! We're going up. We could be arrested for being here. I have a father too, you know, and if I get into any more trouble he will not be happy. And my aunts will try to make him marry me off to someone safe.' She dragged on my hand. 'I'm not going without you.'

I let her pull me to my feet and we set off down the bank with Lanya still gripping my hand as though she thought she might lose me on the way. Back towards the bridge we found some stone steps with a locked iron gate at the top. We scrambled up and squeezed over the wall and through the wire, with only a few scratches.

On the other side Lanya leaned on the wall. She gave me this long look, like there was a lot to say and she wasn't going to say any of it out loud. All she said was, 'You scared me.'

'It'd take more than a stone.'

'You don't know that.'

The guards on the bridge gate were watching us. 'Let's move,' I said. We walked west along the wall, away from the bridge. All round us, the evening's work was beginning: kids hauled pails of water to kitchens, men lit streetcorner fires, women hung lanterns in windows and from porches and conjured meals from scraps. Cookshops and coffeehouses were coming to life.

'Where are you going to go?' said Lanya.

Away, mainly. I said, 'Don't you have stuff you ought to be doing?'

'I'm doing it.'

'Being annoying? This is your job for the day?'

'That's right.'

'Go and tell Levkova I don't need a babysitter.'

'She knows that. She only sent me to ask you to come back. The rest is my own invention. Please tell me what happened this morning?'

'Lanya…'

'I don't want to help. I just want to know.' Which made me smile. She smiled back. 'Well?'

'No.'

'And you think *I'm* annoying. Tell me about the city, then. Oh.' She stopped. Coming down the road towards us was Coly, the toxic little creep whose fight with Lanya had set the whole Remnant takeover in motion. And he had friends with him, three of them. Lanya swore. 'He's seen us.' She dived for the first alley on offer. I followed.

We raced past houses that were boarded up and derelict, but not empty. The families squatting in them hung lanterns in their porches to stake their claims. The first dark porch we came to we ran up the steps and crammed ourselves into the shadows.

Lanya blew out a breath. 'I thought he saw us.' She peered into the alley; her braids fell across her shoulder and the last of the sunlight shone gold on the back of her neck. She leaned back beside me. 'I don't see him, but we should wait a while. I hate him! His father's high up in Remnant. He's just the sort of person my aunts would match me up with.' She shuddered and looked at me. 'Sorry. Family quarrels.' Then she smiled. 'You can have family quarrels now that you have a father.' She patted my arm. 'You've already had one, I think? Don't worry – I won't mention him again. I'm not even supposed to know about him, so I'll just…' She zipped thumb and finger across her lips.

I looked at her smiling face and felt her arm press on mine. I wasn't breathing properly and my throat ached. I looked away, out towards the alley. It was quiet. Coly hadn't followed.

Lanya said, 'What are you going to do?'

'I don't know.'

She nudged me. 'Well, think!'

I took a breath, and tried to ignore how close she was. 'Okay,' I said. 'I have to find Sol. I'm not doing anything until I find him and get him home. Then I guess I could go back over the river. I'll have to steer clear of ISIS because of… you know… him, but there'll be no getting out of being drafted because, well, you just don't get out of that, which means I'll end up fighting hostiles – which is you, by the way, so…' I shrugged, stuck.

'So stay.' She put a hand on my arm. 'Stay.'

I picked up her hand and held it in my unbandaged one. 'You're the one who wants to go over the bridge.'

'I was.'

'…And fight the city. We're at war, remember? You and me.' Her fingers were long and black, light on my palm. Her braids fell over her eyes. The beads clacked as she shook her head. And then I couldn't look at her because my heart was beating so loud I was sure she could hear it.

'Nik?'

'What?'

She put her hands on my shoulders and I bent my head and kissed her.

And she kissed me back.

She smiled. 'Don't tell Coly.'

'No. Do you have a whole lot of brothers who'll have to kill me now?'

Her smile got wider. 'I dare you to risk it.'

I picked up one of her braids and ran it through my fingers. 'I think I could risk that.'

We stayed a while.

Until it got dark and very cold.

Lanya said, 'It's late.'

'Come on. I'll walk you back to base.'

'Just like that? I was busy thinking up arguments about Sol and your father to get you to come back.'

'You've got a funny way of thinking up arguments.'

She punched my arm. 'Are you truly coming back?'

'I guess. I can't let it go at one meeting. Maybe he was having a bad day.'

Maybe.

CHAPTER 37

'**Tasia, I want you to look at this.**' It was him, my father, striding into Levkova's kitchen, holding a piece of paper. He saw me and stopped.

'Of course,' said Levkova. She took the paper and headed out the door.

'Don't go,' he said. 'I need an answer straightaway.'

'And you shall have one. I won't be long.' She closed the door behind her.

He went to the fire and stood staring down at it. I picked at the bandage on my hand. Silence for a while, then he said, 'What happened to your hand?'

'I met Fyffe's kidnappers.'

'Damage?'

'I don't know. My index finger doesn't move very well, and there's parts with no feeling. The doc says nerve and tendon damage, wait and see.'

'You came a long way for this Hendry boy.'

'Yeah, well, he matters to me.' Like family, I almost said, but didn't. I watched his back, his head bent to the fire. I couldn't read what he was thinking, but all that compressed energy of the day before had gone. I said, 'If ISIS had sent me, don't you think I'd have done something by now – tried to go back over the river to report that you're alive, or had a go at killing you?'

Silence.

'Or do you think they're playing a really long game where even I don't know I'm a spy?'

He turned around at that and I thought he might leave but he just looked at me like he had no idea what to do with me. He was probably a man who was used to knowing what to do with people. 'You have questions,' he said. 'Ask them.'

Just that. Questions. Ask them. I could hear Lou saying, *Jump!* He had a deadly imitation of Gorton: *My boy, when the freight train of opportunity speeds by, you gotta jump.* I looked at my father, and thought, yeah, sure – on it, or under it?

'Well?' he said.

I sucked in a breath. 'Did you know about me?'

'Yes, I did.'

'And that I was in that school?'

'Yes.'

'Why was I in that school?'

'I don't know. I was in the Marsh. When I came out, Elena was dead and you were gone. I found out later where you were.'

'Why did you leave me there?'

'It was logistically impossible to do anything else.'

'But isn't that your job? To do the logistically impossible?'

Silence at that. Maybe rhetorical questions weren't part of the deal. Then he said, 'Tornmoor wasn't a school. It was an ISIS training facility.'

'Well, it seemed like a school to me. We did calculus and algebra and geometry and physics and chemistry and...'

'History? Social analysis? Languages? Any of that?'

'It was a science school.'

'Where ISIS trained recruits – why else the assault course on the back field, the training in ciphers and electronics, the laboratories and computer systems beyond anything a school would need, Scripture indoctrination to keep you all in line, and the selection, every year, of an elite to join the Service?'

'So they came recruiting, okay. But it's not like they were in the classroom every day –'

'No?' He ticked names off on his fingers. 'Stapleton, Tremewan, Lewis – all senior ISIS agents; Gorton was retired, Williams was in the Marsh and Burton –'

'Wait! Dr Williams was in the Marsh?'

'Before my time, and not in any senior capacity, but yes. He trained there. All their medics do their psych training there.' He looked at me. 'You know what the Marsh is, don't you? It's where ISIS turns thinking, questioning, rebellious individuals into compliant drones. They do it with drugs in what they like to call therapeutic interrogation. They've been doing it for years. We've lost some of our best people in the Marsh.'

I stared at him. I didn't dare ask what had happened to him in there, but I was starting to think that the reasons he hadn't come for me weren't simple.

'I'm not surprised you didn't know,' he said. 'ISIS prides itself on its control of information, particularly when it comes to indoctrinating potential recruits.'

'And now you think I'm one of them – a city kid, a fascist-in-training?'

He didn't answer.

'Do you?' I demanded.

Finally, like it was wrenched out of him, he said, 'Tasia thinks highly of you. So does Sim. They don't bestow that judgment lightly.' He glanced at his watch and moved towards the door.

I said, 'One more! One more question.'

'Well?'

'Why did you change your mind?'

'About what?'

'About telling me all this.'

He hesitated in the doorway, then he looked straight at me. 'You look like your mother.'

And that was that. Question time was over and he was gone.

I shut my eyes and pressed on them hard with the heels of my hands, and I hurt with an old ache that I'd thought I was done with a long time ago.

A while later Levkova stuck her head through the door. 'Come into the study.'

Commander Vega was there, and my father, and the rest of the CFM leadership who'd been there the day before. Levkova closed the door. 'We're coordinating an operation to retrieve the Hendry boy. He's in Blackbyre. We've learned that much. DeFaux was eager to help, you'll be glad to know. We're sending a squad...'

At last, I thought. He's alive. This will work. 'Can I go with them?' I asked.

'Yes. We want someone who knows him.'

'Then Fyffe can take him home.' Looks were exchanged. 'What?' I said. 'Why not?'

'We can't just let him go,' said my father. 'He's too valuable. We'll set up a prisoner exchange.'

'No!' I looked at Vega but he was staring out the window. 'He's eight years old!' I said.

My father said, 'He's valuable however old he is. We have someone over there we need to get back.'

I said to Vega, 'An exchange. Like with Kasimir? A suicide switch?'

'We can't let an opportunity like this go,' said my father.

'Yes, you can,' I said. 'You can decide that he's only eight and just let him go home.'

'Enough,' he said.

'Is this what you want?' I said to Vega.

'That's enough,' said my father. 'You can go. Now.'

Okay. So I blew that. If I'd shut up and gone along with them and their stupid plan, they'd have taken me to Black-byre and I might've been able to get Sol away from them and back over the river without going through with the switch. As it was, I shot my mouth off and they shut me out of the whole deal.

CHAPTER 38

Next day, a hand-picked squad set off to snatch Sol from under Blackbyre noses. They were ultra-confident of their ability to do this, and that confidence bled through into a staunch belief that they were good enough not only to snatch him but also to make a switch work – never mind what had happened to Vega's son.

They didn't let me near the op. I tried the 'you need someone to ID him' line and they said, 'yes, we do,' and took Fyffe instead. Which left me behind, kicking the doors like a two-year-old.

I sat in Levkova's kitchen, inscribing the top of the table – an old school table – with a blunt army knife, tracing years of grafitti left by bored kids (Deter ♥ Chara. Chara is easi as π...). I scrubbed out π and scratched 3.14159265358979323... to one hundred places exactly, then started to do it all again in binary. Levkova came and

went, and Lanya made flatbread with Max. By midnight
Lanya had finished the bread and was so fed up with me
she went to bed. Around 2am Levkova came to the table
and said, 'I take it you intend to sit there defacing the
furniture all night?'

'Yes.'

'You won't mind if I go to bed then?'

'No.'

She sat down. 'Nik.'

'What?' I stabbed the table. 'You have to stop the
switch.'

She unstuck the knife, folded it closed, and laid it
down between us. 'It's a joint decision, not mine alone.'

'It's barbaric.'

'It's war. And… they started it.'

'They started it? The suicide switch was their idea?
That's your excuse?'

'Don't call it that. Things escalate. It's hard to stop.'

'What about Fyffe?'

'She'll go too.'

'Will she be wired up?'

'I don't know. Probably. The Hendry boy is worth
a fortune. City want him back – they'll make damn sure
he's safe.'

'Will they? What if Remnant decide that if they can't
have him, CFM can't either? It wouldn't take much to
get at the triggers – it only needs the right frequency in

the wrong hands. He'd better be worth it, whoever you're getting back.'

'She. And yes, she is. Suzannah Montier. She's our heart and our future. Her father led the uprising in '87 and brokered the cease-fire. But on the brink of signing a peace agreement, we were betrayed. We think, by DeFaux. Daniel Montier was assassinated; your father was captured and sent to the Marsh. It all came to nothing.

'Suzannah took on Daniel's work, bringing the people together. She is much loved up and down the river. People listen to her, and they will follow her. She's our hope for a united Southside and a just peace. Our leader-in-waiting. We need her back.' Levkova stood up. 'The exchange will go smoothly, you'll see.'

She was standing there, not leaving, so I said, 'What?'

'Your father –'

'What about him?'

'You should understand what it means for him – you coming here.'

'I know what it ought to mean.'

'He's afraid. Do you know that?'

'Of what? Not of me.'

'Of grief, I think.'

I thought about that. 'Because I look like her?'

'Partly. But also, he's lost all the years of your growing up. That's so much to lose. And now here you are, and to look at you is to see all that loss.'

'But that's not fair.' Me being a two-year-old again. 'I'm here now.'

'You are. And the worst of it is you can't help him. Except by being you, and waiting. If you have enough patience to do that. He has to work it out.'

'But what if he never…'

'Never comes round? I can't tell you. I don't know.' She left.

I picked up the knife again and scratched Sol's name, and Fyffe's, into the table.

Sometime later I must have put my head down and gone to sleep because then it was daylight and Lanya was shaking me awake. 'They're back! Wake up! They're back!'

CHAPTER 39

Sol was unhurt, outwardly at least. I'd forgotten how small he was – just a scrap of a kid with straggly fair hair, deep shadows under his eyes, and no meat on his bones at all. He marched up the road, hand in hand with Fyffe, in a well guarded retinue like the prize that he was, and people watched as they went by. But he didn't care because when he saw me he charged away from them yelling, 'Nik! Nik!'

He arrived with a thump and burst into tears on my shoulder. I held him tight and when I could speak, I said, 'Hey! Look at you! Survive anything, yeah?' When he'd calmed down, I stood him at arm's length. 'They didn't feed you much. You okay?'

He wiped his eyes. 'I guess.'

'You're hungry, right?'

He nodded.

'Let's find some food.' I turned to see Lanya looking at me sideways, and I realized I'd been jabbering away in Anglo. 'Sorry,' I said. 'This is Sol. Sol, this is Lanya.'

She bowed and murmured a formal greeting. He sniffed tearily and she smiled at me. 'I keep forgetting.'

'What?'

'That you're… you know…'

'The enemy?'

'Well, yes. You're not living up to expectations at all.'

Fyffe and the squad arrived. I hugged Fyffe and we grinned at each other. Mission accomplished. Almost. But I couldn't help seeing us through Southside eyes – happy families, City-style, courtesy of Breken risk and hardship once again. 'You did great,' I said. 'Tell me everything. And let's find some food for this kid.' I put Sol on my back where he weighed nothing and clung like a limpet, and we headed off to Levkova's.

'Now what?' said Fyffe when we'd put bread and sausages in front of Sol.

I shrugged. 'They're gonna tell you before they tell me.'

'An exchange, they said.'

'Yeah. They tell you any more about it?'

She shook her head. 'Home. At last.' But she sounded more exhausted than excited.

Sol finished his food and we got him cleaned up and

then, because he was sleeping where he stood, I put him to bed in an upstairs room. They'd given it over especially for him and Fyffe as valuable soon-to-be-exchanged prisoners, and there was a guard on the door. Sol gripped my sleeve. 'Stay!'

I sat down. 'I'm not going anywhere. You go to sleep.'

'Are we going home soon?'

'Yeah. Soon. In a day or so.'

'Were you kidnapped too?'

'No. We came over to look for you, Fy and me.'

Long pause. 'I want to go home.'

'I know. And you will.'

He drifted off to sleep.

Fyffe came in after a while to sit with him. 'It's over,' she said to me. 'We did it.'

'Nearly over,' I said. 'This exchange. I have to tell you what it is.'

She was white-faced by the time I'd finished.

'And you?' she said. 'Will you be wired up too?'

'I don't know. It's you and Sol who are valuable. No one over there wants me back the way they want you back.'

'I don't understand. I thought they were friendly, Levkova and Vega?'

'They are. To a point.'

She looked exhausted and she was trying not to cry. 'I won't let them put explosives on Sol.'

'No. Fy, they're sure they can do this safely, or they wouldn't be doing it. They want their person back safely too.'

'Can't you talk to them? You helped save the Commander's life. They *owe* you.'

'I've tried. And I'll try again. You get some sleep.'

As I was leaving, Jeitan peered through the doorway and crooked a finger at me.

I followed him back to the room where I'd first met my father. I looked round when I went in, just in case, but there was only Vega. He saw me looking and frowned. Then he cleared his throat. 'The prisoner exchange –'

'You can't wire them up, Fyffe and Sol. You'll have a hysterical eight-year-old wrapped in explosives on your hands.'

'They won't wire him. It's not my call, but I'm told they'll only wire the girl.'

'Oh, well that's all right then. We can all relax. Can't you stop it? You have to try!'

'I can't.' He looked out the window and I think he sighed. 'They're not the problem. The problem is you. We can't risk you falling into ISIS hands. You know too much.'

I sank onto the arm of a chair. 'And so?'

He shook his head. 'Opinion is divided.'

'Do I get a say?' He didn't answer. I said, 'Is that a No?'

'We're at war. We must ensure our security.'

'And I'm a security threat?'

He turned round to look at me. 'You know you are.'

'I should have stayed a scavenger from Gilgate, shouldn't I?'

'No,' he said. 'I don't think so.' He nodded at the door. 'Is anyone outside?'

I peered out. 'No.'

He beckoned me over, rubbed a hand over his face and said quietly, 'The triggers that detonate the switch explosives…'

'What about them?' I said.

'They can be remotely disarmed.'

'How?'

'There are jamming devices.'

'But?'

'They're locked away.'

'Can you get one?'

'I can. But, there's a problem. Their range is poor – to be effective, they'd have to be used on the bridge.'

'Oh.'

'Yes. The triggermen get searched for jammers and the like, but I think I can get you on the bridge as a calming influence on the boy. And I think I can manage to forget to search you. Do you know how to operate a jammer?'

'Yeah. The fascist-in-training, remember?' He ignored that, so I said, 'Do you know what the frequency range will be?'

'I can find out.'

'For both triggers?'

'For both triggers.' His stare told me not to ask how he was going to discover the Cityside one. 'Well?' he said.

'What if I don't come back?'

'I don't think you want ISIS finding you any more than we do.'

True enough. 'All right. When?'

'The exchange is planned for first light, two days from now.'

'Tell me what to do.'

CHAPTER 40

Mol Bridge. 7am. Suicide switch day. The sun didn't rise that morning so much as seep grayly through thick cloud so that the gloomy light became slowly less gloomy until you could see the other end of the bridge. The giant ribcage of the Mol arched over us gleaming faintly, radiating cold, and the whole thing creaked and groaned like a beast in pain. You could taste the sea on the river breeze.

I took Sol to one side so he wouldn't see the women wrapping his sister in explosives. 'Okay, Sol, now listen. We're going to walk halfway across the bridge. We can't run. We just walk. Then we're going to stop for a minute, right in the middle, then you and Fyffe are walking on, to the other side.'

He thought this through behind wide blue eyes. 'Not you?'

'I'm staying here for a while.'

'Why?'

'Got some things to do. I'll come back later.'

'Okay.'

'Not long to go now. Who do you think is waiting for you over there?'

'Mama.'

'For sure.' I stood up as Lanya came over.

'They're ready,' she said.

'Right. Let's do it.'

She put her hand lightly on my chest. 'God go with you.'

My voice stuck, so I picked up her hand and kissed it, then took Sol back to Fyffe.

I'd thought hard about whether to tell Fyffe about the plan to jam the triggers. Vega had said that no one else should know, besides him and me. If word got out that Southside were doing this, there wouldn't be any more exchanges. But Fy was the one wearing the explosives, not Vega. I told her.

When I saw her on the bridge that morning, wearing the padded jacket, I could tell she didn't think the jamming would make us any safer. She was standing very still as if she was afraid to breathe, and the smile she directed at Sol was brittle and too bright. She held out her hand to me. I took it and squeezed it.

'Ready?' I said. She nodded. 'It'll all be over in fifteen minutes. Can you handle fifteen minutes?'

'I think so,' she whispered.

'Okay.' I took Sol's hand.

So there we stood, Fyffe, me, Sol, hand in hand on the bridge in front of the gate. Behind us stood an armed squad and behind them a crowd of jostling onlookers. Ahead of us, in the middle of the bridge, an ISIS agent held the trigger for the explosives on the Breken hostage, and with him stood the triggerman from Moldam who had gone over to verify the hostage and to hold the trigger for the explosives on Fyffe. At the gate at the other end where the Breken hostage stood there'd be ranks of troops too, and maybe there was a crowd, I couldn't see. I wondered if Dash was watching.

A foghorn bellowed on Cityside and we all jumped. An answering bellow came from Southside. That was my signal. Not sooner, Vega had said. Save the battery. I put a hand inside my coat, felt in the inside pocket for the buttons I'd practiced with. Pressed them. A tiny vibration told me the jammer had winked into life. No outcry sounded behind us. No alarms went off. So far, so uneventful. I grasped Fyffe's hand again and we started to walk. Five minutes, Vega had said. Five long minutes to walk slowly to the middle of the bridge and another five to make the exchange.

I looked down at Sol. 'Okay?'

'Yep.'

I found myself counting steps so I wouldn't freak out.

Even so, everything pushed itself at me: the hardness of the concrete through my boots; the salt of the sea wind on my tongue; Fyffe's hand, slim and tense in mine, and Sol's, small and sweaty; the gulls – there were gulls that morning, wheeling and crying high over the bridge. By the time I'd counted to a hundred, the hostage coming from Cityside was close, the noise of the crowd had faded and all I could hear were the gulls.

Then, the crack of a shot.

We hit the ground.

Panic charged through me.

A second shot split the air.

The silence that followed was as loud as anything I'd ever heard. I lifted my head from my arms, got up on hands and knees. Fyffe was frozen in a crouch, her lips moving, her eyes closed.

Sol was sprawled in a pool of blood.

The world went blank for a heartbeat – then it all came roaring back. Sol's blood spread under my fingers and knees. Fyffe's wail filled the air. I turned Sol over. Blood spilled out of his mouth and down his white face. I gathered him up in my arms. His chest was a pulp of bloody clothes. His head fell back. His eyes stared up at the bridge, at the sky, at heaven, at nothing.

City voices were shouting all around us and comms units crackled with bursts of Anglo. I held Sol close, brushed his hair back, tried to see a spark in his eyes, rocked him and said, 'No, no – it'll be all right. You'll be all right. We'll get you home. I promise. I promise.'

Then, above me there was just one voice, barking orders, and another, quiet, in my ear, while Sol bled his life out on my coat.

The voice in my ear was Breken. A woman had crouched beside me. I remember thinking that she looked like Lanya, but older. She put a hand on Sol's face and whispered a Breken prayer, then men came and stood around us, bristling with guns and orders and marched her back towards the city.

They wouldn't let me carry Sol. They took him City-side on a stretcher surrounded by paramedics as if that would do any good. But they let Fyffe and me walk off the bridge together.

She went straight into her mother's outstretched arms. And I went into the waiting arms of ISIS.

City forces had taken back the hospital near Bethun Bridge. They took me there and put me in a white room that had a chair and a cabinet and a narrow bed and a window too high up to see out of and a small bathroom. They were kind. They checked that the blood all over me wasn't my own and gave me a hot drink and clean clothes. They told me to take my time, get cleaned up, rest. Someone would come by presently to see how I was. They locked the door.

Someone did come by presently, but I hadn't drunk the drink, or got cleaned up or changed my clothes. They said Dash wanted to see me and wouldn't it be better for me not to be covered in Sol's blood when she arrived? They brought me another hot drink.

So I drank it, and had a shower – it was strange to stand under hot water. I put on the clean clothes and stared at myself in the mirror. They'd given me an old cadet uniform: green fatigues and brown boots. Maybe it was all they had to spare.

I should have looked like a standard issue ISIS cadet, but my hair was too long and I was too thin and what I really looked like was a hostile in a stolen uniform. I turned away, picked up my bloodstained clothes and stood holding them. I didn't know what to do with them. In the end I folded them and laid them on the chair. Then I sat on the bed holding my coat, Levkova's coat, and waited for Dash.

CHAPTER 41

My eyes wouldn't open. I was floating and warm and I didn't want to move.

A voice said, 'Hey, Nik. Wake up. You're home.'

I made an effort and opened my eyes. I was on the bed in the white room and Dash was sitting beside me. She looked like a real cadet – fatigues, boots, hair short and severe – but her eyes and smile, they were just like always. 'Hey.' I reached out my hand and she took it. Her smile trembled and she started to cry.

There was nothing to say that would make it all right, so we didn't say anything, just sat together. Eventually I said, 'They told me you were coming but I fell asleep. Sorry.'

'That was yesterday.'

'I slept a whole day?'

She nodded. 'You must be hungry. And you've got

some recovering to do: this knife wound,' she picked up my left hand, 'it's not healing well.'

'How's Fyffe?'

'Shattered. Badly in need of TLC. Like you.'

'How are you?'

She shook her head. 'We came so close. Half a bridge length. He was nearly home.' She took a deep, shaky breath, then picked up her crutches and stood up. 'I have to go and see Sarah Hendry.' Mrs Hendry. Mother of Sol and Lou and Fyffe. I couldn't have faced her right then. Dash said, 'I'll come and see you again soon. They won't keep you here long.'

I nodded. 'How's the leg?'

'Not bad. Mending.'

'Seeing you is – it's… it's… I mean, you look good.'

She smiled. 'And you look half-starved and exhausted. But you're in the right place, now.'

'I guess they'll want to debrief me.'

'Oh, they've done that.'

'No, they haven't. I've been asleep.'

'Yes, but that was part of it. Didn't they tell you? They just drug you slightly and ask questions and you talk. It's quicker than other ways, and more effective – they can get at things you might not remember. They said you spoke Breken the whole time. It really got into your system, didn't it?'

I rubbed my hands over my face and tried to focus.

'Say all that again. Slowly.'

She went through it, piece by piece. She ended with, 'Rest now. You look so tired.' She kissed me, whispered, 'Thank you for trying,' waved at the cc-eye above the door and left. The door locked. I closed my eyes.

They left me alone for the rest of the day.

Everything. That's what I must have told them. That's what they took. Including the subset of 'everything' that is 'everything that matters.' Elements in this subset: my father is alive; this fact is being protected by, among others, Sim Vega and Tasia Levkova; the jamming of the triggers for the prisoner exchange was deliberate; it was Vega who set it up and me who jammed them; Remnant control all the Bridge Councils east of Ohlerton; CFM supporters – who would negotiate a peace – are under siege and in retreat…

A woman came to see me. She had a notebook and wore a white coat and wouldn't answer any of my questions. She took my pulse, shone lights in my eyes, and looked at the gash on my hand.

I said, 'Why am I locked up?'

She said, 'We're here to help. Don't worry. You're safe now.' She wrote notes and left.

Dash came to visit. 'How's Fy?' I asked. 'Where is she? Can I see her?'

'She's with her parents,' said Dash. 'I'll see what I can do. They're taking Sol home the day after tomorrow, and I've asked to go in the escort. I put in a request for you to go too but the chief here said no. She wouldn't tell me why. Do you know why?'

I knew exactly why. I couldn't imagine them letting me out of there until they'd done a whole lot more prying into what I'd told them under the debrief drug.

'Nik? Do you?' The blue gaze, the frown, the lips pressed together – the Dash wordless interrogation, just like I remembered it.

'Do they use that debrief drug on everyone?' I asked.

'I don't know. I guess so. It's harmless.'

'Did they use it on Fy?'

'Why? Does it matter?'

Did it matter? I'd been trying to work this out. Had Fy seen or done anything in Southside that might put her in danger over here? She didn't know about my father. She hadn't been involved in any CFM or Remnant politics. She knew the triggers on the bridge would be jammed, but that was Vega's plan, and mine. There was nothing she could have done about it. I closed my eyes and wished my head was clearer.

'Are you feeling bad?' said Dash. 'I could get a doctor. They told me that drug was safe. That you'd just feel tired and groggy.'

Tired and groggy. I'm sure that's how people usually

feel when they've been busy betraying other people.

'Hey.' She snapped her fingers in front of my face. 'Come back.'

I opened my eyes. 'What do you think happened on the bridge?'

'You were there. You'd know better than me.'

'But what are people saying?'

'That the hostiles jammed the explosives trigger so that when they shot Sol their person couldn't be terminated and had a chance to escape.'

No. No. No. That wasn't why.

Dash said, 'What did you see?'

I looked at her, and then I couldn't look at her. 'I jammed the triggers.'

She went completely still. 'You can't be saying that. Why did you? Did they make you? Did they trick you? How could that happen?'

'I thought it was a chance to protect them both – the hostages – theirs and ours.'

'What do you mean *protect them both*? Why would you protect a hostile? God, Nik, they used you. They used you to kill Sol.'

I sat on the floor in the dark and thought about Fyffe. She knew I'd jammed the triggers. Now she'd be told it was a plot by the Breken to free their hostage and kill Sol. Would she believe that? Did I?

I walked round and round my room thinking about the possibility that Vega set up Sol's murder. I didn't believe it. The whole thing made much more sense if it was Remnant that had sabotaged the exchange. By shooting Sol they'd be aiming for success twice over: deepened divisions between the city and Southside, and the Breken hostage – the CFM leader-in-waiting – blown into the sky.

Next morning an agent appeared at the door. I said, 'Can I see Fyffe?' but she said that such decisions weren't up to her. She took me down white corridors that were gleaming and eerily quiet – even the people hurrying past seemed to glide on silent runners.

The woman she took me to was white and quiet as well. She had black hair streaked with gray swept back from a high forehead, and her uniform was gray not black or green like everyone else's. She sat behind a large desk with her hands clasped in front of her. Her eyes were small and very blue under thin dark brows. She gestured to a chair and I sat down.

She smiled, but to herself rather than to me. Eventually she said, 'You don't remember me.' She seemed pleased rather than offended. 'I'm Frieda Kelleran.'

A rush of images filled my mind: my mother's long dark hair and gold earrings, a room cluttered with books and boxes and too much furniture, a gloved hand and a gray coat and a walk up the school driveway.

'Ah,' she said. 'Now you remember. Welcome home, Nikolai.'

Frieda. Friend of my mother. Who'd enrolled me at Tornmoor, and then disappeared from my life entirely. Here she was. Back.

'Home,' I said. 'Is that what this is?'

'Certainly.'

'Have I done it then?'

'Done what?'

'What you wanted. Led you to my father.'

'Well –'

'It was a good plan. I see that now. Stick me in Torn-moor and you have all that leverage to use against him in the Marsh. But he escapes – probably not in your plan. And then you get reports that he's dead. That's probably more like your plan. So you forget about me, but you leave me there in case, one day, I might be useful. And now I have been. I've led you right to him, and here I am: leverage all over again. Have I got that right? I think you might be disappointed, though, in just how much use I can be. But still – at least you know that he's alive and over there. I've told you that much.'

'You're angry. I understand that.'

'Do you?'

'But we're not the ones you should be angry with. Your father abandoned you to Tornmoor, and then when you went over the river in, I must say, an admirable feat of bravery, he used you. You must have worked this out by now. By jamming those triggers they could kill the Hendry boy and in the resulting chaos the Breken hostage could escape.'

'Why would they do that? They were getting her back anyway.'

'I'd have thought that was obvious. A message to us that they mean to pursue this fight to the bitter end. And it will be bitter. The hostage is still here and we are more determined than ever to punish the insurgency and push it to a satisfactory conclusion. They have made a grave tactical error and they will pay for it.' She peered at me. 'You're one of us, Nikolai. I think you know that. You can do good work here. You have grounding in the field. Facility with Breken. Understanding of their ways. And you know just how warlike and unforgiving they are. We want you with us, working for peace. Surely you want peace?'

'They'd negotiate, you know,' I said. 'Some of them. If you came to the table, with terms, they'd talk.'

'There will be no negotiation with the hostiles as long as they take up arms. It's out of the question.'

She pressed a button on her desk and said, 'Proceed,' to someone; I couldn't see who. The wall lit up with faces: Levkova, Vega, and a host of others. The images were fuzzy, like they'd been taken from a long way off and magnified multiple times.

She said, 'You've given us a commentary on life over the river. I know you didn't agree to do that, and I'm sorry you didn't have a chance to consent, but time was of the essence. We couldn't wait for you to recover.' The parade of faces and figures streamed across the wall. 'We know some of these people. We don't know them all. We're asking you to identify as many as you can, so that we can match them with your commentary. We want to know who's with CFM, who's Remnant, rank, popular status, you know the kind of thing. We want peace, Nikolai. You can help us achieve that.'

I watched them go by, my mouth dry and my heart beating hard and when the wall went blank I stood up. She said, 'You need time to think. I understand that. You have twenty-four hours.' She punched a button and spoke to the air again. 'An escort please.'

She smiled up at me. 'You haven't asked me about your mother. Surely you have some questions. I was a good friend of hers, you know.'

I looked at her composed face and bright, enquiring eyes. I heard my father saying, *When I came out of the Marsh, Elena was dead and you were gone*, and I knew exactly what kind of friend Frieda had been to my mother.

'I do have a question,' I said.

'Yes?'

'When you befriended my mother, did they give you a promotion? Or did you have to wait until you'd delivered me to Tornmoor?'

She absorbed that without a flicker. Someone knocked on the door. She called, 'Yes!' and said, 'A friend of yours, I think.'

No. Not exactly. Jono, and a buddy.

'Escort Mr Stais to his room.' Frieda nodded at me. 'Think well.'

They took me back through the white corridors; when we got to my room the other guy left. Jono made some excuse about catching up with me, and stayed behind. He said, 'Sol's dead. And that's down to you. Happy?'

I hit him.

I remember thinking once that in a fight with Jono I'd come out with fewer teeth than I took in and not so many limbs in working order. But no. Jono had learned how to fight so that he left no marks. Just immobilization for an hour or two.

When I could move again, I crawled into the bathroom where I threw up, then sat under the shower feeling it drum on my body. I thought about the Moldam doctor and his painkillers. About Levkova. Vega. My father. All those people. Lanya.

CHAPTER 43

'Where are we going?' I said to the next agent that arrived to take me somewhere. I knew he wouldn't tell me, but I was going to keep asking questions just in case, one day, one of these people slipped up and said something to me.

He took me to the door of the hospital chapel. I had time to take one deep breath, and then I was standing inside, in a dimly lit space with the smell of polished wood and candlewax in the air.

Ahead of me at the end of the aisle was a small coffin that I knew must be Sol. Standing around it were people I had known for most of my life. Dash and Jono. Mr Hendry. Mrs Hendry. Fyffe.

Seeing them standing there, part of my brain looked for Lou. He was always with them when we were all together, making everyone laugh, or groan, at his latest pun or practical joke. And Sol, who made everyone laugh just because he was a sweet kid.

Mrs Hendry gripped her husband's hand and put her other arm across her midriff, holding herself together, but only just. She was a thin, gray, heartbroken version of the smiling woman who had welcomed me for the holidays when I was seven and kept welcoming me almost every summer for years after that.

Now she looked down the aisle and said in a strained, cracking voice, 'Why is *he* here? Why did they bring *him* here?'

I couldn't move.

I looked at Fyffe and she looked back at me. I thought of all the times in Moldam when it had been too dangerous or too difficult to speak and we'd just looked at each other: over the table in the dining hall, over the body of the dead soldier in the infirmary, across the yard at Goran's, and in the upstairs room with the doctor holding a syringe in his hand. Now Fyffe looked back at me and that gave me ballast, because even though we had failed, I knew the weight of what we had done.

What I didn't know was whether Fyffe was watching me and thinking of all the experience that ran between us, or if she held me responsible for Sol's death.

Mr Hendry put a hand on the coffin, as though he had to protect it and its precious contents from me. He looked past me to the agent standing at the door and said,

'You! What do you think you're doing? Take him away!'

I was about to turn and run when Fyffe walked towards me.

Mr Hendry said, 'Fyffe! Come back here.' Jono hurried after her and took her arm but she shook him off.

She walked all the way down the aisle and right into my arms.

She cried and cried. We both did.

At last, she wiped her face on her sleeve and tried to smile at me.

'I'm sorry,' I whispered. 'I'm so sorry.'

She took a shaky breath. 'Not your fault.'

'Fyffe!' called her father.

I kissed the top of her head and stood back from her. 'Don't get into trouble on my account.'

She tugged my sleeve. 'We're taking Sol home tomorrow night. Come and say good-bye.'

I looked at Mr and Mrs Hendry and shook my head. 'I can't, Fy. I can't.'

Jono arrived at her shoulder saying, 'Fyffe. Your mother wants you.'

She nodded and said to me, 'I don't believe them. What they're saying about you. I don't believe it. I'll come and see you tomorrow, before I go.' She shrugged off Jono's hand and walked alone back to her family.

In my room, when I could think clearly again, I thought

this had been Frieda's doing. Her message wasn't exactly subtle: take what she offered or she would make sure that Mr and Mrs Hendry would hate me for life. But what would Frieda make of Fyffe not following the script? I was afraid for Fyffe.

When Jono came to my door the next morning, I said, 'If you're taking me back to see the Hendrys, I'm not going.'

But Jono stood in the doorway looking straight ahead and said, 'Mrs Kelleran wants you to meet someone.'

Curiosity, and an aversion to getting beaten up again, got the better of me. I followed him. He took me to a white room with no windows and no furniture. Just the eye above the door. A woman sat on the floor. The Breken woman from the bridge. She wore civilian clothes – a gray tunic and black leggings. Her feet were bare.

She stood up, waited for Jono to leave, then held out a hand. 'Suzannah Montier.' So this was her. CFM's leader-in-waiting. She had a warm, quiet voice and a cool grip.

'Nik Stais,' I said.

She raised an eyebrow, then nodded up at the eye. 'They're watching. They want to find out if we know each other.' She bowed to the eye. 'We do not.'

'You're the hostage.' I said.

'I was the hostage, yes.' She studied me. 'You have a famous name.'

'So do you.' I sat on the floor, opposite the eye, so I

could watch it the way it watched me.

Suzannah said, 'My father and Commander Stais were friends. Did you know? The last time I saw them together was at a Crossing, the last Crossing of the '87 rebellion. My father asked Nikolai to speak.' She smiled, remembering, then walked across to the eye and spoke to the watchers. 'Do you know what he said? He said, "Freedom." And "Justice." He said, "We'll feed our families with the work of our hands. We'll build a common life. An honorable life. Not of plenty, but of sufficiency." He said that, and I believed him.'

She swung back to me. 'I still do. Despite all this. So, Nik Stais, who are you and where do you fit?'

'I'm no one. And I don't fit anywhere.' And because it was too hard to think about that, I said, 'Why are you here? Why did you stop?'

'Stop?' She set off around the room on her bare, silent feet.

'On the bridge,' I said. 'You could have run. The triggers weren't working. Why didn't you just run?'

She glanced at me and kept on walking. 'And then what?'

'You'd be free. You'd be home.'

'And that child? Shedding his life's blood in your arms? No. Our people killed an innocent. By the logic of this war, the city must strike back.'

'Well, yes. Exactly that. And now here you are – right

in their firing line.'

'It looks that way.' She leaned on the wall. 'Who jammed the triggers?'

'I did. Vega's idea.'

'You saved my life.'

'CFM want you back. It'll be harder now, to try for talks. The city's digging in. Remnant has CFM in its sights, and it's winning. It must have been a Remnant gunman that shot Sol.'

She nodded and resumed her walking. 'Remnant has won this round. So, how does it stop – this suicide march? This death for a death?'

'I don't know,' I said. 'It doesn't stop. Not till one side's crushed the other.'

'And then what will we have? Will we have peace?'

'No. I don't know. Of a kind.'

'Of a kind.' She stopped in front of the eye. It stared at her, crowding the room with watchers: Frieda, the doctor with her notebook and little torch, Dash, Jono, others, lots of others.

Suzannah watched back for a while then turned away. 'Yes. Peace without justice, if it's the city that wins. Peace without mercy if it's Remnant. Which would you choose, Nik?'

I shrugged. 'I don't get to choose.'

'But you do. You choose where you stand and who you stand with.' She was watching me and reading my mind. 'You can't not choose. To walk away in disgust – that is also a choice. You are entangled, Nik. Like all of us.'

'All right,' I said. 'What about you? Which would you choose?'

'I choose justice.' She looked at me. 'And mercy. That, we can call peace.'

'Hey – unfair. You didn't offer me the box set.'

She smiled. 'No. Why not, do you think?'

'I don't know. It's not possible?'

She nodded. 'It's not possible, if one side crushes the other. But if both sides meet, if both will negotiate, then, perhaps.'

'That's not happening, though, is it? And it's not going to now.'

'No. It won't while we're trapped in this… this dance. The suicide switch is well named, isn't it? We seem hell-bent on killing ourselves.'

'How do you change that?'

She folded onto the floor beside me. 'You asked me why I stopped on the bridge. That is why. To make a chance for the city to break that circle. To say, yes, a child was murdered, but something new can come from that: a refusal to answer a death with a death.'

She looked up at the eye, staring the watchers down. Her hands gripped her knees; her breathing was short and sharp. I wondered if they could see that through the eye. But then she looked at me and smiled. She didn't seem to have an insane spark of martyrdom in her eye.

I said, 'That's one hell of a gamble.'

'It's a way forward. It's the only one I can see right now. There are days, many days, when I cannot see any way forward. It's all too hard; it asks more of everyone than they can give.'

'What do you do on those days?'

'On those days, I tell myself: don't look up, the mountain is too high; but choose for this day, for this moment, that's enough. But, Nik, today is not one of those days. Today, I think, here is a chance to look ahead. Shouldn't we make the choices that will lead us to peace?'

'What if it leads straight in front of a firing squad?'

'It's a risk. I think it's worth taking.'

The door buzzed and an agent came in, a senior agent by the look of him, dressed in black, with an assistant trailing behind him. He nodded to Suzannah, called her Ms Montier, and asked her to go with him, please.

'Where?' I said. 'Where are you taking her?'

His glance passed over me as though I wasn't there, but he spoke to her. 'We wish to discuss the current situation. This way, please.'

Not a firing squad then. Not yet.

Suzannah put a hand on my shoulder and looked straight into my eyes, and that's when I knew she was afraid. But she spoke calmly enough, a Breken parting, 'Peace on your road, Nik Stais.'

Dash came to see me a few hours later. I was back in my room, sitting on the floor, trying to make sense of it all. She was wearing her efficient persona. It suited her; always had. If she ever doubted where she fitted in the world, she never let on. She leaned on her crutches and studied me. 'Well?'

'What?'

'What did you decide?'

'I decided, no, I'm not going to ID those people.'

Her shoulders slumped. 'Well, in that case, they're right to be taking you to the Marsh. No, don't look like that. They say it will help. It will, Nik. I mean, look at you – you look wretched. And that is a wretched decision.'

'I thought the Breken had taken the Marsh.'

'They did. They freed their people and looted it for

medicine. And tried to burn it down. But we've taken it back, and part of it's still operational. Just as well for you. You need help. They dug too deep – you're not you anymore. You speak Breken in your sleep.'

'How do you know that?'

She nodded towards the eye.

'What do I say?'

'They don't tell me that.' She limped to the bed and sat down. 'Look. You're home. You've had a terrible time but now you're safe and you can rest and get well.'

'Being locked up, spied on, and sent to the Marsh – this will make me well?'

'And being used by the hostiles? How does that feel? Face facts, Nik. People here are going to wonder about your loyalties, aren't they? Until you can prove which side you're on.' She took my hand. 'You'll sort it out in the Marsh.'

'Which side do you think I'm on?'

'Ours, of course.'

'*Ours* meaning you and me, or you and ISIS?'

'What's that supposed to mean?'

'It's supposed to mean maybe those aren't the same thing.'

'Now you're scaring me. Don't you want an end to all this? The uprising quashed, no more bombings, safety for our families? Peace! Don't you want peace?'

'Sure, I do. What about the Breken?'

'Disarmed, and back over the river.'

'With the gates locked? And no access to medicine or decent food?'

She frowned. 'They'll be better off than they are now. They're starving, aren't they? They can go back to the way things were if they agree to demilitarization. That's fair, isn't it?'

'Is it? I don't know. You'll have to ask them.'

'Well, I can tell you now, it's the best offer they'll get.'

'Then I think they'll keep fighting.'

'You say that like you think it's okay.'

'No, it's not okay. But what you're offering isn't peace.'

'Listen to yourself!'

'Do you know who I met this morning?' I told her about Suzannah.

She sat and listened and said at last, 'So she wants to be noble. So what? What about Sol? What about Lou and Bella? Shouldn't they be avenged? I would avenge Sol. Show me a hostile, any hostile, and I'll avenge Sol.' When I said nothing, she said, 'Aren't you even angry about him?'

'Jesus, Dash.'

'I'm sorry, but we have to send them a message. They can't just gun us down and get away with it. We have to respond!'

'Sure, you have to respond. But do you have to

respond in kind? And anyway, who's *they*? What if –
think about this – what if it was a Remnant gunman that
shot Sol? What if he shot Sol, and got shot himself before
he could shoot Fyffe. There were two shots. What if there
are people over there worth negotiating with? People who
aren't Remnant?'

'You talk like those are distinctions worth making.'
She grasped her crutches and stood up.

'I think they are,' I said.

'They're hostiles, Nik. That's what they are.'

'It's not all they are. I found my father over there.'

She stopped and looked hard at me. 'What?'

'Over the river. I found my father. I'm Breken, Dash.'

She missed a beat, but recovered fast. 'You can't be.
You're one of us – you've always been one of us.'

I nodded. 'That too. Go figure.'

'This is crazy. Your father's dead.'

'He's not dead. He's a Breken strategist. They took
me to meet him.'

'You didn't believe them, though, did you?'

'Yes. I did.'

'Did you believe everything they told you over there?'

'They had nothing to gain by lying to me.'

'Of course they did. You're a brilliant mathematician.
Anyone would fight to have your brain working for them.
Think about it. If your father was alive and Breken, he
would never have let you grow up in a city school. He'd

have tried to get to you, wouldn't he? To get you out. It doesn't make sense. They lied to you. It's what they do.'

'You don't know what they're like.'

'Yes, I do. And I know what you're like, and this is not you. Go to the Marsh. Let them help you.' The door buzzed and she looked relieved. 'Oh, yes. You have a visitor.'

She nodded at the eye.

Fyffe. I scrambled up. 'Hey.' I gave her a hug. 'How are you?'

'All right. I'm sorry about last night in the chapel. The parents. Are you okay?'

'Yeah,' I said. 'Course I am.'

'He's not,' said Dash. 'We're taking him to the Marsh to recuperate.'

'Oh, no!' said Fyffe.

'He needs help,' said Dash. 'He thinks he's found his father. Over the river. Do you know anything about that?'

Fyffe shook her head, and looked at me anxiously.

'No,' said Dash. 'I didn't think so.'

'Your father?' said Fyffe to me. 'I don't understand.'

'I couldn't tell you,' I said. 'He's wanted by ISIS and he's been in hiding. But now it doesn't matter. They've got me talking in my sleep and I've told them all about him.'

'Oh, Nik. That's what all that business with your name was about?'

'You don't believe him,' said Dash.

'Why not?' said Fyffe.

'You people! What did they do to you over there?'

Fyffe turned back to me. 'What will you do?'

'You mean if I ever get out of the Marsh?'

'Don't be like that,' said Dash. 'We just want you back to your old self. We need you. We need that brain of yours. When you're recovered they'll take you on here, they told me.'

'And you believed them?' I said.

'Of course.'

'Do you believe everything they tell you here?'

'What's that supposed to mean? Don't let's fight.'

The door buzzed and swished open to Jono. He smirked in my direction. 'I just heard. The Marsh. That'll straighten you out. What is this? A school reunion?' He turned to Dash. 'It's nearly 1800. We'll be late.'

'Late for what?' I asked.

'Prayer 'n' swear, of course. You're not invited.' He held out a hand towards Fyffe. 'Fy?'

But she sat down on the bed and folded her hands in her lap. 'I'll stay with Nik.'

'Let's move, then,' said Dash. 'We're late and I'm slow.'

Jono gave me one last filthy look as he punched the button that closed the door.

I sat on the floor by the bed. 'Thanks. You could've gone. I don't need looking after.'

'I know,' said Fyffe. 'But I can pray any time.'

'Can you? Will that help?'

She gave me half a smile. 'It'll help me.'

'Didn't help Sol.' Tears snuck up on me again. I stuck the heels of my hands in my eyes and breathed deep. 'Sorry,' I said.

Fyffe sat down beside me and put her head on my shoulder. 'Don't be. He's worth crying for. I think I'm all cried out for now. Do you think it was Remnant?'

'It must have been. They wanted the other hostage dead. They want the war to escalate.'

We sat there for maybe an hour, talking about Sol and Lou – who they'd been, who they might have been, how we could remember them.

At last I said, 'People are coming for me soon. Are you going home tonight?'

'Yes. My poor parents. I have to help them get through this. I wish we could take you with us. They blame you. It's stupid. You tried so hard to bring him back, and he wasn't even your brother.'

I hated the thought of her going home to that big silent house with only her grief-stricken parents for company. And Jono arriving for weekends thinking she was still his meek little girlfriend, not knowing what she'd done, who she'd been, in Southside.

She looked up at the eye. 'Does it listen as well as look?'

'Yeah.'

She was silent for while, then she said, 'Everything's different now.'

'Everything is.'

'It was only three weeks and it felt like a year. I'm afraid for you. Going to the Marsh.'

'I don't exactly envy you.'

'I won't stay home forever. I want to come back to the city. I want to save a life, two lives, for Lou and Sol.'

With the eye staring at us, I didn't ask what she meant. But knowing Fy, she meant something brave and heartfelt and, now and then, madly reckless.

Dash came back and said it was time to go: a car was waiting to take me to the Marsh.

Fyffe and I stood up and Fyffe said, 'I might not see you for a while.'

'Don't worry,' said Dash. 'He won't be long in the Marsh.'

But that wasn't what Fyffe meant. She kissed my cheek and whispered in Breken, 'Dear Nik. Go home.'

Dash and I sat locked in the back of an armored car, waiting to go to the Marsh. It was dark. The car we were in was practically hermetically sealed. There was no getting out, except through Dash.

'Dash, we're still friends?'

'Course. More than friends.'

'If I go into the Marsh, I won't come out in one piece.'

'Sure you will.'

'No, listen. You have to believe either them or me about this, because only one of us is telling the truth.'

'You only think like that because you've been so… indoctrinated.'

'And you haven't?'

'They killed Sol! They used you to do it.'

'Someone did. I want to find out who. I can't do it from inside the Marsh.'

'We know who!'

'I don't.'

'I want you here, Nik, working with me. We can do good work together. Didn't we always say that's what we wanted?'

'Yeah, we did.'

'Well, then.' She sat back, argument won. She took my hand. 'Kiss me.'

When I didn't move, she smiled and said, 'What's the matter? Forgotten how?'

So I did, I kissed her, and she said, 'Okay, why did that feel like good-bye? You'll be out of there in no time. And when you come out I expect something much happier. That's an order.'

The driver arrived and as he opened the door there came a high-pitched, howling yell – a war cry – in Breken, from somewhere close. Fyffe came running towards the car, crying out. She grabbed the driver's arm and gasped, 'I saw them! I saw them!'

'How many? Which way?'

'Three or four – I couldn't tell.' She pointed away from the gates towards a complex of low buildings.

'That's where you were,' said Dash to me. 'They must be looking for you.' She climbed out and I followed. Dash put an arm around Fyffe and the driver ran towards the complex. I looked at Fy. She looked back at me with a perfectly innocent expression then buried her head in

Dash's shoulder, and while Dash was telling her, don't worry, you're safe, I ran for the perimeter fence.

I hid in the shadows of the fence, watched the guards on the main gate, and hoped.

I hoped Dash wouldn't be punished for taking her eye off me.

I hoped Suzannah would be okay, that they'd see that what she was offering was a chance to change the course of the war.

I hoped I could get out before they found me.

But most of all, I hoped Fyffe would be safe: that ISIS would never work out what she had just done. Her angelic face would help. Who could doubt that face? And having a powerful father, that would surely help too. I desperately didn't want to leave her with ISIS and Jono and her grieving parents. But I couldn't stay. I couldn't waste this brave thing she'd done for me.

I skirted the perimeter, listening for trouble. The place wasn't exactly high security: just a hospital that they'd planted a few extra guards around. Most of the security was inside, not out. Maybe they were more stretched than they were letting on. I came to the south gate where a lone guard was shouting into his comms unit.

'Yes! I heard it! It's hostiles. No, I haven't seen any. Send someone down here. We need to reinforce this gate. No, I told you, there's only me. I don't care! The perimeter's weak here. Get —'

I put a boot into his back as hard as I could. He went down with a grunt, and I kicked him again and pulled his gun away. He lay there gasping. The comms unit screeched. I settled for one more kick and a word in his comms unit, in Breken: 'We're everywhere.'

Then I ran.

I ran about twenty blocks, heading downriver towards the Mol. In the blackout it wasn't difficult to be invisible. What was difficult was the thought that Dash was right: I'd said good-bye, to her and to Fyffe. Maybe forever.

CHAPTER 47

The Mol at sunrise. A haze lay over the river. The bridge creaked in the cold air. Light grew in the sky. Two city guards paced at the bridge gate. I wanted to get past them, and now that I had a gun I could see a way to do that. I stood in a doorway close to the riverwall, took aim at a darkened shopfront across the road and fired. The guards came running. I hid in the shadows and when they'd gone by, shouting into their comms units, I ran onto the Mol.

I was heading for the place where Sol died. I hoped it would help me know what to do next.

But there was something there already. I was close before I saw what it was.

Suzannah. Her body had been dumped in the stain left by Sol's blood. Now her blood ran with his. They'd slit her throat.

There was so much blood over her body and on the

ground that they must have marched her there and done it as she stood in sight of home. No justice. No mercy.

The gun was heavy on my shoulder and thoughts raced through my head about what I could do with a free hand and a loaded gun. I stood there, looking at Suzannah. The slap of the river and the waking sounds of the city and Southside receded into white noise.

I felt Sol's blood warm on my hands, his thin shoulders in my arms and his dead weight on my chest; I smelled Lou's charred bones and his clothes burned to his body. The echo of gunfire rattled the air and explosions and shouting rose up from the river. I saw bodies strewn up and down the Mol and blood running across the concrete, dripping through the bridge and off the bridge and pooling on the surface of the river and flowing down to Port and out to sea. Both sides of the city were burning, and there was me standing in the middle of it, uselessly, with a gun in my hands and dreams of revenge crowding my head, because Lou wouldn't ever sit up now and laugh and say, *Ha! Joke's over!* and Sol wouldn't frown over a number puzzle I'd made for him, and Suzannah wouldn't front up to CFM and say, 'Here is a way forward!' There would be only confusion and shouting and gunfire and smoke and explosions, and the dead.

Then Suzannah came back into focus and I heard her say, 'Some days, you know, some days, I tell myself: don't look up, the mountain is too high, but choose for this day, for this moment; that is enough.'

I moved. Took myself across ground that felt sticky with blood, through air thick with the stink of people burning and the sound of my own breath rasping. I moved to the side of the bridge, gripped the gun, took aim at the river and fired. The noise obliterated all other noise. When the bullets ran out I was deafened and gasping and sick. I lifted the gun high and hurled it into the water. Then I laid my forehead on the side of the bridge and let the cold of the ironwork slide through me until the noises of the world came flooding back. Gulls. The waves. The wind in the ironwork above me.

I went back to Suzannah. Her face was calm, and her eyes were wide and dark. Her feet were still bare. I dropped down beside her and closed her eyes. She was curled towards me like a sleeping child hiding a secret treasure. When I looked closely I saw what it was. She was wearing a jacket packed with explosives. A message from the city to those who would come to take her home to Southside.

A crowd was gathering at the Southside gate. A man left the group and walked onto the bridge. My father. As tall and lean and battle-hungry as he'd been the first time I saw him. He said, 'Ah, no,' and put a hand out to Suzannah's hair.

'Don't touch her,' I said. 'She's dead.'

'So I see.' He knelt beside her without speaking for a while, then he said, 'You got away. That's impressive. We thought we'd lost you.'

'I'm not yours to lose.'

He ignored that and, ever the strategist, said, 'Did you talk to her? Did she tell you anything?'

'Yeah, as a matter of fact, she did.'

'She did? What? What did she say?'

'She wished me peace. She was afraid, and preoccupied with trying to broker a way forward, but she stopped and wished me peace. Then they took her away and killed her and now they've wired her body. A little push, from you or me, and we'll be blown sky high.'

He sat back on his heels. 'Is that a threat?'

'This is where Sol died. See that? It's blood. His blood. This is where we killed him –'

'*We* didn't kill him –'

'– and I'm finding it hard to forgive myself for that. And for Suzannah, since the one followed the other. So you can imagine how I feel about you. But you don't escape so lightly either. They know you're alive now. They drugged me and I don't know what I told them, but it was probably everything. So, you were right – they were playing a long game after all – I was a spy for them and didn't know it. And I met Frieda. She's one of them. I think she always was.'

'Listen to me –'

'Why? So you can tell me that this is war? And that I'm being naive?'

'They won't negotiate.'

'Funny. They say the same about you.'

'We must find a position of strength to negotiate from.'

'And they say that too.'

'They prey on us.'

'I know that. But who do you prey on? Lanya thinks victory will bring peace and justice and food and health and education for everyone. Suzannah thought so too.'

'So don't you want to avenge this death?'

'No!' I heard the yell in my voice and stopped because it wouldn't take much to keep on yelling. I wanted him to understand. I said, 'That's what she was trying to change. That's why she didn't escape when the exchange went wrong. She wanted to give the city a chance: to choose not to avenge Sol's death.'

He thought about that, then said, 'You must understand –'

'What I understand is that I've seen the bodies.'

'You think this is simple? Don't you think if there was a simple answer we'd have come to it by now?'

'No, I think it's very complicated. It's you that's made it simple, you and them between you. You kill Sol, they kill Suzannah. They shell the townships, you bomb the city. They train their children in fear and hatred and killing. You call yours to glory and freedom and death.'

He shut up then. I watched Suzannah.

Minutes ticked by. He said, 'Is there a timer on those explosives?'

'I don't know. I haven't looked.'

'Christ.' He stood up. 'I'm going for a bomb squad. Come with me. Come on!'

I shook my head.

He turned away and whistled sharply. Two guards came running up and he sent them to get the squad. He looked back at me. 'For God's sake. What's to be gained by this?'

'Nothing.' My voice came out quiet and cracked. 'Nothing is to be gained by it. I'm just saying good-bye.'

'You didn't even know her.'

'Nor did you, or you'd have known what she was trying to do. I did know Sol. And Lou and Bella. And Dr Williams. And Lev. And Elena. And I never said a proper good-bye to any of them.'

He stood there a long time, watching me. Maybe he was afraid I'd blow up the bridge if he left. I wished he would go and leave me alone, but when he did finally move he didn't go; he came and sat on the ground beside me. I couldn't, with him that close, say anything at all.

River waves hit the pylons under us with a regular thwack. A breeze off the water ruffled Suzannah's hair. At last he spoke. 'They won't leave you, you know, your dead. You can say good-bye, but they pitch camp in your mind. Sometimes you wish they wouldn't. That they'd come to you on your terms not on theirs. They remind you of what you couldn't do, or be.' He picked up Suzannah's hand. 'They remind you that they're gone.'

He lifted a thin chain from around his neck. On it hung the talisman of the Southside Charter. Silver, like the one the ISIS agent had taken from me. 'Here,' he held it out to me. 'Yours now.' I took it on my palm and he said, 'You are, in fact, ours to lose.'

He stood up to meet the bomb squad.

They arrived at a run. 'Sir?'

'First priority is your team in one piece. If it looks too hard, it is too hard – don't do it. But if you can, we want her back home for a Crossing. And the bridge intact.'

'Sir!' They looked at me. 'What about the boy?'

'His name is Nikolai. He's grown; he can decide for himself.' He walked away down the bridge.

CHAPTER 48

Lanya watched me walk off the bridge. A crowd had gathered at the gate, but it was a blur: all I could see was her, standing straight and solemn and beautiful. People made way for me; she opened her arms, and I walked into them and held on for dear life.

Remnant was toppled by Sol's murder, in Moldam at least. The trail from gunman to Council wasn't hard to trace, and added weight to DeFaux's testimony about Councillor Terten and his plan to assassinate Commander Vega. And since the web of Sol's kidnap spread to Blackbyre, Remnant's fall in Moldam threatened their hold on the Blackbyre Council too, and on others – ripples turned into breakers. All that, in the few days I'd been away.

That night there was a Crossing for Suzannah. Like the one for Tamsin all those weeks ago. The people preparing it asked me to speak to Suzannah's family and I said I would, if that's what they wanted, but were they sure about that, because what could I tell them? That she'd died honorably and needlessly? In the end I met them and told them the bare facts and left them to decide.

Sitting there, watching them – mother, sisters, and brother – I thought of the Hendrys taking the road home to Ettyn Hills. And I thought that one day I'd go there again and see them. Not to explain or excuse. Just to see them and sit with them and tell them what Fy had done in Southside. And if Fy was there, how great that would be. But chances are she'd be away, being true to her word, trying to save some lives. I knew she wouldn't stop at two.

The crowd sang Suzannah off the bridge and down to the pyre that was waiting for her. Commander Vega spoke and told us what we'd lost in losing her. And then we stood in silence. No one urged us on to glory. No one roared or punched the air.

Lanya danced. I watched. She'd wept for Sol and for Suzannah. When I told her what had happened Cityside, and what Fyffe had done, she listened and nodded, then took my hands in hers. 'And here you are. I'm glad. I thought perhaps you wouldn't come back.'

'Well, it was this or the Marsh, which would you pick?'

She smiled. 'No. Once you'd got away you could have gone anywhere.'

But I think that's only partly true. The dead drew me back to the bridge, and the living drew me across it.

The dancers lit the pyre and flames leapt into the night. We stood in silence, watching, remembering our dead.

Thanks to everyone who read this book, or versions thereof, in draft, particularly Bernadette Hall, Frankie Macmillan, Fleur Beale, Morrin Rout, Fiona Farrell, and my fellow scribblers at the Hagley Writers' Institute, and also to Martyn Beardsley for his clear-sighted critique. Special thanks to everyone at Text for their warm welcome and to Jane Pearson in particular for her keen eye and sound advice. To Hugh, Marion, Finn, and Niall Campbell and Barbara Nicholas who read this and other stories, a huge and lasting thank you. And thanks, always, to Paul, who listened and whose problem-solving was terrific.